MY BROTHER'S KEEPER

U. E. Wynn

ISBN-13: 978-1-7320325-2-1
ISBN-10: 1732032521

ABOUT THE AUTHOR

U.E. Wynn

A self-educated, business savvy, humble entrepreneur was counted out at a young age by his peers, teachers, and family members. After enduring life altering events that would destroy and/or diminish any individual, he chose to overcome and excel. He turned what would be deemed a negative into a positive. He reevaluated himself and reclaimed a positive position within society.

U.E. Wynn is the founder of 501C nonprofit, Save a H.O.M.I.E. Inc. and an active activist within the community. He continues to assist disenfranchised youth, feed and clothe the homeless and bring forth literacy to the illiterate. Wynn also helps in providing a positive, productive and social atmosphere for the youth to unwind and enjoy themselves throughout the Carolinas via events, concerts and parties.

This is Wynn's second novel presenting you with a page turning, nail biting, exotic read.

ACKNOWLEDGMENTS

From the heart, Wynn Publications would like to acknowledge the following people...GOD...Joanie Thomas (I know you see me Mama, miss you), Iris Wynn, Lakesha Thomas, Danette Wynn (see Ma, I did it!), Quaneika Thomas (something I did you can be proud of), Jyvonda Marshall, William Little, Dante Brice, Ayanna Sellers, Sonja Bienemy (thanks sis!), Whittney Foster, Javon Bienemy, Anthony Henderson (miss you big bruh), Quanisa Hyman, Donald Collins, Khaila Cammacho, and to all our brothers and sisters caught up in the struggle...This is for you!

CHAPTER 1

It's somewhat unbelievable how the brutal murder of one seemingly hard working, honest family man, affected the lives of so many people. Unbelievable how this one senseless murder set forth a chain reaction of madness and murder; eventually giving birth to a secret organization the city of New York was hardly prepared for. Yes, it's all so unbelievable, yet all so true. The South Bronx is where it all began, August 20th 1993, in P.S. 100 School Park on Story Avenue.

Jahad Copeland, a barefaced lanky thirteen year old, was returning from school shopping on Fordham Road with his gang of childhood friends (Tony, Razor, Derrick, Cream, Joey, and Kwan), unaware that destiny was about to make its first appearance in his young life; a jarring appearance that would set the stage for all to come. Dusk had set, giving New York's skyline a blood colored rust tint, as the sun faded to its high place. Across from the park the fourteen story buildings that made up Monroe projects loomed like gothic sculptured mountains casing enormous phantom shaped shadows over the vibrant avenue.

As the teenagers strolled the sidewalk, shopping bags in hand, fortunate enough to have parents to provide money for new school clothes, they joked over the constant noise coming from the heavy traffic, (blaring horns, screeching tires, and occasionally, a stream of curses from an angry driver), about the upcoming school year. Who would most likely get the most girls (Cream). Who would most likely spend the most time in detention (Joey and Kwan). Who would most likely start the most fights (Derrick). Who would most likely win the most fights (Jahad). Who would most likely go through the whole school term without a single incident (Tony). Who would most likely get kicked out of school for cutting somebody like he did the year before (Razor). Normal lingo for the project raised thirteen year olds.

Suddenly, without warning, gunshots rung out, numerous gunshots, and the joking came to a jolting halt. For a second Jahad and his friends froze, dropping their bags, gripped by fear. All along Story Avenue, near P.S. 100 School Park, people ducked scrambling for cover, some running into storefronts until the gunshots ceased abruptly, leaving an eerie silence.

"What...What was that!" Cream asked lying flat on his stomach beside a parked Honda Accord in front of the bodega.

Jahad glanced at him, smirked, then grabbed his bags. "Get your scared ass up. Ain't nothing but somebody shooting in the park. You act like you ain't never heard gunshots before."

Cream stood brushing off the front of his Nike t-shirt, "You were scared too Jah, don't even front."

"Yeah," Tony pitched in.

Jahad shot them both a warning glance. Since grade school he had established himself as leader of their little clique, and to show or admit to being scared was something he refused to do, "I wasn't scared."

"Yeah right." Derrick mumbled as they began walking towards Monroe projects.

Jahad looked in his direction, but Derrick turned away grinning.

"I betcha' somebody got hit up." Razor said with a sadistic grin walking up beside Jahad, "Ya'll wanna go see?"

Cream quickly shook his head, "I ain't going over there. What if whoever was shooting is still over there. We could all get shot."

"Uh huh!" Joey and Kwan added.

They were about a hundred yards from the park. In the distance, all that could be seen was a grayish murky light coming from the moon, being that most of the park lights had been shot out. No activity whatsoever.

"Ya'll scared or something?" Razor challenged.

All heads turned in Jahad's direction, "What ya'll lookin' at me for?" He scowled, "If ya'll scared go home. C'mon Razor." The two strutted off, leaving the others no choice but to follow or either get teased later.

P.S. 100 School Park, labeled "The Big Park", by those who lived in Monroe projects and surrounding areas, was made up of numerous similar parks, therefore earning its name. By day, its occupants were kids, at night, in moved the drug dealers, crackheads, and stick up kids who claimed the park as theirs.

Entering the park the teenagers looked around and noticed that not a living soul lingered about, not even a crackhead, which was uncommon since gunshots could be heard almost everyday in the South Bronx. The basketball courts crowded only minutes ago were deserted. Neglected basketballs, t-shirts, and water bottles were the only evidence that games had been in progress. At the stone tables where old men usually sat playing chess and feeding pigeons, half bottles of beer were knocked over, still leaking.

It wasn't until they neared the handball court, a Puerto Rican hangout spot, did the desolation of the park become clear. Two men, one Black, the other Puerto Rican, were laid out almost side-by-side bleeding profusely. Jahad, walking ahead of his friends paused at first, his heart beating rapidly as he recognized the gray transit system uniform, then struck out running towards his father leaving his friends behind baffled.

"Dad!" He cried as he reached the body, his knees giving in by the weight of grief.

By this time, Jahad's friends had gathered around looking down at John Copeland horrified.

"Oh shit!" Tony yelled dropping to his knees beside Jahad. "Somebody go call the ambulance and get Mrs. Copeland . . . now!"

Cream, Derrick, Tony, and Kwan ran off while Razor stood fascinated, his eyes fastened to the older Puerto Rican man who's blood poured from the side of his head.

"Oh God no! Dad!... Dad look at me!" Jahad cradled his father's head in his arms as blood pumped freely, a deep crimson red, from the bullet wounds in his chest.

Hearing his son's plea, John forced his eyes open, although he felt himself sinking into darkness. His legs twitched sporadically and he clawed at the concrete with his fingernails desperately trying to hold on. There was something terribly important he had to tell his son.

"I. . . love. . . love you son. You. . . You have. . . have to. . . take care of. . . of the family. . . now," he said with a crooked smile as blood seeped from the corners of his mouth.

Jahad shook his head, his eyes blurry with tears. He couldn't imagine life without his father. No more trips to the P.A.L (the local boxing gym) for his boxing lessons. No more weekend outings to

Manhattan. No more birthdays, Christmases, or Thanksgivings with his father around. No, it was something that he could not imagine. "Please dad, don't die. Please!"

"It's . . . It's my . . . time son," John coughed up a glob of blood, "Lis . . . Listen. Your mother has. . . has a. . . key to. . ."

"Who did it!" Jahad cut his father off overcome by grief. "Who did it Dad? I swear I'll kill 'em. I swear it!"

"No!" John's voice was full of authority, "You . . . You get . . . get that . . ." Another fit of coughs racked his body, and then he grew still, his eyes focused on Jahad.

Jahad blinked a few times until it dawned on him that his father was dead, "NOOOOO!" He roared turning his head up towards the black sky. His cry echoed through the park like a battle cry.

~~~~

Taking his fathers words to heart, Jahad vowed to take care of his family by any means necessary. Michelle, his mother, worked as a nurse at Jacoby Hospital, but her paycheck was hardly enough to keep him, his older sister by a year Latrice, and their baby brother Koran, who was about to start kindergarten, accustomed to the life they were use to living. This began his life of crime. A week after John Copeland's funeral Jahad started planning petty robberies with the help of his friends. At first, they started rolling bums only to learn that it was too much work for so little money; bums fought hard for their dimes, quarters, and nickels. Faced with this, Jahad moved their operation to Mid-Town Manhattan. There, they preyed on Wall Street workers, pick pocketing wallets, or sometimes if Jahad could catch his mark in a secluded area, he would simply knock the man out and strip him for everything. Then came the smash and grabs, where a brick was thrown though a jewelry store window and they would snatch what jewelry they could within two minutes.

Over time Jahad organized two teams. Since Joey, Kwan, and Cream were the most skilled at pick pocketing he sent them off by themselves with Derrick as the lookout man. While he, Tony, and Razor hit the jewelry stores. Soon they were clearing close to ten thousand dollars during each outing. At the end of the day, regardless of who snatched the most jewelry or took down the most wallets, all money was divided equally. The jewelry was fenced off to Budda, an older guy from their projects who gave them reasonable prices for their merchandise. While most of his friends, with the exception of

Tone, went to Fordham Road to shop after every score, Jahad took his money home to Michelle, letting her take what was needed for the family before spending a dime.

For nearly two years, up until he was fifteen, Jahad upheld his promise with a fierce determination until the day a smash and grab went wrong. Tony and Razor were in the process of raking jewelry from a Tiffany's jewelry store window, when Jahad, who was the look out man, spotted two uniform policemen racing up Fifth Avenue towards them. Judging by the distance he knew it wasn't possible for his friends to get away, someone was bound to get caught. Without bothering to contemplate the consequences, Jahad grabbed a brick and launched it at the cop on his left, hitting him directly between the eyes. As the cop fell and his partner advanced, Jahad turned to his friends who were still busy grabbing jewelry.

"Run! Run!" He yelled, turning back to face the cop. "It's the cops!"

Hearing the word "cops" Tony and Razor hauled ass, stuffing jewelry in their pocket without looking back. If they had of, they would have seen Jahad square off with the beefy Irish cop, they would have also seen when the cop bashed Jahad over the head with his black medal flashlight. Jahad awoke hours later at the Tombs in Manhattan with a knot the size of an apple on his head, charged with assault with a deadly weapon and breaking and entering. This earned him three years at Spofford Detention Center for Youths located in the Bronx. Spofford Gladiator School was a more suitable name because that's exactly what it was. Weaklings didn't stand a chance and were tormented constantly. Being a new face, Jahad fought daily for the first six months until he proved he was no weakling by knocking out almost everyone who dared to challenge him. A feat he managed due to his boxing lessons.

Left alone, Jahad focused his time on getting his GED, which only took two months since the test were simple reading and comprehension; except for the math and he had always been good with numbers. With his GED under his belt, he started writing rhymes after hearing a rap session in the bathroom from inmates he went to school with. He figured if they could do it so could he, and soon found out he was pretty good at it, this lead to the dream of owning his own record label. Dreams of being a rap star weren't good enough; he wanted the whole shebang.

Then along came Rahoul Hernandez, and Jahad's troubles started again. A Puerto Rican from 143rd and Amsterdam in Harlem, Rahoul was fresh in for drug trafficking, after being caught on a Greyhound bus transporting four kilo's of cocaine to Albany New York for his older brother. He came to Spofford sporting a twenty five thousand dollar platinum chain, and a ten thousand dollar matching platinum bracelet he wore all of one day. The next day he was robbed of everything, even his brand new Air Jordan sneakers, by three thugs from Brooklyn.

Rahoul wasn't a big dude. He stood 5'5" in his sneakers, and weighed no more than 130 pounds soak and wet. He wasn't a fighter either, had never been in a fight, but he was far from a coward. Whenever he caught one of the guys who robbed him one on one, he attacked, regardless of the outcome, which usually led to him getting his ass beat. This went on for a few weeks until the three thugs got fed up and decided to teach Rahoul a lesson; one he would never forget if he lived through it.

By chance, or maybe it was destiny again, Jahad happened to walk in the bathroom the day they cornered Rahoul with their homemade knives. Stories of the little Puerto Rican who kept getting his ass beat had been circling around, but Jahad couldn't help admiring Rahoul's courage. So when the three thugs made their move, Jahad, knowing he was going against the grain by not minding his business, intervened, making a friend for life. Jahad and Rahoul came out with quite a few shallow cuts. The three thugs from Brooklyn, however, went to the infirmary with concussions and something broke, a jaw, a nose, and an arm.

This drew the attention of Travis Walker, b.k.a. Wolf. The first, but certainly not the last person, Jahad would ever kill. Wolf, an up and coming hoodlum/drug dealer from East New York, was in for manslaughter. At the age of fourteen, Wolf and his younger brother murdered a big time drug dealer in hopes of taking over the drug trade on Blake Avenue in front of their building in the Alabama Projects. Wolf being the oldest by a year, claimed sole responsibility for the body, and freed his brother; who took control of the strip with his own little crew.

For close to two years, Wolf had been the dominating force at Spofford, running a large clique from Brooklyn. Just so happens the three thugs Jahad and Rahoul sent to the infirmary, were members of that clique. Being their leader, Wolf couldn't have a guy from the Bronx, and a little Puerto Rican from Harlem, beating up on his people. It was bad for his image. He heard all about how tough and good Jahad was with his hands. This didn't phase Wolf one bit. He was just as tough and good with his hands. In a match up pound for pound, they were equally stacked weighing in the range of 170 to 180 pounds, but Wolf had one major advantage. An advantage Jahad wasn't prepared for. On the gritty streets of Brooklyn a unique style of fighting was invented, dubbed the 52 Handblock, where hands and elbows were used deceptively to disguise when and where a punch would be launched. Wolf perfected it with a twist of his own.

The first fight took place in the bathroom after Wolf called Jahad out in the chow hall in front of everybody. The Correctional Officer, aware of Jahad and Wolf's reputation as fighters, used the opportunity to place wagers and set it up so the fight could go uninterrupted. The day of the fight, an air of excitement could be felt. If Jahad won, he would be the new undisputed champion of Spofford. Unfortunately it wouldn't be. Wolf knocked him out cold within two minutes, with a right hook Jahad never saw coming. All he remembered was Wolf doing something with his hand, sort of like he was dancing, then waking up on the floor with Rahoul standing over him.

From there Wolf made it his business to beat Jahad's ass whenever the opportunity presented itself. Most of the Correctional Officers approved, since they had bet their money. If only Jahad would have accepted the ass whipping and looked up to Wolf as the other inmates did, Wolf would have left him alone. It wasn't about to happen; Jahad's pride wouldn't let it. So the ass whippings continued until Jahad started learning Wolf's technique; using each defeat as a learning experience.

Finally after five long painstaking months and numerous black eyes and bloody noses, Jahad called Wolf out in the same manner he was called out, in the chow hall in front of everybody. An audible gasp arose from the crowd at his announcement. The Correctional Officers, curious by Jahad's show of bravery, arranged for the fight to go down in the bathroom again. Like last time, bets were placed, only this time on how long it would take before Wolf knocked Jahad out. Jahad heard all this as Correctional Officers and inmates filed into the bathroom, making a circle around the two fighters. Wolf put his hands up in the southpaw stance when they squared off, while Jahad bounced on his toes, his arms hanging loosely at his side.

"Better put you hands up BX, unless you wanna go to sleep real fast." Wolf taunted, weaving from left to right.

Jahad continued to bounce, never taking his eyes off of Wolf's nose. "Sleep is the cousin to death, but you gon' get to know it real well."

"Yeah?"

Jahad nodded, "Hell yeah."

"Let's see then." Wolf moved in, throwing a rapid series of right jabs, dipped to the floor and spun on his knee until he was behind Jahad, then kicked him in the ass, "I'm right here nigga."

The crowd erupted with laughter, piping out jokes and insults directed at Jahad.

"Stop bullshittin' Wolf and knock that nigga the out. I got my money on this shit!" One of the Correctional Officers called out.

Wolf winked, then gave Jahad a twisted grin, "You heard that, it's night night time . . . you ready?"

"Don't talk me to death." Jahad replied, focusing intently on Wolf's nose, patiently waiting to make his move. A move he spent weeks practicing.

Wolf nodded then out of nowhere threw both his arms in the air expecting Jahad to look up. He made a fatal mistake. Anticipating the move, Jahad dropped to one knee and slapped Wolf on the ankle. Just as Wolf looked down shocked, Jahad came up shooting a vicious uppercut directly into Wolf's nose. The force lifted Wolf off his feet and sent his nose bone slamming into his brain. For a few seconds Wolf shook uncontrollably, blood pouring from his nose and eyes, and then Wolf exhaled one last breath.

Jahad faced the crowd still bouncing on his toes, "Any of you other niggas want it? If so step up to the plate. That goes for you bitch ass police too!"

Rahoul broke through the crowd, grinning like a kid on Christmas, and put his arm around Jahad's shoulder. "You heard my nigga, step up to the muthafuckin' plate… And whoever got my jewelry, give my shit back!"

What happened next was a big cover-up. Wolf's death was made to look like a sporting accident, saving Jahad from being charged with murder. The Correctional Officers involved were forced to resign once the snitches related what happened to the Warden who resigned quietly six months later. Jahad didn't go unpunished. For the remaining 18 months of his sentence segregation became his home, but punishment brought forth sweet rewards. There in that single cell room, caged 23 hours a day, he tapped into a talent he fell in love with. Every waking moment rhymes, different concepts, and money schemes filled his mind. With these three companions dreams took shape and form, ideas started breathing life, until he could clearly see each step taken up until his feet were on top of the world. It was destine!...so he thought.

Who controls fate? The "what ifs" and "who could have beens". The two paths, the fork in the road, who decides left or right? And who can resist the lure of destiny?

The story begins.

CHAPTER 2

January 15, 1998

Eighteen red candles flickered on the double layered chocolate birthday cake that sat in the middle of Michelle's dining table. Lauren Hills "X Factor" played on the stereo from the living room, filling the apartment with her heart touching lyrics. The vibe was beautiful Jahad thought looking around at his family and friends from where he stood at the head of the table. Michelle and Koran were at his sides, arms tightly around his waist making him feel an intense wave of love. Three years of being locked away taught him to appreciate the bond between his loved ones. If he could help it, that bond would never be broken again. Beside Michelle, forming a clockwise circle around the table in her small kitchen stood Latrice, Tony, Kwan, Razor, Cream, Joey, and Derrick, with guienine grins and smiles on there faces.

"C'mon jailbird, make a wish," Tony said grinning.

Jahad gave Tony a crooked smile, and then glanced at Michelle, who was overjoyed her oldest son was finally home. During his time spent at Spofford, his friends being loyal, made sure she never fell on hard times. For this alone Jahad's love for them went beyond words.

"You know I'm greedy, so I gotta have more than one wish." Jahad glanced at Michelle again, "My first wish is to get Ma-Duke out these projects, that's a promise tho'. My second wish is for my knucklehead brother here; he palmed Koran's small head, to be the next Johnny Cochran. My third wish," he looked at Latrice cracking a sly grin, "is for my sister to grow some hair and stop rocking those weaves."

Although she wore other people's hair, Latrice was quite pretty, with Michelle's delicate features. Smooth chocolate skin, large soulful sad light brown eyes, long curly eyelashes, thick arched eyebrows, thick heart shaped lips, and a small thin nose. Actually, she and Michelle could almost pass for twins if it weren't for the crow's feet at the corner of Michelle's eyes and the gray streaking through her jet-black hair. Jahad favored his father, more in looks and build, but had Michelle's chocolate complexion and large light brown eyes, which looked almost golden when struck by the light. Jahad's face was close to a perfect triangle; rounded at the corners and carried a strong sharp jaw line, ending at his pointed chin. He had a broad crooked nose, thanks to Wolf, and thick wide lips framed by a thin mustache. The time he spent working out in his cell at Spofford, transformed his 6'2", 210-pound frame, into a mass of hard rock muscle. From his father he inherited his round shoulders, deep wide barrel chest, and "V" shaped torso.

"Chill Trice." Jahad held up his hand laughing, "I'm saying, you a'ight, but what you gon' do if they ever run outta horses?"

Latrice rolled her eyes, "For your information, this is 100% human hair," she shook her long ponytail, "and I don't care what you say, Tony likes it."

Jahad shot Tony a dour glare, "What you mean Tone likes it?"

"What you think I mean?" Latrice shot back with a smug smile.

Jahad glared at Tony again.

"Whoa Jah," Tony grimaced, "We grown now homey."

"A'ight grown, we'll build about that later tho' . . . back to my wishes. My fourth wish is for all my niggas to eat love, love!"

They all nodded in agreement as Jahad blew out the candles while Michelle closed her eyes and said a silent prayer. The last thing she wanted was for Jahad to pick up from where he left off. She knew exactly what he was hinting at with his fourth wish, and had something set up in hopes of steering him towards a different path.

From the kitchen the party moved to the living room, where Jahad opened stacks of gifts, brought by his friends. The whole time Koran sat off to the side admiring his older brother. The three years Jahad had been away, Koran tried his best to assume Jahad's role, doing petty crimes in an effort to bring money home to Michelle. Luckily Tony and the rest of Jahad's friends kept him from getting into too much trouble. Like Jahad, Koran was highly intelligent, but surrounded by drug dealers, stick-up artist, and murders; he had one ambition, to be a thug like his brother.

Once the coming home/birthday party broke up, Jahad dressed in a pair of off black Pelle Pelle jeans, silver Timberlands, a silver black and white Pelle Pelle sweater, and a black Pelle Pelle butter soft leather jacket. A house party was being held in the next building over in his honor, at Tony's mother's apartment, since she was out of town. Before he could make it out the door Michelle called him back, a pensive expression showing on her round face.

"What up Ma?"

"I need to have a word with you before you leave."

Jahad followed her to the living room and took notice of its shabbiness for the first time. The furniture was close to ten years old with patchwork done by Michelle to keep it looking halfway presentable. Knicks and scratches scarred the coffee table from years of use. Across from the couch sat a late floor model television, the knobs broken off, with a picture of his father perched on top like a shrine. The same furniture John bought years ago. It was definitely time for a makeover Jahad thought.

"Jahad," Michelle said drawing his attention back to her, "growing up you never really listened to me, feeling you had to do whatever it took in order to help take care of us, but you need to listen to me now and take my advice to heart. I understand you want us out of these projects, but I don't want you doing anything that might risk your freedom again. I've been in these projects nearly thirty years and I'm making out just fine. Koran and Latrice are too, you . . ."

"Ma, I . . ."

"Shhh! Listen to me Jahad!" Michelle snapped, "You may not know this but Koran worships the ground you walk on, so what you do reflects on him. Do something he can be proud of Jahad, instead of having him risk going to jail or worse . . . Now you may not like this but I have a job set up for you with a friend of mine. It's a furniture moving company and he'll be expecting you to show up in the morning. All I ask is that you give it a try. I want you to save some money, and I'll save some, so we can see about getting you into college. You know your father always wanted you to go to college. Will you do it?"

Jahad dropped his head and glanced at the picture of his father. Before John Copeland was murdered, college was something Jahad looked forward to, but that was then. Now he had to figure out how to accomplish his goal and keep Michelle satisfied at the same time. None of what she said went along with his plans. The first thing he wanted to do was get her out of the projects. Working and saving money for college wouldn't get it. Still, the thought of Koran following in his footsteps opened his eyes to a bigger picture. Koran had the opportunity to be someone important, someone great, and what Jahad had planned wasn't the example he wanted for his little brother to follow, not the beginning phase anyway. With that thought he decided to give the job a try, but in the back of his mind another plan was forming. One that could make his dreams a reality.

"A'ight Ma, I'll take the job, but I still want you outta these projects, so lets forget about me going to college and concentrate on Koran. Can you go for that?"

"Do I have a choice, with your stubborn self." Michelle smiled sadly, "Now don't get in no trouble tonight and don't get too drunk. You have to be at Joe's moving company at eight in the morning. It's on 161st and Calhoun Avenue, not too far from Starbucks."

"This friend who's giving me the job, he your boyfriend or something?" Jahad asked with a grin but his eyes were serious.

Michelle giggled, "No boy! Joe's wife and I are friends."

"Oh."

"If I did have a boyfriend, what about it?" She teased.

"I don't know. I'd probably beat him up or something. That's if he wasn't good enough for you." Jahad laughed and kissed her on the cheek, "I'm about to get up outta here."

Just as he stood to leave, Koran bounced in full of energy, "Let me go Jah." He asked eagerly.

Michelle smacked her lips, "The only place you're going is to bed. You know you have school tomorrow."

"C'mon, Ma. It's only nine o'clock"

"Only nine o'clock my butt. You have an hour before bed time."

"I'll be home before ten." Koran whined looking at Jahad.

"Nah, peanut head. I'll hang out with you tomorrow tho'." Jahad punched him lightly on the shoulder.

Koran sighed loudly, murmuring curses under his breath as he stormed off.

"See what I'm talking about," Michelle said looking after him shaking her head, "he's hot headed and stubborn just like you."

"Don't stress it Ma. I'll make sure he does the right thing. Now I'm out, I'll be home in a few hours."

"You better."

On the way to the house party, Tony filled him in on what had been going on since he had been gone. For a while after Jahad was arrested they continued their petty crimes in Manhattan, then gradually crossed over to the drug selling. Budda, their old fencer, introduced them to Hector and Jose', two Puerto Rican brothers known as the Coco Twins, who controlled most of the drug trade in the South Bronx. After explaining that the youngsters were trying to make some fast money, the Coco Twins had one of their lieutenants supply each of them with five hundred dollar packs of crack for a 70/30 split. Two and a half years later they were up to getting two thousand dollar packs for the same 30% split. Jahad listened without saying a word or showing any emotions, but inside he was steaming. Whoever the Coco Twins were, they were getting over on his friends big time. This didn't matter though, because it wouldn't be long before things changed. Jahad would make sure of that.

~~~~

The next morning, Jahad showed up at Joe's moving company at little after eight with a slight hangover. The building sat in between an electronic store and a seamstress shop, with a advertisement sign posted in its dusty window, stating Joe's offered the lowest rates throughout the Bronx. Stepping inside, he looked around at the dimly lit interior, which was no bigger than a small bedroom. Behind the waist high counter to his right, a black man sat paging through a Sports Illustrated magazine. On the far wall facing the counter was an orange couch dated back to the 70's, with a small round coffee table placed in front of it.

"You Jahad?" The man asked moving from around the counter. Around five eight, built like a retired wrestler with a thick neck, massive arms, and shiny bowling ball baldhead, he looked Jahad up and down frowning.

"Yeah, what up?"

"I'm Joe, your boss if I decide to keep you. And it's twenty minutes after eight, that's what's up. You s'pose to be here at eight o'clock." Joe barked, his face resembling a pitbulls. "I'll tell you now, I know all about your past and I don't tolerate no damn stealing. When we go in these people's houses, don't be fucking with their shit. You understand?"

Jahad screwed up his face. "Yeah, I understand, but since you know all about my past, let me say this. I did what I did for one reason, to feed my fam'. I ain't no fuckin' thief."

Joe held Jahad's stare, then nodded, "That's all I wanted to hear. We have four deliveries today, two in the Bronx and two in Harlem. I pay $75.00 for each delivery. Now let's go."

Jahad followed Joe through a side door that opened to a large storage area, where old couches and dressers were stacked against the front wall near a small office. Two yellow moving vans were parked one behind the other, facing a garage-sized doorway.

"I won't ask if you have a license, but can you drive?" Joe asked, walking to the lead van.

"Yeah."

"Good . . . Hope you have a strong back."

"Don't worry 'bout my back. Just have my dough when we finish this shit." Jahad glanced around. " Hold up man, it's just you and me? You don't got no more workers?"

"They quit, couldn't handle the work. Tomorrow I got somebody else coming to help out." Joe tossed Jahad a set of keys.

Throughout the day the conversation between the two was kept at a minimum, but Joe came to respect Jahad for his hard work. By three o'clock all their deliveries were out of the way, two hours ahead of schedule.

Impressed with his work performance, Joe gave Jahad an extra fifty dollars. Although he was tired, when Joe counted off the three crispy big-faced hundred dollar bills and a wrinkled fifty, he couldn't help from smiling.

"Remember, eight o'clock tomorrow Jahad. We have six deliveries."

Jahad nodded, holding back a slick remark, then jogged outside where his cab was waiting. Twenty minutes later he was dropped off on Story Avenue in front of his building. Exhausted, he half walked, half stumbled into his building with two thoughts in mind, a hot shower and his lumpy bed. On the elevator after pressing the button for the tenth floor, he leaned against the wall and closed his eyes, taking no notice when the young woman walked in.

"Looks like you're working hard for the money."

Jahad snapped his eyes opened and was jolted by the sight. Before him stood one of the prettiest women he had ever laid his eyes on. Her complexion, the color of sunrays, large almond shaped emerald green eyes, silky honey blonde hair that hung to the middle of her back, framing her oval shaped face. She wore a tan Baby Phat sweatshirt, the top hugging her melon sized breasts, the pants clinging to her round hips, and a pair of white Nike Air One's on her small feet. Jahad took all this in while his eyes stayed glued to her face; feeling like someone had put an Energizer battery in his back.

"You just don't know Ma, I'm working too damn hard." He flashed his crooked grin. "What's your name gorgeous?"

"Janet, and there's nothing wrong with a little hard work. It's good for a man."

"Janet. Miss Jackson if you're nasty, huh?"

Janet blushed.

"So I take it you be feelin' hard working dudes?"

"Maybe. All depends on who the dude is."

"Well my name is Jah' gorgeous, and I been working my ass off. What other qualifications do I gotta fill?"

Janet looked him over from head to toe, liking what she saw, then held up her hand to count on her fingers, "Let me see, a hard worker, single, handsome . . .oh, no kids."

"I'm good then." He glanced down at his sweaty sweatshirt and scuffed Timberlands. "You can look at me and see I be bustin' my ass. As far as being single, right now it's just me, myself, and Jah. I'm as honest as Abe, got movie star looks although I ain't conceited, and I definitely don't got no seeds. So I'm good, right?"

"I don't know yet, but you're fitting the description. How about I give you my phone number and see where it goes from there?"

Jahad smiled so hard, his bottom lip was on the verge of splitting. "I'm with that. If you want you can write it across my teeth, since I can't stop smiling."

Janet laughed. "You're funny. That's another qualification, you have to be able to make me laugh."

"You want me to do my Bernie Mac impersonation? Shit, I'll take it back and hit you with the Bill Cosby."

Janet laughed again, holding a hand over her mouth. "No, no. You can save the impersonations for another time." She said as the elevator stopped on the tenth floor.

"You live in this building?"

"No, I live in 1760. I'm over here to visit a girlfriend, she lives on the twelfth floor."

Building 1760 was the next building over, Tony's building.

Once they exchanged numbers, Jahad strutted off feeling rejuvenated. His day was turning out to be pretty good he thought as he entered his apartment and the smell of garlic bread and tomato sauce filtered through his nose, making his mouth water. Following the aroma to the kitchen he found Latrice standing over the stove, dropping spaghetti noodles into a pot of boiling water.

"What you burning?" He asked sitting at the dining table.

"Your dinner so shut up before I burn it for real." Latrice answered looking over her shoulder. "How was your day?"

"PSSS! That nigga Joe had me lifting all types of couches and dressers. He hit me off tho'. I made three fifty."

Latrice gave him a sweet smile, "Let your big sis' hold something. I'll pay you back."

"Yeah right." Jahad snorted. " You know damn well you ain't gon' pay me back, but here," he peeled of the wrinkled fifty, "I expect a hot meal everyday when I get off work."

Koran walked in with his book bag hanging off his shoulder, just as Jahad passed Latrice the money. "Where's mine Jah?" He asked holding out his hand.

"Damn, I'm getting stuck up without a gun. You'll have to wait until I get some change and I'll hit you with twenty dollars, but when I need something ironed, that's you. Now let me go wash my ass before I get robbed for all my dough."

"Tony stopped by earlier, he wants you to meet him in the park."

Jahad nodded. He needed to see Tony too. "What's up with you and Tone?"

"That's her boyfriend." Koran blurted out, cutting his eyes at Latrice.

"Mind your business Koran, don't you have some homework or something to do."

"Don't worry about my homework, answer Jah's question."

Latrice wrinkled her face at Koran before answering, "We been going out for about a year now."

"Why nobody ever told me? Before I got sent up, ya'll couldn't stand each other."

She gave him a wicked smile, "Times have changed."

"So I see . . .Ayo, you know a chick named Janet, who lives in Tone's building?"

Latrice took a second to think, "Janet . . . I think I know who you're talking about. Light skinned girl with green eyes and long hair?"

"Yeah, and a bangin' ass body."

She rolled her eyes, "I don't really know her like that, but I be seeing her around. Why?"

"None of your business. You ain't tell me what was up with you and Tone. Now get my food ready. O-yeah, you better not use that dough I gave you to cop some horse hair." He laughed walking out the kitchen with Koran on his heels.

Michelle was home from her nursing job by the time Jahad finished showering and dressing. The same job she held since he was a kid. She sat at the kitchen table massaging her feet, a glass of wine in front of her when he walked in.

"What's good Ma-Duke?" He kissed her on the forehead before taking a seat. "They worked your ass off today too, huh?"

"Did they. I've been on my feet all day. How was your day?" She asked with a tired smile, taking a sip of her wine.

"Joe worked the hell outta me, but he paid me a'ight." Jahad reached in his pocket and gave her two hundred dollars. "Put that up for whatever . . . Check it Ma, I'm a try this out for a while, but I ain't gon' be working like a slave forever."

"You won't have to if you take your butt to college. It's not too late Jahad. You have the mind to be anything you want to be. You know this too."

Jahad shook his head, "We already talked about this Ma. My first obligation is to get you outta these projects. That'll solve the problem with Koran too. From there, I'm a do me. I'll be careful tho'."

"Jahad, don't . . . "

"C'mon Ma, work with me." He said quickly, "Trust me, I know what I'm doing. I thought it all out, plus I won't be mixed up in what I plan on doing for too long."

Michelle gave him a grave look, "I see that look in your eyes, so I know there's no talking you out of whatever you have in mind. I want you to remember this though; you're not the only one who's at stake. If it wasn't for Tony and the rest of your friends, I don't know what I would've done with Koran. Keep that in mind."

Jahad nodded as Latrice and Koran walked in preparing to serve dinner. With what he had planned, Koran would never know what he was up too. He could set a good example and still do what he had to do on the side.

CHAPTER 3

On Jahad's way out the door to meet Tony in the park, Koran hovered around his legs like a hyper puppy. Out of Michelle's kids, Koran took after their father the most. A high yellow complexion on the brink of being red, long, broad nose, wide, thick lips, and triangle shaped face was all John Copeland. The only feature from Michelle was his large light brown eyes. For a ten year old, he was short for his age, standing only five two in his sneakers, but showed signs of growth by his big feet.

"Can I go Jah?" He asked unable to be still.

"Yeah, c'mon little nigga. I need to talk to you anyway."

As they walked to the elevator, Koran tried to imitate Jahad's easy strut, fumbling over his big feet a few times before he finally got the rhythm right. As the elevator closed Jahad cornered Koran, giving him a mean stare. "What you been doing since I been gone, don't lie either?"

"I ain't been doing nothing." Koran replied innocently with a mischievous grin, "Going to school, getting good grades and whatnot."

"So what's this I hear about you wilin'? You think the shit I went to Spofford for was cool? You think having to fight everyday, eating nasty ass food, and having my freedom taken was cool . . . huh?"

Koran looked down at his sneakers, "I wasn't doing it to be cool. When you left I had to take care of mommy like you did."

Koran's response was like a punch to Jahad's stomach. He definitely had to be careful how he went about reaching his goal. "You know, I can't be mad at you for that, but Ma had my homies holding her down. From now on tho' I don't wanna hear about you getting in no shit. I mean that. Now that I got this job I'm a make some moves to get ya'll out the P.J.'s, so cool you lil' ass out; You heard?"

"You coming with us?"

"Not for a while. I gotta stay here so I can get some music stuff poppin' off."

"I wanna stay with you then. I won't get in no trouble, I promise." Koran said with pleading eyes.

"Nah Kay, this ain't no place for you."

Koran screwed up his little face, "I'm telling you now, if you make me leave, I'll start wilin' for real."

"I'll fuck you up too." Jahad grabbed him by his collar.

"So! It won't stop me!" Koran shouted defiantly. "I wanna stay here with you. I told you I won't get in no trouble."

They held each other's glare until the elevator reached the bottom floor, bouting will against will. Jahad was seriously thinking about beating Koran's ass right then and there, but the look in Koran's eyes told him it would be meaningless. Koran's mind was set on staying. He could beat the blood out of him and it wouldn't change a thing. Finally, Jahad blew out a frustrated breath as the elevator door slid open, "I should beat your ass, but we'll see. If mom is cool with it, and you stay your little ass outta trouble, I just might let you stay."

Koran suppressed a grin following Jahad out. He wasn't going nowhere.

School kids were leaving the park in herds as Koran and Jahad crossed the busy avenue. It was an unwritten rule that at the first signs of nightfall the park belonged to the nightlife, despite the drug free zone signs that were posted. Ever since the 60's, the Big Park had been a drug zone and it wasn't about to change unless the government stopped drugs from entering the United States, which was impossible.

Tony, Razor, Cream, Joey, Kwan, and Derrick were sitting on a park bench across from a group of crackheads, who were on the basketball court arguing over a hit when Koran and Jahad walked up. About thirty yards away, Spanish music blared from a boom box where the Puerto Ricans hung out on the handball court, the same handball court where John Copeland was murdered.

"What up Jah?" Razor stood to give Jahad a hug. "Heard you were a nine to five nigga now."

25

Jahad laughed, "That ain't a job, that's some slave shit Duke got me on... What up with you niggas?"

"Ain't shit." Derrick said taking a nickel bag of weed from his North Face coat pocket handing it to Tony who was splitting a White Owl cigar. "We out here scheming on this paper."

"You hustling?" Jahad looked surprised, "I figured you'd be out here robbin' niggas."

Out of the seven friends, Derrick was the most belligerent. Having a fierce temper, his temper always got the best of him, because once mad, he couldn't think. Tony was the thinker, a natural hustler who always thought a situation out before making a move. Unlike Derrick, he tended to stay away from violence, although when push came to shove he could rock with the best of them. Joey and Kwan who were brothers, Joey the oldest by a year, were both jokers, often underestimated because they were always clowning.

When it came time to get busy though, the joking came to a stop and those who underestimated them usually became the butt of their jokes. Cream was the pretty boy, accepted first by the others because he could always provide them with girls, being he had a string of them. On the other hand, when it came to standing up for himself, one of the others usually had to come to his rescue. No matter how many times they tried to teach him how to fight it just wasn't in Cream.

After a while they all accepted that he was a coward, but he was their coward and anybody who messed with him had to answer to them. Razor was the psychopath, often cutting people for simply looking at him, but to his friends he showed nothing but loyalty. Like his name, he kept a razor in his mouth at all times and was more than happy to use it. Jahad was an enigma. He could be as vicious as a hungry lion when it was called for, and at the same time, diplomatic and docile. That's when he didn't let his stubbornness cloud his judgment, which was his only flaw.

"Ayo Jah, let me build with you Sun." Tony stood after rolling the blunt, and began walking a few feet away from the bench.

"Tone, what up with my blunt?" Derrick called out.

"Roll another one. I'm taking this to the face."

"A'ight nigga, but you gon' cop me another bag. Word up!"

Jahad shook his head grinning as he followed Tony. His friends were still the same.

"Jah, what you gon' do man? You serious about this job shit?" Tony asked with a straight face.

Jahad smiled, he was expecting this question. "It ain't 'bout what I'm a do, it's 'bout what we gon' do. Now this is how it's going down. I'm a stay with this job for a few more months to keep my moms from beefin', plus, scrams is paying me a'ight. Until then, I'm a stack my dough . . . how long does it take ya'll to move a pack?"

Tony's face lit up with a smile. "You got something planned don't you nigga? That's the Jah I know. We were wondering if Spofford had turned you into a square nigga."

"Never that. Now how much dough ya'll be seeing?" Jahad asked, all business.

"We all move a pack in like three days. We could do it faster if it wasn't for all these other dudes." Tony looked around, hustlers spread out in the park. "We can't move on 'em tho' because they all hustle for the Coco Twins."

Jahad nodded, thinking, who in the hell are the Coco Twins. "Ya'll keep fucking with them Goya eating muthafuckas until I get my shit together, then we'll do our own thing like before. I ain't feeling how them niggas pimpin' ya'll. I'm surprised you went for it ... anyway, once we get our bellies full we'll get on some different shit." You with me?"

"You know I am. I'm telling you tho', the Coco Twins got shit in a chokehold. They on some shit like if you ain't moving their work, you don't eat."

Jahad's temper flared, "I don't give a fuck what they got in a chokehold. We were born and raised in these damn projects and we gon' eat out here. All we need is start up money for this other shit and they can have this damn park. Until then, we getting some of this cake. So fuck them niggas!"

"A'ight Jah, don't spazz out on me," Tony held out his hands, "you know we with you. What's this other shit you talking 'bout?"

"It's way down the line, but I'm talking 'bout dipping in the music industry. Look at Fat Joe, Jay and the WU, they started right here where we at, the hood. I wrote mad rhymes when I was on lock down at Spofford, enough for everybody in our clique to spit..."

"You ain't the only nigga who can rhyme. Me and Derrick get busy too. We be having ciphers out here every now and then."

"Word! That's what I'm talking 'bout," Jahad said excitedly, "we gon' take the money we make out here and start our own label."

"I'm feelin' that, how long you plan on doing this job shit tho'?"

"Long enough to stack some for my moms, and save a nice chunk, so I can go see my man Rahoul."

"Rahoul?"

"Yeah. Puerto Rican cat I met at Spofford. He put me up on the coke game when we were locked up. Supposedly his brother is doing big things in Harlem. I want us to rock with 500 grams off top, feel me? If ya'll seeing two gee's a piece every three days, together we can see twenty thou' or better a week. You don't gotta tell me either, I know ya'll be trickin' mad paper, but that shit gotta stop. I'm setting up a kitty starting this week. I want each of you to drop in at least a buck fifty a week. That way when I go see Rahoul we can cop crazy coke. Everything will be set up like before with an even split for us all, but keep in mind, until we get this music shit off the ground, we stackin'."

"No doubt. Like I said, we with you."

Jahad hesitated a moment before speaking, "Check it Tone, you ain't gon' be feelin' what I'm 'bout to say, but whatever you and Trice got going on, dead it."

It took a second for Tony to comprehend what Jahad was actually saying, "Dead it? . . . Hold up Jah, I know that's your sister and all, but she's my shorty Sun."

"Was your shorty," Jahad replied coldly, "you my nigga Tone and I love you like a brother, but Trice is my sister. What ya'll got going on will only end up fucking up our friendship."

"How?" Tony asked angrily. "What the hell does me and Trice have to do with our friendship?"

"Because I can never hear about you cheating on her or disrespecting her in any kind of way, for real. So let me rephrase how I said it. Out of the friendship and brotherly love we have for one another, will you fallback from my sister... for me?"

Tony gazed at Jahad long and hard weighing out his love for Latrice, against the love he had for Jahad. He knew exactly what was beneath Jahad's words, knew Jahad wouldn't hesitate to take whatever action he deemed necessary to protect his sister's honor. When John Copeland died, Jahad became the man of the house in every sense. Tony remembered the many fights, and people, Jahad cut and stabbed over Latrice whether she was right or wrong. He also remembered how Jahad always put himself on the line for his crew against any odds, whether they were right or wrong. That thought alone helped sway his decision.

"A'ight Jah, but damn nigga, you act like Trice was just another chick. It was deeper than that Sun."

"Believe it or not Tone, I know she wasn't just another trick out of the respect we have for one another. On the same token, I know we gon' be chasing mad chicks together like old times . . . you remember Tracy from 12A?" Jahad asked grinning.

Tony smiled at the memory of the girl they use to sex together after sneaking off from the rest of their friends. "Do I! Shorty turned our asses out. If I ain't mistaken she still lives on the same floor."

"Word! ...You see what I'm sayin' tho' right. Trice is my blood. How I look going to knock off another chick with you or seeing you spit at another chick, then be all up in Trice face? You know I don't rock like that. If the shoe was on the other foot I would never try to play one of your family members out of respect for you."

Tony nodded, "I feel you Sun."

"Good." Jahad gave Tony a crooked smile, "So what's up, how 'bout we go pay Tracy a visit for old times sake."

"I don't think you wanna do that Sun. Tracy be turning more tricks than a magician. She strung out on that shit."

"Damn, so much for that fantasy... what's been up with Koran? Moms said he been wilin'."

"That lil' nigga is a mess. We use to have to chase his little ass out the park. He was out here selling feens candle wax." Tony laughed shaking his head, "He's smart as hell tho'. He took our pick-pocketing scheme to a whole nother level, word up. I caught him one day standing out in front of the Bodega just watching traffic, when I was coming out the chicken spot. So I watch his little ass 'cause I see it on his face that he's up to some bullshit. A few minutes later this white dude comes through, pushin' a big body Benz. Koran runs in the street, bumps the side of the car, then fall out like he's fucked up. The white dude stops to see what's up and Koran is lying there like he's fucked up. I know he was frontin' tho. To make a long story short, he got dude out $900.00. When he gets the money in his hand the lil' nigga hops up and starts skippin' down the street. A week later, I catch his ass in the same spot watching traffic, but I ran him home. That's a funny lil' dude. One thing I can say about him tho', he be on some dolo shit. Kay don't fuck with nobody."

"I gotta get his ass outta these projects before he get caught up in some shit." Jahad cut his eyes at Koran who was play boxing with Razor. Then again maybe that wasn't the answer either he thought. His threat to act up if he was forced to leave wasn't a threat at all. It was a promise.

~~~~

Later that night before going to bed, Jahad dug Janet's number from his jean pocket with a silly grin on his face. Through out the day, fragments of their encounter flashed through his mind; her mischievous smile and sexy green eyes. Most of all her silky voice that echoed in his ears like a song stuck on repeat. After dialing her number he propped himself up against the bed board, then closed his eyes imagining her face as the phone rung.

"Hello?"

"Is this Miss Jackson?"

Janet giggled, "Maybe. Is this Mr. Working man?"

"And you know it Ma. What you doing?"

"Sitting here doing my nails. I was wondering if you were gonna call."

"That's something you never had to wonder about. You too pretty for me to play hard to get."

"What if I played hard to get?"

"Then I'd have to go hard, 'cause I'm a get you, believe that?"

"O-Yeah? What makes you so sure?"

"If I told you, you'd probably take me as being arrogant."

"How about you try me and let me judge for myself."

"A'ight. It's because I'm me... I'm Jah."

Janet laughed, "And who's Jah?"

"That's something you'll have to find out for yourself. Telling you will take all the fun outta it."

"UM... I see you're on top of your game."

"No doubt, and I play rough. Now, can I see you tomorrow?"

"Sure, but will you have enough energy? If you be working as hard as you claim, then you may be too tired."

"Oh, it wasn't a game Ma, but one look at you had me feeling like I could work another ten hours without a break."

Janet blushed; Jahad was saying all the right things. "Since you put it like that, when you wanna see me?"

"Whenever I get off work. It'll probably be around four or five."

"Okay, it's a date... where you work at anyway Mr. Working man?"

"This furniture moving company over on Calhoun Ave, and you?"

"I'm a beautician."

"Oh word. So that's how you be looking all fly. I thought it came naturally."

"It is natural," Janet snapped, "don't get it twisted."

Jahad laughed, "Well pardon me Ma. I would never want to get you twisted. Not in that sense anyway."

"And what sense would you be talking about?"

"You really want me to go there?" Jahad asked with a smile in his voice.

"Nah, Nah," Janet giggled, "I see where your mind is at."

"Right now my mind is on you with your pretty self."

She blushed again, "Flattery will get you everywhere."

"Really? Well tomorrow be prepared to be flattered and some."

"I hear you."

"Word up. If I could see you now you'd see."

"You can see me. I'm only a skip and a hop from you."

Within seconds Jahad grew hard, "Don't play with me Ma."

"Playing is for kids, and I'm twenty years old. But before you get the wrong idea, when I said see me, I meant just that. You gets no nooky, maybe a few smooches."

Jahad smiled from ear to ear, "I'm on my way then. I ain't had a good smooch in a while. Where you at?"

"9-B. If you hurry I'll have some cocoa waiting for you."

"Say no more," Jahad hung up, jumped out of the bed and grabbed his jeans tugging them on as fast as he could, then walked to his dresser which was in between his and Koran's bed, and slapped on a dab of cologne.

"Where you going?" Koran asked raising his head before Jahad could make it out the door, "I thought you had to work tomorrow."

"Let me worry about that. You suppose to be sleep anyway."

"Koran squinted his eyes, "You going to get some pussy ain't you?" He asked jumping from the bed pulling his pajama top over his head. "I wanna go."

Jahad burst out laughing, "Nigga if you don't get your lil' ass back in bed. What you know about pussy anyway?"

"Nothing, that's why I wanna go, maybe I can learn something."

"I tell you what, right now just worry about keeping your grades up. I'll see what I can do 'bout getting you some pussy."

"Word!"

"Yeah, word... Nigga you don't even have no hair around your little shit, talking 'bout some pussy."

"Uh-huh," Koran made a motion to pull his pajama's down.

"Whoa! I don't wanna see your shit. Crazy ass dude." Jahad laughed as he walked out. Koran was definitely a mess.

"Jahad!" Michelle called out when he tried to slip past her room.

Caught, he backed up and stood in her doorway, "What's up Ma?"

"You know its eleven thirty. Where you going?"

"I'm just going out for a little while."

Michelle frowned, "Don't tell me you gave up the job already?"

"Nah Ma. I'm going to work in the morning, so don't stress that. Right now I gotta go check for this shorty I met earlier. If I'm lucky I won't be back tonight."

Michelle rolled her eyes, "If you do stay the night, she must not be worth nothing."

"Oh, she said I wasn't getting no nooky, but you can best believe I'm a try to change her mind. You gotta think about it Ma. I been gone three years, that's a lotta pressure.

"Boy, get your butt out of here." Michelle laughed.

CHAPTER 4

Things were going well. Jahad debated on taking the stairs after waiting five minutes for the elevator. Finally just as he was about to walk off, the elevator arrived and a little old lady stepped out carrying two large grocery bags looking as if they were weighing her down. She was dressed in a light blue polyester dress, a white hat, and a brown wool overcoat. Her steel gray hair was pulled into a tight bow stretching some of the wrinkles from her face. She wore thick bifocals that magnified her brown eyes to the size of Kennedy fifty-cent pieces.

"Mrs. Harris!" Jahad said smiling. Emma Harris was his old babysitter and played the role of his grandmother since the day he was born.

Emma looked at him a moment, slightly confused until she recognized who he was, "Sweet Jesus! Jahad is that you?"

Jahad couldn't help from feeling like a kid again. "Yeah, it's me Mrs. Harris."

"Look at you. You done got so big. C'mere boy and give me a hug."

"Let me help you get these bags to your apartment first. What you doing out this time of night anyway?" He took her bags and led her to her apartment, which was only three doors away from the elevator, and three doors down from his own apartment.

"I'm coming from church. They helped me with my groceries this week."

"Helped you with your groceries?" Jahad asked frowning as they reached her door. "What, you doing bad Mrs. Harris?"

"It gets rough from time to time, but Jesus makes sure I'm taken care of." She replied fumbling through her keys until she found the right one.

Jahad didn't like the idea of Emma having to depend on other people for groceries, "I'm home now, so whenever you need something you let me know a'ight. In fact," he went in his pockets and gave her forty dollars, "I'll bring you some more tomorrow when I get off work. You shouldn't be carrying these heavy bags either. It's nice and all for your church to buy your groceries, buy they could a had somebody help you with 'em. From now on when you need a grocery run, let me or Koran know, okay?"

Emma nodded with tears on the brim of her eyes. "Thank you baby. You were always a good boy, just made some bad decisions. Now you listen to me, don't let them streets have you Jahad. Your father wanted better for you. You have a good head on your shoulder, use it baby."

"I plan to do just that Mrs. Harris. I gotta go now. Gotta date waiting on me. You have a good night, a'ight." He kissed her on the cheek then shot out the door before she could keep him any longer. He had some hot chocolate waiting and hopefully something else hot.

~~~~

The street lights cast a dull grayish light over the projects when Jahad stepped out of his building into the bitter cold night. It was a brisk twenty-five degrees out, but felt more like twenty-five below with the wind chill factor. He bunched his collar up around his neck, and then stuck his hands deep in his pants pockets, trying to shield his bare skin from the freezing wind that seemed to seep down to his bones. Unbelievably, across the street in the park, crackheads and hustlers moved about like it was spring. Drug dealers dressed in North Face goose feathered coats, thick jeans, and Timberland boots. Crackheads dressed in layers of clothes, unconcerned with how they looked, as long as they got their crack and were warm.

With the cold biting into his skin, Jahad picked up his pace to a light jog and made it to Janet's building in under thirty seconds. Once she buzzed him in, he blew hot breath through his hands to restore the feeling on his way to the elevator. A few minutes later the door slid open and he stood face to face with a tall slim Puerto Rican who looked as if he could be a model. Black wavy hair hung to his shoulders like a woman's, slanted green eyes set back in his oval shaped face, sharp and alert, a neatly trimmed five o'clock shadowed beard sketched his sharp jaw line, and he had a long sharp nose that stopped right above his rosy red lips. His attire was straight out of a

GQ magazine. Brown lizard skin boots, thick brown wool pants, and a full-length brown mink coat with a fur hood.

"What up homey?" Jahad spoke moving past to get on the elevator.

The Puerto Rican looked Jahad up and down arrogantly, like he was dirt, then strutted off. Jahad's face instantly screwed up, as old Spofford thoughts filled his head. The mink coat and lizard skin boots would look good on him. "You got away pretty boy. If I catch you again tho'..." He mumbled to himself with a sneer.

Turning his mind back to Janet, butterflies fluttered in his stomach thinking of what might happen. What he prayed would happen, despite her remark about getting no nooky. It had been three years, three long years, and the thought of what he could do to her curvy sensuous body made him so excited his third leg attempted to walk. When he made it to her door he knocked, then stuffed his hands in his pockets to keep from fidgeting, feeling almost like a virgin again. A few minutes later Janet opened the door with a scowl on her face until she saw it was Jahad.

"Hi there working man. I was about to give up on you." She smiled holding the door open for him.

Jahad made no motion to move, letting his eyes wander from her face down to her pretty toes. The green silk nightgown she wore that matched her eyes clung to her body like a wet t-shirt. It only took a matter of seconds for the fantasy of peeling the nightgown off to play through his mind.

Janet gave him a probing look, glanced down at the huge bulge in his jeans, and shook her head, "Stop it because it's not going down like that. Now come in and have your cocoa." She turned adding an extra twist to her hips, knowing he was watching.

The apartment smelled of jasmine, as he followed her into the kitchen, small but tidy. A small dining table with a cloth flower design covering, sat across from the stove, matching the colorful flower designed wallpaper. Janet pulled out a chair for him to sit, then went to the stove and poured two steaming mugs of hot chocolate. Jahad watched, enchanted, while she placed a mug in front of him with only one thought in mind. Sex!

"Don't get quiet on me now Mr. Flattery," she said sitting across from him.

"You'll make any nigga speechless gorgeous."

Janet laughed, "Okay, I see you're back on track."

"If you only knew what I really wanna get on," Jahad held her eyes taking a sip of his cocoa.

"I won't even follow up on that because I see where your mind is at," Janet replied giving him a sexy smile. Her mind was there too, every since seeing the bulge in his jeans, if he played his cards right he would get some nooky and a little something extra.

"I'm sayin', you'd be horny as hell too if you went without sex for three years. That's why I'm looking forward to those smooches. They might get me a little closer to what I need in my life."

"Three years!" Shocked, Janet sat her mug down. "Where you been, a monastery?"

"Hell nah, I was biddin'."

"Bidding? You mean you were locked up?"

"Yeah, I just touched yesterday. My moms set me up with a job and whatnot."

"What you do?"

"Don't stress that. I ain't no rapist."

"Never said you were. I'd still like to know."

Jahad exhaled an audible sigh. He didn't like speaking about his past, "I got knocked for a smash and grab and rockin' a cop when I was fifteen."

Janet took time to take a sip of her cocoa, then said something that turned the night sour, "Don't take this personal, but I don't usually deal with criminals."

Jahad held up his hand, "Whoa Ma. How you gon' come off on me like that? You don't even know me."

"I mean you were locked up, right? And to get locked up you had to commit a crime. But anyway, is it true about what they say happens in there?"

Jahad let the insult go, well, his third leg let it go not wanting to mess up the chance to get some exercise. "What you talking 'bout Janet?"

"You know, about the guys... you know. I don't want to say it."

Confusion was written on his face until he realized what she was getting at. In an instant, his calm expression was gone, replaced with a twisted sneer, "You trying to say I'm a faggot or something? What the fuck you smokin'!"

"I was..."

"Save that shit man," he stood and grabbed his coat, "I'm a bounce before I say some really disrespectful shit 'cause you got me all fucked up," he walked off, shrugging on his coat, muttering curses under his breath.

Just as he opened the door, Janet grabbed him by his shoulder, "Wait a minute Jah, I didn't mean for you to take it personal."

Jahad stared at her long and hard, then without saying a word, pulled her in his arms and kissed her roughly. At first she protested, pushing hard against his chest until he slipped his tongue in her mouth. All at once, her body melted against his as their tongues intertwined like vines. Heat shot through her loins, causing her to grow wet feeling his huge erection pressing into her lower stomach. Slowly she moved her hands over his chest, down to his crotch, and gripped his manhood.

"Tell me it's real," she said in a husky voice.

Jahad wasted no time whipping out his ten inch slightly crooked python, "I can show you better than I can tell you."

Janet gasped, "Damn boy! You..."

He cut her off with another kiss, while his exposed manhood brushed up against her thigh. Janet took hold of him, using his pre-cum to lubricate his plum sized head with her thumb in slow circles. The feeling made him suck in a deep breath, "You better chill Ma before I bus' off in your hand. I told you it's been three years so it won't take much."

Janet continued to stroke him while moving his hand between her legs so he could feel her heat, "I wanna see it."

Jahad almost came when he palmed her moist mound. Lifting her nightgown, he slid a hand into her panties and used his middle finger to penetrate her thick hairy lips, which seemed to suck his finger in. "Damn Ma, you dripping down there." He whispered against her ear, easing his finger in and out then added his index finger pushing, deep inside her. Janet moved bucking her hips and spreading her legs wider so he could go deeper while speeding up the rhythm with her hand, stroking the length of him. Jahad positioned his hips to her hand, riding the feeling until his eyes rolled back in his head and his knees buckled.

"Oh Shit Ma!" He yelled blasting her hand and the front of her nightgown with his seed.

Janet looked at him with lust glistening in her eyes, "You were loaded weren't you? Let's get you hard again so we can do this the right way."

Jahad smirked and removed his hand from her panties, wiping his sticky fingers on her nightgown, and then stuffed his limp dick in his jeans. "If I ain't mistaken, you don't fuck with criminals. Thanks for the nut tho', and don't take it personal." he said opening the apartment door.

"Jah, I..."

The door slammed in her face before she could finish the sentence. She stood stunned, mouth wide open, with cum dripping through her fingers. Never had she felt so humiliated in her life. Who in the hell was he to just leave her like that she thought. Anger pushed her to go after him. As she reached for the doorknob she realized that her hand was still full of cum and shook with fury.

"That muthafucka!" She screamed rushing off to the bathroom.

~~~~

The next morning, Michelle was sitting at the kitchen table, drinking a cup of coffee when Jahad walked in still half sleep. Sleep didn't come easy the night before, not with Janet crossing his mind every few minutes. He even had a dream about her, one that woke him in the middle of the night, and made him have to change his sheets.

"Well lover boy, I guess you didn't get lucky last night." Michelle said with an impish grin.

"Huh?" Jahad yawned then cracked a crooked smile, "I got lucky; she didn't."

"What you mean?"

"Sorry Mommy. I don't kiss and tell."

"Um huh."

On his way to work, as the cab maneuvered its way through the congested morning traffic, Jahad stared out the window, still unable to get Janet off his mind. Who in the hell did she think she was to judge him? Criminal! Damn right he was a criminal, would be one all over again before he accomplished his goals. He figured she wanted a nine to five dude who brought his paycheck home to her every week. Well, he wasn't that dude and wasn't about to be that dude, just so he could please her. Then again, he did want to please her, only in a different way. But, that was a dead issue now. Snickering, he thought of how she looked when he let off in her hand, and told her he was leaving. She didn't deal with criminals but she sure knew how to get a criminal off.

Twenty-five minutes later, the cab dropped him off in front of Joe's moving company. Joe was behind the counter when he walked in, with a tall light skin dude. He looked to be around Jahad's age, maybe a couple of years older. He wore his curly black hair in a tapered Afro, had small wide set brown eyes, a blunt wide nose, and a square chin with a dimple in the middle. His face was set in a scowl, as he looked Jahad up and down, sizing him up. Jahad did the same, his mind state automatically flashing back to his time spent at Spofford. This is how it usually happened before fists were thrown.

"What up?" The slim light skin guy asked more in the form of a challenge, stepping from behind the counter.

Jahad bunched up his fist, "What up with you nigga? Something wrong with your fuckin' eyes or something?"

"Hold up! Wait a damn minute," Joe shouted from behind the counter to stand between them, "Eric, this is my new worker Jahad I was telling you about. Jahad this is my nephew Eric, the help you asked about. He's recently out of jail too, so I guess this is a male bonding thing you two have going on, but it won't happen in here." Joe said firmly, looking from Jahad to Eric, "At the end of the day when we finish working, I won't give a damn if ya'll beat each others brains out, but for now we have a lot of shit to do. If we can finish by six, I'll throw in a little something extra. Now let's get the hell out of here. Time is money!"

Jahad and Eric held each other's scowl a second longer before following Joe to the storage area. The reason behind the friction was simple; they were too much alike and shared some of the same experiences. Whereas Jahad served three years at Spofford, Eric had served close to three years at Rikers Island for attempted murder. Luckily, the charges were dropped or he'd be in Green Haven doing a three to five year sentence. Also, just as Jahad had to fight everyday, Eric had to fight and carry a razor everywhere he went. The only difference between the two was their looks and ages. Eric was three years older.

"Eric, you ride with Jahad so ya'll can get better acquainted," Joe said as he approached his van, "and I'll tell you like I told Jahad, don't be fucking with these people's shit."

Eric looked at Jahad and arched his eyebrow questionably,

receiving a shrug as Jahad hopped into the driver's seat.

"Where you from?" Eric asked when Jahad turned on the Major Deegan, following Joe's maniac driving.

Jahad cut his eyes at Eric, "Story Avenue; Monroe Projects. Where you rest at?"

"Oh word. I'm from Bronxdale; right up the block from you... Uncle Joe said you did a bid. Where were you, up north?"

"I ain't been up north, I did a juvey bid at Spofford. You been up north?"

Up north was the term used for New York's state prisons.

"Nah. Them crackers kept me on the Island for two and a half years." Eric answered, then his mouth curved into a sly grin, "When you walked in the shop you looked at me like you could fuck me up or something. What up with that?"

"Nah, it wasn't like that. You gave me an ice grill, so I gave it back. I did think I was gon' have to tap your chin tho'."

"You said that like it would be easy."

"I'm sayin', I ain't one to talk about my knuckle game. If you feel up to it tho', after work we can go a round or two in the alley. Whoever loses gotta cop the 40's and trees. What up, you with it?" Jahad asked with a crooked smile.

Eric laughed, "Hell yeah I'm with it. Free weed and beer, shit, I can't pass that up."

"Free huh? We'll see 'bout that."

With the ice broken, the similarities between the two became evident. They both had a deep love for Hip-Hop, dreams of making it out the hood, and knew that working for Joe wasn't going to get it. He paid good, but the strenuous work would have them broken down by the time they turned thirty. It was when Eric told Jahad how he wanted to get into the music industry that Jahad really started liking him. Jahad went on to tell Eric his plans of making money to start his own record label.

"Oh Word!" Eric said excitedly, "If you lookin' for a hot MC, I'm that nigga."

"Psssst. You can't rhyme nigga," Jahad taunted.

"Who can't rhyme? Why you think I was on the Island for? I was battling this nigga, chewing his ass to pieces and dude took it personal, so I had to spark his ass for real... I'm telling you Sun, I'm that nigga."

"Let me hear something then, since you that nigga."

Eric's face lit up with a silly grin, "A'ight. Check it out, this the rhyme that got me locked up... Ayo, your block is my block/ And your coke is my rocks/ And your dough is my knot/ And so forth and whatnot/ And your wife is my chick/ She sucks on my dick/ I be pushin' your whip/ And loungin' in your shit/ I fuck in your bed, different positions/ I throw up her legs without your permission/ I eat in your kitchen/ Drink out your glasses/ Do all this shit and hell no I ain't askin'/ 'Cause your weed is my weed/ I'll smoke all your trees/ And drink all you Kris/ Me and your bitch/ Your connect is my connect/ And your gun is my Tec/ And your rings and your chain, I rock on my neck..."

"Oh shit Sun, that shit is blazin'! I see why scrams took it personal," Jahad laughed slapping the dashboard. "Ayo, word up, I'm a draw up the contract for your ass now."

"I told you nigga, I'm bound to blow. You ain't heard shit yet tho', I got anthems. So what's up?"

"You know what's up. You keep writing rhymes and I'm a make sure we get our foot in the door. Let me hear something else."

Throughout the course of the day, Eric and Jahad talked nothing but Hip-Hop. Their fervor even affected Joe, who was a big fan of Cool Hurk, Grandmaster Flash, the Furious Five, Rakim, and to their surprise, Biggie Smalls. By the time they made their last delivery, they had named almost every rapper who had ever made a record and all the local legends that never made it.

After work, once Joe paid them adding an extra hundred dollars, being they finished at five 'clock, Jahad made his way behind the counter to use the phone when Eric tapped him on the shoulder grinning.

"You forgot about our bet didn't you, or are you too tired to take this ass whipping?"

Jahad laughed, "Feelin' yourself, huh? I'm a try not to break your jaw so you can keep practicing your flow. C'mon."

In the alley, Joe addressed them both where he leaned against the building, "I don't care which one of you gets knocked out, but you both better have your asses here in the morning. Matter of fact, I'll time it. Ya'll got two minutes to do whatever ya'll gon' do and it's over." Joe turned to Jahad, "I ain't trying to scare you young buck, but my nephew ain't no slouch. He might knock your ass out."

"Oh word? Since you put it like that, I got $300 on myself. If I'm on my ass at the end of two minutes, the dough is yours. If your nephew here is on his ass I want $300 and a day off with pay."

"Wait a minute. If he do knock you on your ass, I want $300 and a free day of work."

"Bet." Jahad said glancing at Eric, "I hate to do it to you homey."

"You did it to yourself... Uncle Joe, I want half of that dough." Eric put up his guard leading with his left. Jahad did the same but kept his hand in constant motion, patting his arms and chest. "What the fuck you think you doing, pop locking? We suppose to be boxing nigga."

"I'm a box your ass a'ight. C'mon." Jahad urged with a wicked grin.

Eric moved in, throwing five rapid short jabs followed by a right hook that Jahad slipped easily while pivoting, until he stood behind Eric.

"Over here homey." Jahad tapped Eric on the back of his head, "What, you trying to make this easy for me?"

Eric turned astonished, "How..."

Jahad laughed, nodding his head, "Yeah, you done stepped in some shit... Joe, how much time we got left?"

"Forty five seconds!" Joe called out, praying Eric would still be standing.

"You heard that, right? You got about forty seconds before I lay your ass down." Jahad said doing the Ali shuffle.

"Don't speak about it, be about it." Eric faked a left and launched a mean overhand right.

To Eric and Joe's amazement, Jahad caught the punch between his right shoulder with his left hand and kissed Eric's fist. Caught up in the move, Eric paid no attention to the right upper cut Jahad shot up that connected with his chin snapping his head back. Jahad was in the motion of following up with a left hook, but pulled the punch short when he saw that Eric was already on his way to the concrete.

"Goddamn!" Joe shouted, "Boy what was that shit? That wasn't no regular damn boxing."

"Nah, a little something I picked up at Spofford."

Once he got himself together, Eric stood and shook Jahad's hand, "You got your shit off. I want a rematch tho', as soon as you teach me how to do that shit."

"No doubt, I'll put you on," Jahad replied, turning to Joe, "Let me get my money before I knock your ass out."

"Hey, I don't want no problems," Joe smiled holding up his hands then pulled a wad of money from his pocket and peeled off three one hundred dollar bills, "Eric get a good night's sleep, cause I'm a work the hell out of you tomorrow."

"A'ight Uncle Joe, just because Jah knocked me down, don't mean you can."

"Don't underestimate the old man, I ain't fucking with you though... Tell you what, since I worked the hell out of you today, and you got your ass beat, you can have tomorrow off too. I'll get one of my lazy ass sons to help me tomorrow. Thursday morning, I want both ya'll here at eight o'clock. Now get the hell out of here.

"Ayo Eric, c'mon and bungee with me so I can plug you in with my mans. It's a weed spot around my way too."

Eric laughed, "A'ight nigga. I'm serious about you teaching me that 52 shit tho'; I always heard niggas talk about it, but that was the first time I seen it done." He rubbed his chin.

"A nigga from Brooklyn taught me, well, I taught myself after he kept fucking me up. I bodied his ass once I got it down pat."

Eric's eyes grew wide, "Word!"

"Word up," Jahad nodded "using the same shit he used on me. Fucked around and did almost two years in the Bing behind that shit. I'll show you tho'. It ain't hard once you get the hang of it. Sorta like free styling, only you free style with your hands, but always keep 'em up so you can block your face."

Eric nodded, "Yeah, I wanna learn that shit. I'm a body me a muthafucka' with the knuckle game."

CHAPTER 5

Story Avenue was lit up by traffic and street lights when the cab dropped Eric and Jahad off in front of his building. Instead of going to his apartment, Jahad led Eric across the street into the park where Tony and the crew were sitting around their usual park bench hustling. The park was crowded with people selling drugs, smoking drugs, or either looking for drugs while rap music came from someone's radio in the distance.

Tony stood as they approached and gave Jahad a thug's hug, "What up?"

"Ain't shit, just got my ass off work... this is my man Eric," Jahad nodded towards Eric, who's attention was on a group of young project chicks walking through, "Eric!"

"Yo, what up?" He turned, grinning, "Ayo, them bitches got some juicy asses."

Jahad laughed, "Let me find out you a sucka for love ass nigga... these my mans Tone, Razor, Derrick, Joey, Kwan...where's Cream?"

"Probably out fuckin' something," Tony said shaking Eric's hand. "What's up Sun?"

"I'm good Tone," Eric went on to shake hands with the rest of the crew.

"Me and the Homey work together. Sun is sick with the flow too," Jahad patted Eric on the back, "this is the next Jay right here."

"Word, Sun can spit?" Shit, let's have a session then. We need some more trees to'." Derrick said, reaching in his pocket for some money.

"I got it Dee," Eric pulled out his money and counted off fifty dollars, "c'mon, let's troop it to the weed spot."

"Nah, chill Sun," Tony looked over at a crackhead who was over by the monkey bars, with his head down, searching for a hit. "Ayo Luck! Make a run to the weed spot for me, I'll bless you when you get back."

The crackhead quickly ran over.

"Ayo, don't try no slick shit Luck. We live in the same building, so I'll see your ass eventually," Tony motioned for Eric to give the crackhead the money.

"I worked my ass off for that dough, so if you fake a move, I'm a fuck you up personally." Eric said before handing over the money.

"I put the Homey up on our money scheme," Jahad said addressing his crew once the crackhead left, "I was dead ass serious when I said we signing him. Ayo, Eric, spit some of that hot shit for 'em."

On cue, Razor started beating on the table while Joey and Kwan harmonized a Hip-Hop melody.

"Ayo, Ayo, Ayo," Eric said catching the beat, "I buy niggas like slave traders to spray haters/ Niggas claimin' they players, but my game's greater/ I never trick on a slut, yo what the fuck/ I keep a dime in my truck/ don't do the ducks/ With pussy good like fruit loops, a good screw/ I ain't spend no cash, I'm a pimp duke/ My bitches call me the shit just like I'm do-do/ But I smell like roses/ My neck and wrist is frozen/ I be pimpin' my hoe's man/ And movin' them O's five hundred a pop/ You coppin' a lot the prices might drop/ You never know, so get your weight up, your outta state up and you just might blow/ And when I flow, it's sorta like a money machine cause every time I spit it equals dough..."

Tony cut in picking up the rhyme, "I see so much paper dog my eyes are green/ Started out on fifth avenue snatchin' wallets and chains/ followed up in the park selling dimes to feens/ I smartened up, stopped trickin', started stackin' my cream/ then my man came home, he rebuilt the team/ He said Tone just watch we gon' do our thing/ And not long after that we started slingin' them things/ No more digital scales, we using triple beams/ Now all them block niggas, yo, they cop from me/ So get your cake up it's twenty a key/ Break it down and make fifty/ Maybe a little more, my coke is pure/ On the whip up, you get your shit off/ My coke is raw..."

Derrick came in next with his aggressive flow, "You don't gotta like me, you gon' respect me tho'/ Or expect it when I pimp smack you like a hoe/ Put my finger in your face, all up in your nose/ Let you know I ain't the one, you fuckin' stupid/ I don't do a lot of talkin' I just do it/ I'm only talkin' now because I'm makin' music/ Don't give a fuck about your man's or who you move with/ them nigga's bitches and you know they ain't gon' do shit/ Don't really care, if you go and find a new clique/ 'Cause like I said before them niggas ain't gon' do shit/ I keep the gat Duke and I keep two clips..."

To everyone's surprise, Jahad grabbed the beat, "Ayo, I plan shit for hours/ Study 48 laws of Power/ Then watch me blow niggas like the Twin Towers/ I'm crazy 'noid, keep the biscuit like I'm mixing flour/ Hardly smile 'cause the hood I'm from is crazy sour/ I know you know about them cold nights and lonely days/ On the Ave. serving feens like you fuckin' slaves/ Don't want a job, you'll be hustling 'till you in a grave/ But I'm a rob you 'cause it's in my fuckin' DNA..."

"Oh shit! Jah, you been holdin' out on niggas!" Razor said excitedly, stopping the beat, "Word up Sun, that's that bullshit."

Jahad laughed, "I do a little something; keep that beat going tho'."

As the rap session continued, people from all over the park crowded around in a massive circle. Soon it turned into a mini concert. Every few minutes a new rapper would break through the crowd, set on showing his skills. The drug dealing, stick-ups, and everything else that usually went on was forgotten as the essence of Hip-Hop took hold of the crowd, their energy radiating like heat waves. The rappers fed off this energy, soaked it up like a sponge, then gave it right back to the crowd with hot bars and slick metaphors.

Three hours later, after close to twenty nickel bags of weed were smoked, the session finally broke up. Razor's skin on his right hand was raw from beating so long, but he was still willing to keep the beat going. The session was just that hot. Eric stole the show. His animation, versatility, and delivery was live enough to raise the dead, plus he could freestyle at will. When Jahad looked at him, not only did he see a friend, he saw dollar signs. Once they got their feet in the door, Eric was the ticket to take them straight to the top.

~~~~

Once everybody went their separate ways, Jahad walked to his building still high and keyed up from the rap session. His thoughts were filled with fantasies of his record label: Money Getting Records or Black Market Music or …it all came to a halt when he keyed himself in and saw Janet posted up by the elevator, scowl on her pretty face, arms folded tightly across her chest. She wore a pink sweater, tight black Polo jeans, and a pair of pink Timbalands, with her honey blonde hair pulled back into a ponytail. The second she saw Jahad she pushed herself off the wall, her green eyes blazing with anger.

"You self-centered bastard! You don't do no corny shit like that to me. You know how many niggas be begging for this pussy?" She spat stepping in front of him.

Jahad kept his face impassive, as if he didn't hear her and side stepped towards the elevator. He wasn't use to confrontations unless fists were thrown, and he wasn't about to hit her. Deep down he wanted to have a repeat of last night. On the same token, he wanted to slap the shit out of her for suggesting that he was gay.

"Don't ignore me muthafucka," Janet spun him around by his shoulder, "Who in the hell do you think you are!?"

Jahad's patience evaporated, she just wouldn't leave him alone, "I'm Jah bitch, that's who in the fuck I am!" He yelled inches from her face, "The same nigga who got up in the middle of the fuckin' night to come see your stuck up ass, only to be fuckin' insulted! Yeah, I did three years in jail, so fuckin' what. I did it to feed my damn family and I'll do it again if I have too. You or none of the other muthafuckas who think like you gon' make sure my family eats. So fuck your opinion and fuck you!"

With that, he turned and walked off towards the staircase, leaving Janet lost for words. A few minutes later he exited the staircase on his floor, out of breath from running up ten flights of stairs and pissed off for still having Janet on his mind. He didn't care about the guys who begged for her pussy. He wasn't about to be one of them, although the comment struck a nerve. He'd see what she had to say when he was CEO of his own record label he thought as he stopped and knocked on Emma's door. At the moment she would be the perfect distraction to help take his mind of Janet.

"Hold on, hold on. Ole Emma is coming." She called out. A few seconds passed before she opened the door wearing a white apron over a gray cotton dress. In her hands was a pan of oatmeal cookies, straight out the oven. "Hey baby. I know you ain't just getting off work?" She asked looking at his dirty clothes.

Jahad thought he caught a whiff of marijuana mixed in with the cookie aroma, but was too embarrassed to ask if she was getting high, "Nah Mrs. Harris, I came by to drop off this dough. You a'ight with groceries?"

"Yes baby, and I don't need any money. I have everything I need for now."

"You can never have enough money." He said digging in his pocket, just as Janet bent the corner after stepping off the elevator.

"Jahad, can I speak with you please?" She asked meekly.

Emma and Jahad turned their heads in her direction. Emma giving her a warm smile, "How you doing young lady? I'm Mrs. Harris, and Jahad ain't going nowhere until he comes in and have some of these cookies, so you may as well come in too."

Jahad didn't even bother to glance at Janet as he followed Emma inside. He said all he had to say and wasn't in the mood for arguing. She could save that drama for one of the guys who begged for her pussy.

In the kitchen, Emma pulled out two chairs for them to sit, then went to the refrigerator and took out a gallon of milk. Janet gave Jahad an inquiring look, smelling the strong odor of marijuana, but he ignored her.

"Jahad, I know you like ice in your milk. How about you young lady... What's your name baby?" Emma asked over her shoulder while taking an ice tray from the freezer.

"Janet, but I'm not in the mood for cookies Mrs. Harris. Thanks anyway."

"Oh, nonsense. There's no such thing as being in the mood for cookies. Now do you want ice or not?"

Janet giggled, "Since you put it that way, yes ma'am. I'd like some ice."

"That's more like it." Emma smiled as she poured two glasses of milk. After placing the milk and a platter of cookies on the table, she pulled a chair out for herself and sat beside Jahad taking hold of his hand. "How was your day baby?"

"It was A'ight. I worked my ass... butt off. Everything was good after I got off, then I bumped into this certain person," Jahad cut his eye at Janet, "who approached me with a bunch of bullsh-... nonsense after calling me a criminal and suggesting that I was a homo."

Emma shot Janet a scowl, "Well whoever this person is, must not know you too well."

"See, we on the same page Mrs. Harris." He kissed Emma on the cheek, and then gave Janet a smug grin.

"That's why I came up here, to apologize. I'm woman enough to admit when I'm wrong."

Emma looked from Janet to Jahad, enjoying her role as a peacemaker, "Now you see there Jahad, that's a lady for you. You don't see many these days. Being the man you are I know you'll accept her apology."

Jahad mumbled something under his breath.

"What you say baby?" Emma asked just as her phone rang. "Ya'll go 'head and finish the cookies, I'll be back in a few minutes."

Once she walked out they sat in an uncomfortable silence. Janet staring at Jahad, Jahad keeping his attention on the cookies he kept stuffing in his mouth. He finally broke the silence when there were no more cookies to eat. "So you came to apologize, huh?"

"Yes, I was way out of line; I didn't expect you to take what I said the way you did though."

"How else was I supposed to take it? That criminal shit, I let slide, but a homo? C'mon Ma, the only thing funny about me are my jokes."

"I never said you were gay."

"You were hinting at it tho'!" Jahad snapped. Two words he refused to be called were a snitch and gay.

"And I'm sorry," Janet replied calmly, "You can't accept my apology?"

He studied her a second before grinning, "If you weren't so pretty, no. How 'bout we start over... my name is Jah and you are?

A smile lit up Janet's face, "To you it's Miss Jackson."

"Oh word? Does that mean we gon' get nasty?"

"Come back to my apartment and you'll see."

Jahad placed two fifty-dollar bills under the cookie platter, then grabbed her hand, "You don't have to ask me twice. C'mon, lets blow this joint before Mrs. Harris comes back and hold our ears hostage."

Emma was on the telephone talking to someone about a church convention and took no notice when they crept by the living room. Jahad closed the door softly, leaving out and headed towards his apartment.

"Where we going? The elevator is the other way."

"I can't go to your crib all dusty and shit. I gotta wash my ass and change clothes. I ain't checked in with my mom's either."

"Oh. How about you grab some clothes so we can take a shower

49

together at my place?" She asked with a seductive smile as he opened his apartment door.

"You sure do know how to apologize. Give me a second to grab my gear."

Before he could close the door, Michelle and Latrice came rushing up the hallway towards him. Michelle smothered him with a hug, "Boy where you been? I called every last hospital and precinct in the city looking for you."

Jahad shook his head and glanced at Janet, "My moms thinks I'm a criminal too."

"What you do Jah?" Latrice asked frowning stepping in front of Michelle.

"What you talking 'bout Trice? I ain't done nothing."

"Why is Tony saying he can't be with me no more then?"

"I don't know. Maybe he's tired of you rockin' that weave," Jahad laughed, but Latrice didn't find his joke funny. She swung a wild right at his face that he caught with his left hand and gave her a shove backwards, "You been drinking or something? Ma, you better get her?" He said when she tried to rush him again.

Michelle quickly stepped between them, "Latrice Copeland, if you don't stop! What's wrong with you girl?"

Latrice glared at Jahad hostilely, "I know it was you! I know it! Everything was fine before you came home." She shouted with tears pouring from her eyes, "I don't get involved with your love life, so stay the fuck out of mine!"

Jahad held her glare, feeling like shit, knowing he was the cause of her pain. Still, when he thought of what was at stake he felt like he made the right decision. "I don't know what you talking 'bout Trice. If you and Tone got beef then that's between ya'll. I ain't got nothing to do with it." He lied, walking off, leaving Janet to fend for herself.

When he entered his bedroom, Koran was laid across his bed with his face buried in a book.

"Where you been?" He asked swinging his feet to the floor, "Ma thought you were locked up."

"So that's how ya'll think of me, huh? I'm just a common crook?"

Koran glanced up from his book grinning, "Nobody said you were a crook. A thug maybe."

Jahad laughed, his mood lifting. "What you reading?"

"I got a test coming up in Minority Studies …give me some money."

"I just gave you twenty dollars yesterday lil' nigga."

"I copped a fitted with it. The money you give me today is going towards a Sean John sweater to go with the hat."

"You meant to say, if I give you some money. I tell you what tho'. I'll cop you the whole Sean John outfit with some sneakers if you make a hundred on that test."

"That's a bet," Koran said quickly, "I'll make a hundred easy."

"Oh, it's easy? Well I gotta better deal for you. Every time you make honor roll, I'll take you shopping for the fly shit. You'll get four outfits with the sneakers, but you gotta make all A's and no B's.

Koran's eyes lit up, "A'ight, but I want my shit when I make honor roll."

Jahad laughed, "You'll get your shit, just make the grades. Don't be brining me no bogus ass report cards either. I know how slick your little ass is. Tone told me how you were doing that crazy shit out in front of the Bodega too. If I catch you, it's on."

"I got you Jah, it was easy paper tho'. I was killing 'em out there."

"You lucky you didn't get killed. What were you doing with the money anyway?"

"After I hit Ma and Trice off, I'd go shopping. There's this bad chick at school I'm feeling so I gotta stay fly." Koran brushed off his shoulder.

Jahad shook his head smiling, "From now on let me worry about you staying fly and keep your grades up. If I see or hear about you doing that dumb shit again, you'll get nothing but a beat down. I'm serious."

"A'ight Jah, I said I got you... where you going with your clothes?"

"I got some unfinished business to handle. What you need to be stressin' is that test."

"I got the test. When you gon' take me to get some pussy? That's part of our deal too."

"Breathe easy lil' nigga," Jahad laughed walking to the door, "I'm a take you to get your little dick wet."

Walking past the living room on his way to the kitchen, he glimpsed Janet and Latrice talking. He imagined Latrice was pouring salt on his name to get back at him. He didn't care what skeletons he had in his closet, Janet already knew about them.

Michelle was at the sink washing dishes when he walked in, "Is there any truth to what Trice said?" She asked wiping her hands on a dishtowel.

"Truth to what?"

"You know what I'm talking about Jahad. Don't play stupid with me."

Jahad sighed and ran a hand over his face, "Yeah Ma, I had my reasons tho'. The two of them being together, it won't work... it's too close."

"It was working fine before you came home. What's the difference now?"

"You don't understand Ma. Tone is like my brother so to keep any beef from poppin' off, I asked him to back up. It'll keep down a lot of confusion."

"I understand, but that doesn't mean you have the right to interfere with people's lives like that. You don't know how they felt about each other so that wasn't your choice to make. It was Tony's and Latrice's."

"It ain't like I made him do it. I asked him so the choice was his."

"So Trice had no say so in the matter?"

Jahad didn't answer. Instead he went in his pocket and put three hundred dollars on the table. What was done was done and he saw no reason for discussing it anymore.

"You're ignoring me now?"

He sighed again, "No Ma, but I did what I felt was best for both of 'em. Blood is thicker than water, and nobody, friend or not, is gon' play my sister. I'll kill a nigga for even trying. So I rather Trice be mad at me for a while, instead of her hating me for life if Tone did something stupid and I ended up killing him. That's why I said it was too close. Tone and me are too close. It's best that she dates someone else, so if it goes down I won't feel bad about it. She might not like it, but that's the way it's gon' be. Pops told me before he died that I was the man of the house and I'm a carry it the way I feel he would carry it. If I'm wrong all I can say is forgive me." He said with emotions thick in his voice, with no idea that Janet and Latrice were standing behind him.

"Nothing you just said changes the fact that Trice should've been there when you had your talk with Tony. Whether you were right or wrong, she should have been included. She probably would have taken it better," Michelle said looking past him at Latrice.

"I'm sayin'..."

"Yeah, instead of acting like you're my father, you could've mentioned it to me," Latrice said drawing his attention, "I ain't a little teenage girl, in fact, if I'm not mistaken I'm older than you, so how can you call yourself being responsible for me anyway?"

Jahad's face twisted into a snarl, "If you ain't mistaken? Well, if you ain't mistaken, after Pops died who in the hell bought your school clothes? And who gave you money to put that weave shit in your head, huh? Who in the hell helped feed your ass?" His voice rose with each question, "Who you use to run to when you had beef, or one of them nothing ass niggas you to use fuck with hurt you... huh? Who spent three years of their fuckin' life in jail for trying to take care of your ass! Who..."

Michelle grabbed his arm, "Jahad, that's enough!"

He took a deep breath to calm himself before continuing, "Check it Trice, maybe I went about it the wrong way but you know how I am when it comes to ya'll man. You also know Tone is like my brother, if he hurt you tho' I wouldn't hesitate to... I won't even say it. So I'm asking you now, will you let it go out of respect for my friendship with Tone... Please?"

Latrice nodded, fighting back tears, then silently walked off.

"See, that's all you had to do in the first place."

"I ain't perfect all the time Ma, just most of the time." Jahad smiled and kissed her on the cheek.

"You too much boy. Now who's your friend?"

He placed an arm around Janet's shoulder, "This is my shorty Janet. Janet this is Ma-Duke."

"How you doing... Ma-Duke?" Janet said hesitantly.

"It's Michelle honey, and I'm fine," she smiled looking at Jahad, "you bring her in here and leave her at the front door. I taught you better manners than that."

"Yes, that was rude." Janet added.

"I was trying to get away from Trice before she could beat me up... Ma, I'm a crash at Janet's crib tonight. And before you start screaming about work, Joe gave me tomorrow off... with pay."

"And how you accomplish that?"

"A little something I learned being a criminal. And no, I didn't break no laws. See Ya!"

CHAPTER 6

Janet's view of Jahad changed considerably after witnessing the scene in his kitchen and proved her intuition to be right. When they first met she had a feeling there was more to him than what appeared on the surface, and had lied about her attraction to hard-working men. She was actually attracted to powerful men, suave, confident men. Jahad was definitely confident, and possessed an aura of raw untamed energy, she felt as soon as she stepped on the elevator. He was also composed of many different complex layers. This she glimpsed during his confrontation with Latrice. At thirteen he took sole responsibility for his family and accepted all the consequences for his actions. Now he was back again to provide for them with a fierce loyalty. These thoughts played through her mind as they walked to her apartment arm in arm.

"So I'm your Shorty now, when did this happen?" She asked with a smile once they entered her apartment.

"After tonight, I guarantee you won't have no beef carrying that title."

"It's like that?"

"I ain't one to talk about it. I can show and prove gorgeous." He answered following her to the bathroom.

Janet smacked her lips grinning, "I'm holding you to that, but I bet I'll turn your ass out. Go on in the shower. I'll be in there in a minute."

Jahad's eyes stayed on her ass until she stepped into her bedroom, "I'm a tear that ass up!" He said to himself, grabbing his crotch.

In the bathroom, he undressed while taking in its classy design. Unlike most project bathrooms, Janet's had a sparkling white tile floor, white and gold striped wallpaper matching her shower curtain, and a brass faucet and shower set. For a minute he forgot that he was still in the projects. After adjusting the water temperature to his liking he stepped in the bathtub and let the hot water run over his head. A few minutes later, Janet stepped in behind him and brushed her taut nipples up against his back. In a matter of seconds blood rushed to his dick and made him stand at attention. Turning to face her, he drew in a sharp breath, mesmerized by her nakedness. She had the body of a goddess. Perky breasts, the size of grapefruits, bronze colored nipples, and a flat stomach with a diamond butterfly navel piercing. A thin hairline traveled from below her navel, down to her neatly trimmed pubic hair in the shape of a heart. Her thighs were thick but well toned; legs slightly bowed curving to her small feet.

Jahad took a step towards her, intent on having her right then and there. Anticipation wouldn't let him wait.

"Uh uh," Janet said backing away, "first things first. When we're finished washing we can get into that. Now turn around so I can wash your back, then I'll work my way around."

Whiled she soaped up the washcloth; Jahad placed his head back under the shower and put his hands on the wall. She started at the back of his neck, moving the washcloth in slow circles down over his broad shoulders. Her other hand snaked around to massage his dick focusing her strokes around the head."

"A'ight Janet," he moaned humping her hand, "you saw what happened last time. I'm telling you, it won't take much."

"Yeah, but you aren't going nowhere this time."

Once she finished washing his back, she maneuvered the washcloth over his ass then between his ass cheeks when he spun with lightning quickness, and grabbed her wrist.

"Whoa Ma! Ain't none of that poppin' off. I ain't into all that kinky shit," he scolded.

"All I was doing was washing you," Janet replied innocently trying not to laugh, "You have to wash there."

"You just said the key word 'you' as in me," Jahad took the washcloth from her and quickly washed his ass then wrenched it out before handing it back, "the ass is clean, you may proceed?"

"What difference would it have made if I did it?" She asked as he turned back around.

"I don't know, you might've tried to slip a finger up my ass with it being so slippery and shit."

"I wouldn't do nothing like that," she giggled, "you can turn around now since you don't trust me with your butt."

"It's my turn," he said, taking the washcloth, "let me see how you like it when I wash your ass."

Janet moved under the showerhead turning her back to him, "That's what I'm waiting for."

Jahad looked down at her ass wanting desperately to enter her. His dick rested on top of her butter colored cheeks throbbing for release. He fought to control his lust as he began washing her breast, pinching her nipples lightly as he did so. Janet arched her back, grinding against him while he trailed the cloth over her stomach down between her legs washing gently. Bending to kiss her neck, he slid his soapy middle finger deep inside her and heard a low moan, bubble up from her throat. She covered his hands with hers, urging him to speed up his rhythm, which were moving achingly slow. Sensing her need, he plunged another finger deep, and worked to the movement of her hips.

"What... Whatever you do... don't stop. Keep... keep... ohhhhh!"

She moaned gripping the shower head.

Jahad kept his fingers buried inside her until her orgasm abated then positioned himself so he could enter her. He held his dick to her slippery lips, and moved the head between her slit, watching as hot water, along with her milky cream, flowed around them.

"C'mon Jah, push it in me... I want it."

Needing no further encouragement, he gripped her hips and eased into her until Janet reached around and placed a hand on his hip to stop him. Seven inches were buried deep inside her, more than enough she felt for the time being; "Work with that baby until I get use to it. Feels like you're in my stomach already."

Jahad smiled, working his hips in a slow steady motion. After about ten strokes he sped up, engrossed in the feeling while moving a hand around to caress her breast.

"More!" Janet moaned, pushing back into him, "Give me more!"

"I'm a give it all to you... you want it all?" He asked pounding into her with short powerful humps.

Screaming like he was killing her, Janet grabbed his hand and moved it to where they were joined, placing his finger on her clit. His touch sent her over the edge triggering a series of orgasms.

"UMMMMM!" She screamed reaching around to hold him deep

inside her so he couldn't move.

After a few seconds Jahad's patience wore thin. He gripped her hips intending on reaching his own climax, but Janet pulled off him leaving his dick pointed towards the ceiling. "What you doing Janet? ...C'mere."

"Uh uh," she teased with a devilish grin, "I never got around to washing the front of you so you'll have to wait."

"Wait? Let me get this nut and you can wash all you want."

"Nope."

"C'mon Janet," Jahad begged, yearning to be inside of her, "You know this shit ain't right. You up two on me already."

"Good things come to those who wait. Trust me."

Positioning him beneath the showerhead, she washed his face, neck, shoulders, and under his arms as if he were a child. When she finished the top half of him, she dropped to her knees and took hold of his dick in her left hand. While washing the length of him, she stroked him slowly until pre-cum began leaking from the head. Caught up in the feeling Jahad closed his eyes and worked his hips to her strokes, until he felt something hot and moist engulf him. A shiver shot through his spine as he looked down and saw Janet's lips wrapped around him."

"Damn, Ma, you were dead ass about turning me out, huh?"

"You like that?" She asked, licking the bottom half of his shaft.

"Why you stop?" He pouted sounding like he was about to cry, "Stop teasing me."

Janet smiled and took him back in her mouth, taking only a few inches in before raising off. Gradually she began sinking down further while speeding up the momentum.

"Oh shit! You doing it now Ma," Jahad moaned placing a hand on her head to control her rhythm.

She continued to suck him, while massaging his balls, until he was on the verge of coming then moved her mouth.

"A'ight Janet. I'm getting tired of this teasing shit. I need to cum before I go fuckin' crazy," he said frowning.

"You wanna cum baby?" She stood wrapped her arms around his neck, then opened her legs placing one on the base of the tub, "C'mon, put it in me then, so you can cum."

Jahad bent his legs slightly to enter her then raised both her legs around his waist. Janet grunted as she sunk down onto him, moving her hips in slow circles, but Jahad anxious for release, wanted to speed up the process. Placing his back against the wall, he commenced to bouncing her up and down off him, frantically burying himself up to the hilt with each thrust.

"Oh my God, Jahad!" Janet screamed digging her nails in his back, "Ohhhh... you fucking me baby! I never had it like this... never!"

Her screams caused him to piston his hips and slam her down onto him even faster. It wasn't long before the moment he had been waiting on arrived. Trembling like a sick heroin addict, he exploded inside of her, keeping himself lodged deep, while Janet convulsed in his arms, her sex gripping him like a vice.

~~~~

An hour later, after another session in the shower they finally made it to her bedroom. Like her bathroom, it had a stylish appeal. Plush white carpet, new plush white carpet, so soft it felt like he was walking on mattresses. A queen sized bed against the far wall, flanked by two oak night stands, which held twin gold and white lamps. On the wall directly across from the bed was a small oak dresser with a vanity mirror attached. The dresser held numerous bottles of perfume, lipstick, and other cosmetic products, all stacked neatly.

"I'm feelin' your spot," Jahad said once he was in bed looking around, "beauticians get paid a'ight I see."

"Somewhat," Janet snuggled up against him, intertwining her legs with his.

He gave her a mischievous grin, "Or did a nigga trick on you?"

"For your information, I don't need a nigga to trick on me," Janet replied sharply, "I make my own money, so I can trick on myself. And to be honest, I prefer not to be tricked on because I'm not a trick."

"I ain't sayin' you a trick, but what you just said is bullshit."

She sat up so she could look at him, "Why you say that?"

"Because all women wanna nigga to trick on 'em. It's the law of nature. Ya'll even got a holiday for it, Valentine's Day. And a nigga, regardless of what they say about being pimps and shit wanna chick they can trick on. She gotta be that chick tho', you feel me?"

She stared at him a moment, "You're different."

"I'm different?" Jahad chuckled, "Nah, Ma, I'm Jah, and I'm just keeping it funky with you."

"Since you're keeping it funky, what about all the women who have men to trick on them, but still aren't happy?"

"That's a whole nother story. Material things alone won't keep a chick happy. It's a combination of things. Trickin', the pipe game, making her feel protected, and keeping the quality time poppin' off. If a nigga can't do that, most likely a dude like my man Cream will be blowin' her back out."

Janet smiled, "How long have you been a love doctor?"

"Oh, I'm far from one, but being locked up for three years gave me time to figure certain things out. For instance, you the first chick I been with since I came home, so more than likely if I keep fuckin' with you, you gon' have me strung out."

Her smile vanished, "What you mean if? You have no choice in the matter, so prepare yourself to be strung out."

Jahad sat up. "What you mean I don't have a choice? I mean..."

"Like I said!" She snapped, cutting him off, "I'm not into the one night stands. I would have never slept with you if I felt that's all it would be."

"So what you sayin? I'm your man now?" Jahad asked incredulously.

"Damn right! Unless you do something stupid. Why are you asking questions you already know the answers to anyway? I would never have apologized if I didn't have plans on getting to know you better. Smart as you claim to be, you should know this."

"Know what? Getting to know you and me being your man are two different things. What you sayin' is you wanna commitment off top, but you don't even know me Ma."

"I know enough to know that I want to have something with you. Now if you don't want to be with me, or have plans on being with someone else, let me know right now." Janet said, holding his eyes.

"You putting the pressure on me like that Janet?"

"It's no pressure. I just want to know what to expect."

Jahad sunk back down into the pillow, feeling as if he had been pushed into a corner. He liked Janet, he liked her a lot, but she was asking for his total dedication. Being the man he was, if he committed himself to something he was committed 100%, and this she was asking after knowing him two days. Then again, if that same commitment and dedication was returned he had no problems with it. He sat back up with that thought and stared her directly in the eyes, "A'ight, you got yourself a man, but let me say this. If it's gonna be me and you, it's gonna be me and you to death. I'm crazy loyal to the people I let get close to me, but I expect that same loyalty, so from this day forth, don't ever give my pussy away and don't ever cross me Janet... ever. I'll make you this promise now. I'll never fuck around on you and I'll always hold you down through whatever. You can count on that."

Janet nodded, "I give you that same promise; I mean it. Now what's your plan?"

"Huh?"

"Your plans. I mean you don't strike me as the type to be breaking your back everyday. Not saying there's anything wrong with it, but you give off a vibe like you're... what's the word I'm looking for?" She asked herself, "Ambitious, like you're very ambitious."

He looked at her surprised that she read him so well, "I'll say this, I ain't really no nine to five nigga. I'm doing this now on the strength of my moms and little brother. Why you wanna know my plans for?"

"So I can mold my plans with yours."

"Oh, word? What if my plans involve getting a little dirty before I get clean?"

"Then I guess I'll have to get a little dirty with you. But first I want to know the overall plan once we come from the dirt."

Jahad screwed up his face, "Hold up, so what you sayin' is you're down for whatever, right?"

"Something like that."

"So what up with that, 'I don't deal with criminals' shit you gave me then?"

"I said that before I caught a glimpse of the man beneath the criminal. Tonight at your apartment I saw something in you that you probably didn't even see yourself."

"And what might that be?"

"Strength, leadership, ambition, and a fierce loyalty to those you care about. With those qualities, I see you doing anything you set your mind to. So if you say you have a plan, then I want to be a part of it. If you don't have a plan, then together we can put one together."

"Oh, I have a plan, a big plan." He went on to explain.

~~~~

Janet woke Jahad the next morning at ten o'clock surprising him with breakfast in bed. Fried eggs sunny side up, turkey bacon, buttered toast, and a tall glass of orange juice.

"I get the V.I.P. treatment?" He asked yawning.

"After that demonstration you put on last night, you better believe it. Just wait until you finish your breakfast. I have something else for you." She winked as she left out.

For the better part of the night, after Jahad laid out his plan, they discussed the best way to get the record label off the ground in regards to studio time, Mix CD's, and promotions. A dedicated street team was essential in order to move their underground CD's. A website would also be needed to expand their exposure. The key factor to everything was money, which he kept to himself how he planned on getting.

On a more personal level, Jahad spoke of his life before his father died; his dreams of going to college and moving his family out of the projects. Like Michelle, Janet voiced that it wasn't too late, but he shrugged if off. Janet in turn spoke vaguely of her past, mentioning that she had older brothers she didn't get along with. Then spoke finally of her father telling funny stories of how he use to take her and her baby sister to see the Yankee's play religiously in rain, sleet, or snow. By the time she was twelve, she knew baseball well enough to become a sports announcer.

What astonished him and made Jahad feel closer to Janet was when he learned that her father was killed the same year as his father. They both grew up with the pain of losing a parent, although it affected them differently. Jahad became a man at a young age, accepting the responsibility of taking care of his family, while Janet strived for her independence and had moved out on her own as soon as she graduated from high school.

"Thanks for the breakfast sexy," Jahad said when Janet came to take the dishes away, "next time, it's on me."

"You can cook?"

"Picture that. I'll hit up the chicken spot for you tho'."

"Well, ain't that sweet of you," she kissed him on the lips then took the dishes away. A few minutes later she returned and cuddled up in bed beside him, "You talked my ears off last night about your record label, so let me hear something."

"You want me to rhyme?"

"Yeah. Let me see if you have any potential," she said, putting her hands over her mouth making a beat.

Jahad burst out laughing, "Ayo, you crazy girl, but keep that beat going. I'm a hit you with a lil' something... C'mere you sexy thing you / can I claim you / I wanna do a lot more than just bang you / I'm not a player no more, Joe said it / So all them chicks in the past don't sweat it/ I settled all a that / deaded all a that / Put my black book away boo, I'm here to stay / Ain't trying to play with your mind, just wanna spend some time / Wine and dine and soon you'll find / that I'm the diamond in the ruff, plus I'm tough / Street thug cat that'll keep you tucked / Keep you safe and keep them corny niggas out your face / I'll keep you laced with fine things that suit your taste..."

Janet squealed happily, "You can really rhyme! You just made that up didn't you?"

"Yeah, I freestyle a little. I'm nicer with the pen tho'. You should hear my nigga Eric. Sun is bananas."

"You'll have to introduce me one day, but for now I wanna hear something else," she bunched her long Minnie Mouse t-shirt up around her waist, and straddled him.

"Word," Jahad grinned gripping her hips, "what's that?"

"You saying my name while I'm giving you this good nooky."

CHAPTER 7

By the first week of March, Janet and Jahad were officially living together. It started out gradually, going to her place, after he went home to take a shower once he got off work. Then he brought his toothbrush and deodorant over so he wouldn't have to make trips home in the mornings before going to work. Over time, with him bringing a change of clothes to her place, a few of his outfits got mixed up in her laundry and before he knew it, most of his clothes were at her apartment. Finally, Janet insisted he move in, since he spent his nights there anyway. Jahad went along with it after they agreed that he would foot half of the bills. He still paid a daily visit to see Michelle, dropping off money for what they had set up for Koran and getting her out the projects. Most days he had to wait until she came home from work, which meant he was left alone with Latrice, who was still mad at him. For a while she wouldn't even speak to him and would go out of her way just to avoid him. Jahad feigned indifference, although deep down it irked him to be given the cold shoulder. Latrice was making a big deal out of nothing, he felt. He broke her relationship up, so what. It wasn't like she couldn't find another boyfriend; she was definitely pretty enough. What he couldn't understand, mainly because he had never experienced it, was the power of love. Latrice was depressed, angry, and scorned; all symptoms of a broken heart and the blame she placed on Jahad. He felt she should be able to turn her feelings off and on like a light switch, something he was good at. This would soon change though, as he would experience the power of love, first hand.

On a brighter side to his visits, Koran had made a complete turn around. No longer did he hang out looking for people to scam, he didn't have the time. Since the day Jahad promised to take him shopping, he poured himself into his books, intent on having his shopping spree. Learning came easy. Without really applying himself he maintained a B average. So when he did take time to study he excelled. The day report cards came out, to make sure Jahad didn't renege on their deal he stood out in front of their building until Jahad got off work. Jahad upheld his end, but found with all his new responsibilities, saving money for his other plans would be hard. This sparked the thought to go see Rahoul.

Together with the kitty he started with his friends, they had close to three thousand dollars. Originally he wanted to wait until they had enough money to buy 500 grams, but at the rate they were going that could take another month or two. Anxious to get the ball rolling he figured he'd go see Rahoul now so they could start turning what they had. He also had something in mind where Janet could be used without knowing the street side of his operation. Something he thought long and hard about.

It was Thursday afternoon when he brought up the subject. He had just returned home after dropping some money off at Michelle's, sweaty, smelly, and in desperate need of a shower. Janet met him in the hallway as she usually did, gave him a kiss then stepped back wrinkling her nose.

"You stink Boo."

Jahad pulled his sweaty sweatshirt over his head, "Stink ain't the word. Funky is more like it. Joe had us moving furniture for some stinkin' ass Iranians out in Queens. That shit got all in my clothes."

"Let me run you some bath water then, because a shower won't work." Janet turned to walk off.

"Hold up Ma, we need to talk."

Janet caught another whiff of him and shook her head, "Uh uh. We can talk after you wash your butt. C'mon."

Jahad laughed, tempted to hug her so she could smell funky along with him.

In the bathroom before she let him say a word, she ran his bath water adding some of her bubble bath, made him undress, put his clothes in a trash bag, and then gave him a bar of her scented soap. "Okay, what is it you want to talk about? She asked, once he was sunk down in the tub.

"C'mon Janet, I wasn't that funky."

"Ha," she snorted, "tell your boss, if you're gonna come home smelling like 'you know what', you need a raise. A big raise, now what's going on?"

"When you said you would get dirty with me, did you mean it?"

"If I have to smell like you were smelling, no," she wrinkled her nose again.

"I'm talking 'bout what we spoke about with the record label. You remember?"

The smile left her face, "Of course I remember, and you don't have to ask if I meant it. I'm here for you baby, so just tell me what you need me to do."

ZAP! ...Right then, love struck Jahad with a sudden jolt. Since their relationship started nearly two months ago, he had placed a shield around his heart in hopes of preventing what had just happened, but Janet's declaration somehow broke through his defenses. Along with the feeling came an intense wave of fear he felt in the pit of his stomach. For a while he held her eyes without really seeing her trying to understand the feelings flowing through him. Joy, pain, doubt, and fear were all wrapped together putting his mind in a state of turmoil.

"What is it you want me to do?" Janet asked again.

He blinked a few times to clear his mind, "When I finish washing my ass, we're going to see a friend of mine in Harlem. After today tho', I want you to be the one who goes to see him. Do I need to say more?"

"Not unless you want too."

"Good. Now how 'bout you get in here with me and help me get this funk off."

"Uh uh," Janet pinched her nose, "get the funk off first."

~~~~

On their way to Harlem in the Black Lincoln Town Car cab, Jahad stared out at the Hudson River's choppy waters still trying to sort out his feelings. To have someone as beautiful, sexy, and smart as Janet on his arm made him feel like the luckiest man in the world. At the same time, he hated the possessive feeling he felt every time he looked at her. Feeling as if he had to have her, couldn't live without her, was a slave to her love. Most of all, he hated that he trusted her completely, although she gave him no reason not to. Since his father was murdered the only people he allowed himself to trust were his family and childhood friends; being they all grew up like brothers. He only trusted them to a certain extent. Anyone outside of that circle earned no trust period regardless of how close they thought they were to him. Now Janet was a part of his circle and he had only known her two months. The main factor based on the new emotions coursing through him was control. He was so use to regulating his emotions, but now love had taken over and he no longer had that ability which explained his fear.

"What's on your mind Boo?" Janet asked taking notice of his thoughtful expression.

Jahad turned away from the window frowning, "Since you asked, you."

"What about me?"

"That's exactly what I'm trying to figure out. I ain't use to this shit, and to keep it real with you, it's got me feeling uncomfortable."

"I don't understand. Why or how do I make you feel uncomfortable?"

"What I'm trying to say is... I mean... I ain't use to wanting somebody the way I want you. I ain't use to trusting... forget it," he turned back towards the window.

"Wait a minute. You got me, so what's the problem?" Janet asked confused.

"No man... No!" He half shouted frustrated because he wanted her to understand without having to say those three words, "This feeling, it makes me uncomfortable."

Janet shook her head, "You're losing me Jah. What feeling Baby?"

He let out a loud sigh, "Why you making this shit hard for me? You know what I'm trying to say."

It was then that Jahad realized that love was a weakness. Never had he felt so exposed, so vulnerable. The only way he knew how to put an end to everything he felt was to leave her alone completely. The thought made him sick. Picturing her with someone else, giving another man her time, her attention, her love, was a thought he couldn't stand. One he had to push from his mind before he turned green.

"Jah, I don't know what you're talking about Baby. I really don't. " Janet took hold of his hand, "What am I making hard..." Her words trailed off as it suddenly dawned on her, "Are you trying to say you're in love with me?"

"Give the lady a prize." He said sarcastically before turning back towards the window.

"Oh Jah!" Janet's face lit up, "You have me ready to cry, I love you too Baby, so you don't have to feel uncomfortable."

He grunted without looking at her.

"It's true, so look at me," she forced his head around, "I've been in love with you since the second day I laid eyes on you. You're dedicated to those you love and you give me that same dedication. Then there's that aura of strength you give off. To be honest it's everything about you. I love myself some Jah."

Jahad blushed, "Stop it Ma, I'm already feelin' myself."

"How about I do some feeling of my own." She ran her hand over his crotch.

"A'ight, you better chill before I have you back here bent up. When we get home it's on tho'. I might even let you teach me how to eat seafood."

"Seafood?"

Jahad glanced down at her crotch and licked his lips, "Yeah, seafood."

Janet screwed up her face, "Uh uh, you got it twisted. Ain't nothing fishy about this nooky. If anything I'll be teaching you how to enjoy the taste of honey. As a matter of fact I will, since you're talking about seafood. Where you get that shit from anyway? You been with someone who smelled like seafood or something?" She asked wrinkling her nose.

"Hell, nah! I'm just going by what I heard. I ain't never did no shit like that. Never had too. My jumpoff is big enough to satisfy any woman."

Janet rolled here eyes, "I can't argue about that, but your jumpoff better only be satisfying me, or I'll take a few inches off."

"Whoa!" Jahad winced, "Don't be talking 'bout the jumpoff like that. Besides, good as that thing is, you don't gotta worry 'bout that."

~~~~

By the time the cab stopped at the corner of 141st and Amsterdam, the sun had faded and streetlights lit up the block. Two story brownstones lined both sides of the street. Puerto Rican's stood along the block in groups, some sitting on the curb, while others leaned against broken down cars that sat on cement blocks.

Overall the atmosphere was carefree. This was until Janet and Jahad stepped from the cab. In a matter of seconds they were surrounded by a group of Puerto Ricans all holding their hands under their coats.

"Que estus haciendo aqui?" A tall Puerto Rican with golden brown skin and wide set light brown eyes barked at Jahad, inching to pull out whatever he had concealed under his coat.

Jahad bunched his fist, "I don't understand that shit man. Speak English."

"He wants to know what we're doing up here." Janet said clutching his arm.

"You speak that shit?"

"Yes, my dad was Puerto Rican?"

"Well tell him I came to see my man Rahoul."

Janet faced the tall Puerto Rican, "El vino a vor a su amigio Rahoul."

"Como conoces a Rahoul?" The question was directed to Jahad.

"He wants to know how you know Rahoul," Janet translated while the others watched Jahad with sharp eyes.

Tell him that's my homey. We bidded together at Spofford."

"Ese es su amigo. Elles estaban en prision juntos."

"Tu tienes una pistola contigio?" The tall Puerto Rican looked to Jahad's waist.

"What he say?"

"He wants to know if you have a gun on you."

"Nah, I wish I did tho'."

He studied Jahad a moment then barked, "Ven y sigueme."

"He wants us to follow them." Janet said wrapping an arm around Jahad's waist while the others followed within arms reach.

"Damn, they act like we going to meet the President or some shit." Jahad snarled glancing over his shoulder.

Conversation on the block ceased and all attention stayed focused on Jahad and Janet as they walked surrounded by Puerto Ricans. At the middle of the block the tall Puerto Rican motioned for them to stop, then ran up the steps of a brownstone to their right.

"Rahoul, tu tienes compania aqua!" He called out knocking.

A few minutes later the door opened and Rahoul stepped out onto the small porch dressed in a gray Sean John velour sweatsuit wearing a pair of gray and white New Balance sneakers. Short and slim standing at five-five his skin was a shade lighter than bronze, his long black hair cornrowed in braids that hung nearly to the small of his back. He had a narrow face, close set bluish green eyes, and a short stubby nose. A year older than Jahad, Rahoul was already a drug Kingpin. Actually, he was born a drug Kingpin since selling cocaine had been the family's business for three generations. While most fathers expected their sons to go off to college or join the armed services, Rahoul's father expected only one thing from him. Learn the family business.

"Oh shit, my nigga Jah!" Rahoul bounced down the steps and embraced Jahad in a bear hug, "When you get out?"

"I been out like a month and some change now," Jahad said grinning, "got a job and all that."

"You working? Pleeease. You probably stuck up four or five niggas already."

"Nah Rah, I'm on some different shit now. Not sayin' I don't plan on getting my hands dirty. That's why I'm here to see you."

"You came to the right place then," Rahoul said, then turned his attention to Janet. "Who you have with you?"

Jahad put his arm around Janet's shoulder, "This is my Shorty Janet. Janet this is my homey Rahoul."

"It's nice to meet you Rahoul," Janet extended her hand.

"The pleasure is mine mamacita." Rahoul took hold of her hand and kissed her knuckle.

"Ayo, go 'head with that Don Juan shit Rah."

Rahoul laughed, lacing his arms around Janet and Jahad's shoulders, ushering them inside. His living room screamed money. Everything coordinated, beige carpet the same color as the beige leather furniture, a large oval glass coffee table with matching glass lamps. A chandelier hung from the ceiling with sixteen lights patterned in an intricate design, casting a soft light around the room. Across from the couch perched above a black marble fireplace was a 60 inch flat screen television. On the opposite wall, a large silver crucifix hung dead center surrounded by pictures of Rahoul's family.

Once seated a beautiful Puerto Rican woman with long flaming red hair framing her small exotic face entered and Rahoul stood and grabbed her hand, "Jah, this is my beautiful girlfriend soon to be wife if she acts right, Maria."

"You better act right," Maria punched him lightly on the arm.

Rahoul kissed her before continuing his introductions. "Maria this is one of my best friends Jah, and his lady Janet."

After introductions were made, Rahoul turned to his girlfriend, "Maria, pidele ha mi amigo's algo de tomar."

Janet stepped beside Maria, "If you don't mind I'll help her while you two talk."

"You understand Spanish?" Rahoul asked surprised.

"Yes, I'm half Puerto Rican, so you never know, we may be related," Janet smiled, kissing Jahad before following Maria into the kitchen.

"You picked a good one Homey. Puerto Rican women are the best creatures on earth, and loyal, very loyal," Rahoul said, sitting on the loveseat across from Jahad. "So what you trying to do?"

"Like I said, I'm holdin' down this job, but it ain't producing enough dough to take care of everything I'm trying to do. So I bought a little dough with me to cop something to start flippin'. I was gon' chill until I had enough to cop 500 grams, but I got mad other shit on my plate right now. When I come back, or when Janet comes back, everything I make on the flip I'm spending with you."

"Keep your money, I got you this time around. You held me down at Spofford so you know I'ma hold you down. Is that all you need, coke?"

Jahad thought how he felt when Rahoul's people surrounded him. Being without a gun made him feel the same vulnerability he felt being in love. "Nah, I need some heat. Your fam' put mad pressure on me when I came up here. Made me realize I was slippin'."

"They were only holdin' down the block. Some dudes came through two weeks ago and robbed my brother. He's still in the hospital. But you won't have to worry about that anymore... What you been up to tho'? Besides the job and whatnot?"

"I'm trying to pop off this record label. That's my reason for fuckin' with the coke. I gotta ill team already, we just need to get our foot in the door."

"Oh word, you still writin' rhymes?"

"I ain't wrote nothing lately 'cause I been working my ass off. I got a log of material I wrote when I was at Spofford tho'. Shit, I wrote five albums when I was in the Bing."

"Yeah I can see you on Rap City," Rahoul said as Maria and Janet came from the kitchen, each carrying a cup of cocoa. After placing the cups on the table they returned to the kitchen speaking rapid Spanish, "I see they're getting along well. Where you find her at."

"She's from my projects. I met her like two months ago and she got me fucked up already."

Rahoul laughed, "Puerto Rican women will get you every time. Why don't you stay for dinner and before you leave, I'll get you right?"

"I'm cool with that. Tell me you got some tree's tho'."

"You know I do, some exclusive shit too. We'll get toasted then get our bellies full."

"Bet."

After dinner Jahad and Rahoul sat in the living room reminiscing over old Spofford days while the women did the dishes. Around eleven o'clock, full, and high as hell, Jahad called a cab. They had seven deliveries tomorrow and he didn't feel like hearing Joe's mouth for being late. Before he and Janet left, Rahoul walked outside returning a few minutes later with a medium sized brown paper bag and a glock, 40 calibers.

"This should keep niggas from crowding you. In the bag is 500 grams of that butter to keep your block pumpin'."

Jahad tucked the gun in his waistline, his eyes full of gratitude. "Good luck Rah, word up! What you want me to bring back?"

"Nothing, that's you. You think I forgot what you did for me? One hand washes the other. All I ask is that you spend your money with me on the next trip."

"No doubt homey. No doubt."

CHAPTER 8

Jahad was in a pensive mood on the way home, trying to figure out the best way to move the coke. He had never sold drugs a day in his life; his hustle had always been robberies, so logically the thing to do was to turn that side of the operation over to someone who knew what they were doing. Tony instantly came to mind since he was the most business minded in the clique. There was still something that Jahad felt that he was forgetting, but every so often Janet would speak while he was trying to think and break his train of thought. Each time he would turn from the window and put a finger over her lips to shut her up, which in turn earned him a bite on the finger.

"Stop doing that!" Janet shouted after he did it for the fifth time. "Next time, I'll bite it off."

"Chill Janet, I'm trying to put some shit together here man." Frustrated, Jahad turned back towards the window.

"Maybe I can help."

"No you can't, because what I'm putting together is none of your concern. All you need to stress is going to see Rahoul when it's time to."

"So you're telling me that we're in this together, but I'll be in the blind about certain stuff?" She asked frowning.

"That's exactly what I'm telling you. It'll be better in the end."

"For who?"

"Everybody involved, so I'm keeping this whole thing separate. If you happen to get bagged and Po-Po puts pressure on you, pressure you can't handle, then you won't know what's going on, so my homies will be safe. If one of my homey's got bagged they won't know nothing 'bout you, so you'll be safe. So it works out on both ends."

Janet screwed up her face, "You think I would tell on you?"

"I'm sayin', if you did one of my mans would probably merk you so I hope you wouldn't. If it did go down like that tho', I'd be the only one to feel the heat."

She looked at him, shocked and hurt by how he spoke of her death so easy, as if it meant nothing. "How can you say you love me when you don't even trust me?" She asked on the verge of crying.

"Whoa Ma," Jahad wrapped an arm around her shoulder, "the reason I'm telling you this is because I do love you. I'd be wrong if I didn't put you up on the stakes. And as far as me trusting you, I wouldn't be sitting beside you right now if I didn't trust you. I gotta be prepared for the unexpected tho', Spofford taught me that. The same way I'm doing it with you, I'm doing with my mans, so don't take it personal."

"You shouldn't be like that Jah."

"Nah, you wrong. It's the only way to be. You never know who'll snake you. The hardest nigga will fold under enough pressure if he ain't sharp. Trust me, I've seen it."

"I'll never snake you." Janet replied as the cab parked in front of their building.

Jahad smiled devilishly, "I'm sure you won't, but how 'bout I put this snake on you when we get upstairs."

"I wanna see if you can work your tongue like a snake. Don't think I forgot."

"I'm glad you didn't," he flickered his tongue out making Janet laugh, "It better taste like honey too."

Once they made it upstairs, Jahad had just enough time to put the gun and coke away before Janet hungrily snatched his clothes off and drug him to the shower. After adjusting the water temperature, she stepped in the tub, placing her back against the wall under the showerhead. Hot water streamed over her head, matting her long hair to the sides of her face and over her heavy breasts, leaving her nipples peaking through like tiny eyeballs. Jahad watched from where he leaned against the sink hypnotized, his dick extended out like a third arm while Janet ran her hands over her breast, caught up in her own lust. Slowly, her hand traveled over her stomach until finally she plunged them between her legs and began stroking herself. Absentmindedly, Jahad starting doing the same, his eyes focused to where Janet manipulated her clit.

"Come taste me, Jah," she licked her lips seductively and placed a foot on the base of the tub, then used both hands to open her sex, exposing her pink love button, "c'mon baby, I want you to taste this honey."

His heart raced with arousal as he stepped inside the tub and dropped to his knees in front of her. Embarrassed, he looked up at her not knowing where to begin.

Janet smiled, "Kiss it baby, like you would kiss me."

He glanced up again sheepishly, and then kissed her clit, hearing her moan softly. Satisfied that he had done something right he concentrated on her clit, kissing the little knob, while holding her hips as she bucked against his mouth.

"Ohhhh Jah!" Her hips moved in quick small circles. "It feels so goooood! Make me cum baby. Please make me cum."

Hearing the desperation in her voice, Jahad greedily covered her with his mouth and used his tongue to dart in and out of her love tunnel. He tasted what Janet called honey which to him tasted more like a salty peach, although he savored the taste just the same. After a while, it got so good he cupped her shapely ass in his hands, trying to bury his tongue inside her as deep as he could. Janet willing to help, grabbed the back of his head and used her hips to bear down on him. A few seconds later, her grip tightened as her dam burst and filled his mouth with her hot cream.

"Ummmmm!" She screamed trembling, her hands clamped on his head refusing to let him move.

Jahad jerked away, outraged once she loosened her grip and spit the warm liquid from his mouth, "Ayo! What the fuck is wrong with you man? You shot that shit in my mouth! That shit..."

"Shhhhh," Janet placed a finger over his lips, "I'm about to return the favor, now lay back." She used her foot to push him back into the tub, then knelt between his legs and engulfed his swollen manhood.

Jahad's anger faded with one loud sigh. Doing her best to please, she held him by the base of his dick; taking as much as she could fit in her mouth before raising up to the head in long slow bobs. "Damn Janet, you know what you doing don't you," he said when she took his balls in her mouth while stroking him.

Sensing he was on the verge of exploding Janet returned to his dick, licking the length of him before taking him back into her mouth. She sucked the head, making slow circles with her tongue while pumping the rest of his massive erection. Jahad's toes curled as he humped her mouth and gripped the side of the tub, almost hard enough to leave his fingerprints engraved.

"Oh shit Janet! I... I... I..." His words trailed off as his eyes rolled back in his head, until only the white could be seen, and he filled her mouth with his load.

Janet continued to suck him, swallowing what she could, the rest seeping from the corner of her mouth. Soon he grew stiff again, and before he could say a word, she straddled him, sinking down until he was buried deep inside her. For leverage she gripped the side of the tub, then began riding him in a frenzy, her clit brushing against his pubic hair with each thrust.

"You know you drive me crazy right," Jahad said pumping up into her, "and I'm telling you, don't ever give my pussy away... ever! You'll fuck around and make me kill a nigga!"

"Never baby. Never," she moaned feeling herself about to climax again.

~~~~

Later that night (well early that next morning, being it was going on three o'clock), before they fell asleep, Janet rolled over on her side to face Jahad and ran a hand over his chest, her mind on the conversation they had earlier in the cab, "Jah."

"Huh?" He moaned sleepily.

"I know you said what you're planning is none of my concern, but can I make a suggestion, something that might keep the heat off of you."

Jahad raised up on his elbows, "Yeah, make your suggestion, but since you won't let me sleep, I want something in return."

"What's that?"

"Go 'head and say what you gotta say. You'll see."

"Uh uh baby, I'm too sore."

"You shoulda thought about that before you woke me up."

"But you weren't sleep," Janet pouted.

"Save it Janet, it's too late now."

She smacked her lips, "Well whatever you have planned, I think you should keep your job. Like I said, it might keep the heat off you."

"I can't believe it, you're a genius!" He mocked with a grin.

Janet scowled and punched him hard on the arm.

"I already thought about that Sexy. I'ma hold this job down for a

"That's what I thought." He smiled as she wrapped her legs around his back.

~~~~

"C'mon Joe man, put some back into it. We can't move this heavy shit by ourselves," Jahad grunted, as he, Eric, and Joe heaved the grand piano up the steep steps to an apartment building on Park Avenue. Weighing close to a thousand pounds, the piano had their muscles tensed to the limit, their veins looking like earthworms protruding from their skin.

It was four o'clock and temperatures were barely above the freezing mark, a rigid wind blowing off the East River. Dirty smog polluted mist fell from the grayish sky like dust, dampening their already sweat stained sweatshirts, but the wetness and cold was their last concern. What mattered was getting the piano up the steps before they dropped it, or it fell back on Jahad who brought up the rear.

"Hold it Jahad! Hold it!" Joe yelled when Eric faltered backing up the steps and shifted most of the weight on Jahad, causing his knees to buckle.

"I got it!" Jahad said straining to straighten out his legs, "Get your ass around and pick up the damn weight."

Joe quickly moved from the middle to help Eric on the other end, but most of the weight was still on Jahad. Using the last of his strength, he carried the piano up the remaining seven steps to the platform and felt a sharp pain shoot from the back of his neck to the middle of his back as he sat it down.

"Ah shit!" He winced standing up straight, "Ayo word up Joe, you need to get some more help. My back won't take too much more of this shit."

Joe mumbled a curse as he walked pass going to his van.

"I'm dead ass Joe! I don't mind working, but this shit is crazy. I ain't no damn robot."

"Word!" Eric added, walking around the piano to stand beside Jahad.

Joe nodded knowing they were right. They were doing a six man job all by themselves. He usually hired drug addicts, despite his no stealing policy. They were cheap and didn't give him too much lip. The problem was they only lasted a few days before the work broke them down. Truth be told Jahad and Eric were invaluable to his business. With them he was able to almost double his deliveries. This is the main reason he paid them so well.

"Alright with ya'll whining asses. Give me a couple of days and I'll get us some more help. When I do ya'll can take a few days off. In the meantime, let's get this shit done. C'mon Eric, move your ass!"

~~~~

After work on their way home Jahad told Eric to start looking for a studio they could use, but said nothing about the drugs. That part of the operation he wanted Eric to have no parts of, so he saw no reason to tell him. Eric had one purpose and one purpose only in Jahad's scheme of things, to make hit songs.

It was dark when the cab dropped them off across from the park. Tony along with the rest of the gang were sitting at their usual park bench, smoking blunts when they walked up.

"Let me hit the blunt, you pretty as nigga." Jahad smiled addressing Cream.

"Oh you think I'm pretty? Bitches think I'm pretty too, you Mighty Joe Young lookin' muthafucka." Cream laughed, passing the blunt.

"Shit, I'd rather look like Might Joe Young then Lil' Kim. I could put your ass in a dress, shave off your mustache and make some money off your pretty ass. Call you hot Cream."

Everybody laughed as Cream's face turned beet red, "A'ight Jah, you got that so chill with the pretty shit."

"A'ight you pretty ass nigga." Jahad laughed turning his attention to Tony, "Ayo, let me spit at you for a minute homey." He said walking off a ways from his friends.

"What up?" Tony asked thinking Jahad was about to question him about Latrice. Since their break-up he tried his best to duck her, not trusting himself to keep his word. Whenever they happened to bump into each other on the street they acted cordial, but there was no way they could deny what they felt for one another. They were still in love and nothing Jahad could do or say could stop it.

"Ayo, it's on nigga!" Jahad said, a crooked grin stretching across his face.

"What you talking 'bout Jah?"

"How much work you niggas got left?"

"We still holdin' a little something. We re-up tomorrow. Why?" Tony asked confused.

"Forget about reing up. Meet me at my mom's crib at nine and I'ma hit you with 500 grams of some raw. You can..."

Tony's eyes lit up like light bulbs, "Say, word!"

"Word nigga. I told you it was on... Now check it, I'ma stay with this job for a while, but I want you niggas to bubble. In between time I'll be working the other end with the studio's and whatnot. If it's poppin' out here like you said, we should be able to re-up with a brick a week easy. You said those Puerto Rican dudes were giving ya'll eight hundred off a two thousand pack, so we'll keep it rockin' like that. The only difference is the dough ya'll hit me with will be going towards making us all rich; You heard?"

"No doubt," Tony said then hesitated, "the Coco Twins won't like this shit, but..."

"Fuck what they like!" Jahad snapped, "If they have any questions, tell 'em we got some family shit poppin' off. Better yet, send 'em to me and I'll tell 'em... Do you niggas got burners?"

"Razor got a old ass trey-eight."

Jahad laughed, "I shoulda known that crazy ass nigga had a burner. Give me a few more weeks, and I'll have hammers for us all. On the coke tip, you handle all that, as far as passing it out and picking up the money. I'll meet you every Friday at my mom's crib to hit you off and pick up the dough." Jahad glanced over at his friends, "Now you know I love my niggas to death, but I want all this to stay between you and me. They'll probably suspect that you're getting the work from me, don't say shit tho'. I want us to go about this without taking a lot of risk or putting anybody under a lot of unnecessary pressure if someone gets bagged, feel me?"

"Yeah, I feel you. How's it going down with the music? We going at it as a group or what?"

"Yeah, sorta like Wu-Tang was rockin'. We'll put Eric out there first; at the same time flooding the streets with crazy underground CD's to get our name buzzing. That raw Bronx shit!"

Tony nodded dreamingly, while picturing himself in the studio with an ill beat booming in his ears.

"It starts right here, Sun," Jahad continued caught up in his own enthusiasm, "Once niggas get a sample of that real Hip-Hop, it'll be like crack. I'ma cop like five or six CD burners, get the fly cover design, then we gon' sell our shit like you niggas be out her pumpin' crills!"

"Word! I see your vision Sun."

"Its gon' take some time tho' Tone, and in between then some shit might happen so you gotta keep me on point. You know how I be spazzin' at times. If I happen to go there, remind me of our goals to keep me focused, you know?"

Tony smiled and gave Jahad a hug, "No doubt Homey. No doubt."

Not long after that inspiring day, money came pouring in hand over fist. Tony with his gifted business mind, within a month had the clique moving close to two kilo's a week, selling nickels two for five dollars. In the process, they were soaking most of the money up that came through the park and drawing customers from nearby spots, thus drawing the attention of the notorious Coco Twins. And just as Jahad predicted trouble was headed their way, but it was all destine.

CHAPTER 9

Hector stood behind the bar mixing Apple Martini's in his Brownstone on Beach Avenue, while José paced back and forth across the living room mumbling obscenities under his breath. The Brownstone was one of five Hector owned spaced out through out the Bronx. They were all decorated exactly the same with brown suede furniture, tan carpet, 100 gallon aquariums, sixty inch flat screen televisions, and fully stocked bars. Hector occupied all five, alternating his time between three baby mother's, a live-in girlfriend, and one just so he could be by himself when he chose to.

Hector walked from behind the bar and handed Jose a drink then sat back in his recliner, "José will you please sit down, you're making me tired."

"Why let him live Hector? Why?" José asked desperately, his face flushed red, "Being who he is should be the end of it."

For the past two months the argument had been going back and forth as to why Jahad was allowed to live, and secretly José was in the process of planning his death despite the strict warning from Hector to let him be. José had a legitimate argument. For years the Coco Twins were the sole controllers of the Big Park, The South Bronx period when it came to drugs. If a hustler didn't work for the Coco Twins, then they brought their drugs from the Coco Twins. If they did neither, they didn't sell drugs in the South Bronx. That was the law, had been the law every since their father laid it down years ago. Now Jahad was on the scene blatantly breaking the law seemingly without a care.

José's hatred for Jahad went deeper than the situation with the park though, a lot deeper. The park only added fuel to the fire. His original hatred stemmed from the fact that Jahad was a part of the Coco Twins foundation, right at the core. A part José wanted to cut out.

"Let me handle this José," Hector replied calmly taking a sip from his drink, "you're making a big deal out of nothing."

"Nothing!" José shouted, "How can you say it's nothing? In a matter of weeks we went from pulling sixty thousand a week out the park, to a measly ten thousand dollars. Six of our workers have jumped ship to make money for the same muthafucka moving in on us, on top of that we both know who this Moreno bastard is and you say it's nothing!"

Hector smiled, "That's exactly what I say."

Jose smirked and shook his head, "And I say you're getting soft. You know the history with this muthafucka just as well as I do, so why in the hell are you protecting him?"

"Stop thinking with your emotions José and use your head. Don't you see the potential he has? In less than two months he's managed to supply the park straight out of Spofford, and it doesn't stop there. I have someone close to him, watching his every move. Our friend is on the brink of getting into the music business. That's millions José. I want some of those millions!"

José finally sat down across from Hector on the couch, "How we do that?"

"Simple. We pull Manual from the park and officially turn it over to Jahad. From there we ease our way into what he has planned with his music."

José shook his head frowning, "You're playing with fire Hector, I feel it, and if you ain't careful, we all get burnt. We don't need his millions, or anything else you think he can offer. We should just kill him and be done with it."

"No!" Hector yelled, slamming his drink down on the coffee table, "You don't see what I see José, understand what's really happening. Think about it, it's all coming back around. You said being who he is should be the end of it, you're wrong. Being who he is should inspire us to use his talent. I want him and I'm gonna get him or at least try. Believe me, if I see on sign that he might rebel he's dead. Killing him is simple being who he's with. The challenge is, keeping him alive so it can work in our favor."

What you mean, who he's with?"

Hector smiled mischievously, "I told you he's being watched, and it just so happens we have an ace in the hole. So stop worrying so much. I have everything under control... trust me."

CHAPTER 10

By the beginning of May, Jahad and Eric were both fed up with shopping around for studio time. Money wasn't an issue; it was the studio owners. They refused to rent out whole weekends, claiming the slot time was already taken. Eric, eager to get his music out, suggested they build their own studio. His cousin Anthony, who went by the name Atomic, was a DJ/Producer who never really had a chance to make it big, would happily produce tracks for them, so all they needed was a building and the equipment. Jahad just as eager to get the ball rolling went along. From there they struck a deal with Joe to keep working for him part-time, in return for him renting a building under his name. Joe agreed only after being assured that he wasn't getting involved in anything illegal and rented a abandoned bodega on Webster avenue. It was small inside, but perfect for what they had in mind. Using one of Joe's vans, they hauled the old counter aisles and coolers out, and then had carpenter's come in to build a soundproof booth and slots for the studio equipment, which Jahad bought hot off the street, going through his old fencer Buddha. The SSL AWS 900 switchboard, Open Lab Neko 64 keyboard, API Lunchbox, AKGC 414 B-XLII microphones, and other equipment Atomic hooked up through a Microsoft computer.

Wanting the studio to have a gutter Hip-Hop appeal, the walls were painted black then a graffiti artist came in and tagged the walls. Afterwards, posters of Hip-Hop legends were hung. Rakim and Eric B., Biggie Smalls, Tupac, KRS-One, Big L, A.G. and Showbiz, Fat Joe, Big Pun, Cool G. Rap, Slick Rick, and The Sugar Hill Gang to name a few. A disco ball hung from the ceiling bouncing colorful red, blue, silver, and yellow lights off the walls and black carpet. Jahad bought expensive second hand furniture off an old white couple from Long Island after making a furniture delivery to their ten room mansion, finding they were putting it in storage. By the time the studio was complete, over a hundred thousand dollars had been spent.

Rap sessions in the park had almost become a daily event. It was there that they came up with material to be used in the studio after Eric started taping each session. The day before the studio would officially be opened; tired but excited, Jahad and Eric made their way to the park after work for one last session.

The songs for their first underground CD were complete. Twelve hot songs would shake up underground Hip-Hop. Eric had six solos, Jahad had two, Tony had two, and the other two were collaborations with the whole clique. Some of the material from their last session would possibly be used for a bonus track.

As they approached their friends the first thing Jahad noticed was the grim looks on their faces. Derrick paced back and forth in front of the bench; his hands bunched up into fist at his side. Razor sat at the end of the bench; his eyes glued on Tony maliciously. Tony sat on the other end away from Razor; his head down in his hands. Kwan, Joey, and Cream sat on the other side with their backs turned to Jahad and Eric.

"What the hell wrong with you niggas?" Jahad asked addressing Tony, "Ya'll act like ya'll got robbed or something."

Razor pushed himself off the bench without taking his eyes off Tony, "Tell him what's up Tone, since you on that sucka shit."

Tony stood quietly and advanced on Razor, but stopped in his tracks when Razor spit the Gem Star from his mouth.

"C'mon nigga!" Razor taunted holding the Gem Star, ready to strike. "You wanna set it on me, but won't do shit when a nigga fucks with fam'. I'll be happy to buck-fifty your shook ass."

"Ayo, hold the fuck up!" Jahad yelled moving between them, "What the hell is going on?"

"What you scared?" Derrick said standing beside Razor, "Tell him what happened nigga!"

Tony shook his head dismal, as Cream turned to face Jahad. Both his eyes were purplish black and swollen almost completely shut. His lips looked light giant slugs split down the middle, a gap where three of his top teeth were missing.

"What the fuck!" Jahad shouted, "Ayo, who did that shit... you

Tone?"

"Tha' go go wins 'uiet..." Cream began pitifully, looking as if he were about to cry before Jahad cut him off.

"What the fuck he trying to say?"

The clique turned their attention to Tony, waiting for him to answer.

"The Coco Twins lieutenant Man-Man and Cream got in a fight."

"What?...When?"

"About an hour ago."

"Out here?"

Tony nodded.

"Ya'll were out here when he got his ass beat?"

Tony nodded again.

Jahad squinted his eyes, "So why the fuck is Cream fucked up and you niggas ain't? Or did ya'll fuck the nigga up who did it?"

"Tried to. Tone let Man-Man fight Cream knowing he's softer than baby shit." Derrick said looking at Tony disgustedly, "It ain't like we ain't try to step up to the plate. Tone was on that other shit."

"You niggas don't understand!" Anger and pain burned in Tony's eyes at being looked down on by his friends. "The Coco Twins are too strong. Look over there. Look!" He nodded towards the handball court where around twenty people were gathered, "All them muthafuckas over there rock with the Coco Twins, and that's only a small part of their crew."

Jahad looked over at the crowd, and then back at Tony, his face full of scorn, "Oh, I understand. Them Puerto Rican niggas got you shook. How in the hell can you just sit around and watch your man get stomped out?"

"It was a one on one Jah!"

"I don't give a fuck what it was. You don't let it go down like that!" Jahad yelled, stepping towards Tony raising his hands.

Eric grabbed his arm, "Ayo, chill Jah. That's your man."

Jahad glared at Eric, but held his ground, "Yeah, that's my man, but that's that bullshit." He turned back to Tony, "This is how it's going down, I'm 'bout to go over here and fuck that nigga Man-Man up. If them other niggas wanna get it, so be it, but ya'll better hold me down."

"Jah this..."

"Jah what!" He screamed. The thought of someone beating up on Cream while his friends watched infuriated him. "Bring your ass on. Cream you bring your soft ass too."

Eric fell in line as they began walking, but Jahad stopped him, "Chill Sun, this ain't your beef. I'll meet you at the studio tomorrow."

Eric laughed sarcastically, "What the fuck you mean it ain't my beef? You buggin'."

Jahad gave him a brief smile and faced his clique, "You niggas got hammers on you?"

"I got mine." Razor pulled up his sweater exposing a .45 automatic.

Tony shot him a sideward's glance, "You know damn well we ain't suppose to be holding hammers out here when we hustling. You know how the police is."

"I ain't trying to hear that shit. What's the use in having a damn gun if you ain't gon' have it when some shit pop off."

"Good point," Jahad agreed, "but hopefully we won't need it. C'mon."

Together they crossed the park with Jahad in the lead. From all directions, every living soul in the park who wasn't high on crack focused their attention on them. The tension could be felt, radiated in waves, and clogged the air like spring pollen.

"Which one is Man-Man?" Jahad asked scanning the crowd who were equally watching them.

Derrick stepped up, "The dude in the middle leaning against the wall in the blue and white Averix. Want me to rock him?"

"Nah, I got him." Jahad said, sizing Man-Man (Manuel) up from the distance. He guessed they were around the same height and build, but knocking him out wasn't his concern. What bothered him was the fact that they were out numbered three to one, with only one gun. His mind screamed, leave and re-group; his pride pushed him forward though. "Check it, I'ma try to get scrams to go head up with me, but if the guns come out you niggas better die with me!" He said fiercely before turning his attention to Razor. "Ayo, if it go down like that body as many of them muthafuckas before they do us."

Razor nodded, "I woulda did that earlier if Tone wasn't on that chill shit."

"You damn right I said chill!" Tony exploded, "These Puerto Rican niggas don't shake me man. We gotta think about the future tho'; remember Jah? We came too far to fuck it up now."

"I feel you, but when it comes to fam' certain shit can't be avoided."

Tony shook his head, "You ain't thinking Jah."

Jahad ignored him, focusing his attention on Manuel, as they approached the handball court. "Ayo Man-Man or whatever the fuck they call you, me and you need to build on some grown man shit."

Manuel studied Jahad while his crew formed a semi-arc around him, "I'm right here, so what's up? And who the fuck is you anyway?"

"I'm Jah, that's who I am. And the nigga you fucked up, that was my fam'. Now it can go do one or two ways. We can get busy with our hammers and whatnot, some of my people gon' get hit up, some of your people gon' get hit up, but in the end some of us gon' get sent up North for bodies. Or, you and me can shoot the one and whoever wins win. In fact, I'll fight all your mans head up. However you wanna do it, unless you only beat up on niggas who can't fight."

Manuel laughed, "You can't be serious. You hear this dude?" He asked looking around at his crew, "On some real shit, I'll fuck you up out here man."

"That's exactly what I wanted to hear," Jahad cracked a smile looking behind Manuel at the rest of his crew, "any of you other dudes want next?"

A big black dude with long dreadlocks' looking like he could play professional football, walked up beside Manuel, "Yeah, I want next, since you talking so damn much, I'ma break your jaw if my man don't break it first."

"Promises, promises," Jahad said, his smile still in place. "Peep this Man-Man, my mans won't get involved but if they see one of your people reaching its gon' be fucked up out here for both of us. So tell 'em to chill."

"As long as your mans don't make no funny ass moves when I knock your ass out, you have nothing to worry about."

Jahad laughed, "Vice versa, but you talking won't knock me out so let's get busy." He started bouncing on his toes.

"Ayo, watch this shit Sun." Eric whispered to Tony.

"What?"

"Just watch."

Manuel took off his jacket and from his waist pulled a Ruger 9 mm. He placed the gun and jacket on the concrete beside him, and then put up his guard. Judging by how he held his hands guarding his face, his elbows tucked tightly again his sides; Jahad knew Manuel had some boxing experience. It didn't matter, this was a street fight, not a boxing ring and Manuel had no idea what was about to be thrown at him.

Before Manuel could even throw a punch, Jahad pivoted around him, and just as he turned released a flurry of short left jabs, twisting his wrist with each thrust to make sure every blow that landed, cut like a razor. Manuel stumbled back, shaking his head, but Jahad didn't let up. He moved in, ducked, and started at Manuel's stomach with hard lightning fast lefts and rights, raising up until the last punch to the middle of his forehead sent him falling back into the arms of the big black dude.

"If I wanted I could make it quick. I'ma punish your ass tho', like you did my man." Jahad said backing up. "Get him ready big boy, and you get ready 'cause you up next."

The black dude glared at Jahad as he helped Manuel to his feet, while off to the side Razor eased the 45 out and held it behind his back.

Once he got himself together, Manuel stayed out of range of Jahad's right hand, his confidence fading. He was tempted to say fuck it, and get his crew involved, but Jahad's warning about them both catching a bad end was stuck in his mind. Summoning his wits he used his left jab to keep Jahad from coming in, then threw a quick overhand right followed by a left hook. The punches fell short as Jahad weaved to the side and released a hard straight right. The blow connected with Manuel's nose and shattered the bone with a loud Crunch! Manuel dropped to the concrete on his hands and knees, while blood poured from his nose and splattered the ground like fat rain drops.

"Stay there until you get your shit together. When you get up I'll go 'head and knock your ass out... I promise."

Manuel shook his head back and forth, fighting to stay conscious. While he recovered, Jahad kept a steady eye on his crew, praying they wouldn't pull their guns. If so, his only option was to try and reach Manuel's gun before he got hit otherwise he would be in a hell of a bind.

"You ready?" Jahad asked after about three minutes, as Manuel started getting to his feet. "If so, I give you my word that I'ma put your ass to sleep real fast."

Manuel glanced at Jahad, then cut his eyes at his gun, which was only a few feet away, wondering if he could get to it before Jahad reached him.

Reading his mind, Jahad shook his head, "Don't even think..."

"BOOM! BOOM! BOOM! BOOM! BOOM! BOOM! BOOM!"

Gunshots erupted behind Jahad, paralyzing him with fear until he noticed Manuel scrambling towards his gun. Feeding off the fear, he dove to the ground and drove his fist into the back of Manuel's head just before he reached the gun. With his head tucked low he crawled until reached the gun then aimed blindly towards the last spot he saw Manuel's crew standing. To his surprise everybody was gone except for the big black dude who was lying not too far away clutching his stomach.

"What the fuck happened!" Jahad shouted over the ringing in his ears.

Razor looked at him grinning from ear to ear, holding the 45 at his side. "I saw Duke flinch like he was reaching so I gave it to him and a few more of them muthafuckas before they ran off. Scrams took most of 'em tho'. Casually he walked over to the black dude and aimed at this head, "Say night, night."

"No! Don't do that shit Razor!" Tony rushed over and pushed the gun in the air, "What the hell is wrong with you? You can't merk that nigga out here like that."

Razor snatched away, screwing up his face, "Why the hell not? It's on now anyway. Shit, he might be the nigga in the long run to body me. Now get the fuck out the way before I shoot your ass!"

"Ayo chill Razor, he's right." Jahad said moving between them, "It's too many eyes out here, but I feel you. Now let's get the fuck outta here before the police get here. We'll go up on my roof so we can build 'cause if it's gon' be war, then we gon' be prepared."

As they walked off, the crowds in the park followed them with their eyes all having the same thought. Who in the hell were these dudes to have the heart to start beef with the Coco Twins? The answer to their questions would go unanswered, but who these dudes would become in the future would be the product of some of their nightmares.

Ten minutes later they were on the roof standing near the ledge, watching as police strung yellow police tape around the handball court. From the distance, the police looked like ants moving about busily, questioning the few people who were still lingering around, mainly crack heads. Two ambulances were parked at the edge of the handball court while attendants wheeled Manuel and the big black dude to it's' back doors, which were flying open.

Jahad turned from the ledge with the weight of their situation bearing down on his mind. The way things looked, there was no way out, blood had already been shed. If the Coco Twins wanted to maintain their street reputation, which was a very important part of their business, they had to retaliate. Another thought struck Jahad; he couldn't back down. If he or any of his crew showed any sign of weakness, the Coco Twins would definitely keep the pressure on. What they had to do was keep striking. Show the Coco Twins there was no fear, and that they were down for whatever. With that thought he turned to Tony.

"How many people the Coco Twins got on their team who's really built like that?"

"I can't say for sure, but it's a lotta them muthafuckas."

"That don't mean shit. Strength ain't really in numbers, it's the individual. We saw that a few minutes ago."

"Yeah, but I'll tell you what I do know. They're probably more than eighty deep so it's bound to be some niggas mixed up in there who get busy. We're what, eight deep, seven excluding Cream."

Cream frowned, "I bus' I 'un…"

"Shut the fuck up, Cream!" Tony snapped, "You fam', but in some beef I'd rather Koran hold me down."

"Ayo, give Sun a break Tone," Jahad said, feeling sorry for Cream. It wasn't his fault that he was a coward. He was born that way. "On some real shit tho' Cream, if it comes down to it you will have to bus' your gun 'cause we 'bout to take these muthafuckas to war."

Tony's eyes grew wide, "You know what you sayin' Jah? Ain't no way in hell we can go up against the Coco Twins and win."

"I ain't say shit about us winning, but the way I see it, once we show 'em that we ain't puss' and they can't make no money in none of their spots, then they might come at us on some peace shit."

"And if it ain't, how you see it?"

Jahad shrugged his shoulders, "Then we gon' have to kill 'em before they get us. Now check it, from sun up to sun down we gon' be in the studio. When it gets dark, we set it. Tone, you said they had spots on Ftelly and Commonwealth Ave, right?"

"Yeah, Beach Ave too."

"Tomorrow night we'll hit up the spot on Ftelly, then chill a few days and hit the one on Commonwealth. I'ma see if I can get you niggas some vest. The one I got cost fifteen hundred, so bring your dough to the studio in the morning so I can go see my man. And keep your guns cocked at all times. Until this beef is over we gon' keep coming until they wanna squash it, we kill 'em, or they kill us; feel me?

Everybody nodded, except Tony, "Jah this is suicide man. We got a chance to make it with this shit. We can make it. You know I don't give a fuck about dying with you, but over this crazy shit." He glared at Cream, "We right at the door Jah. Right there!"

"What the fuck we supposed to do Tone? Bow down to these Puerto Rican niggas, cop deuces? When have we ever copped deuces?"

Tony didn't answer; his pleading would be in vain. Jahad's mind was set and nothing he could say would change it.

"When it's on homey, it's on." Jahad continued putting an arm around Tony's shoulder, "Whatever the outcome it'll be known that we held it down and didn't go out like suckas. So chill with all the stressin'. The only thing you need to be stressin' is laying down your verses tomorrow."

CHAPTER 11

From the roof, Jahad went straight to Michelle's apartment to drop off some money. With all the drama he had been through Michelle was just the person to help clear his mind. Emma could do the trick too, but there was no one like his mother.

Over the past month, Michelle's apartment had undergone an expensive makeover, compliments of Jahad. The living room was decked out with a brand new white leather sectional, a large oval shaped glass table, decorated with crystal ornaments, and a forty-two inch flat screen television posted on the wall across from the poster size picture of John Copeland that Michelle had enlarged. The shabby beige carpet had been replaced with white carpet, the walls painted the same white shade.

The kitchen now held new appliances and a second hand dining room table Jahad bought from the same white couple he bought the furniture for the studio from. The carpenters who remodeled the studio came in and tore out the old gray tile floor replacing it with yellow and white tiles that coordinated with the new wallpaper.

All three bedrooms had new carpet, beds, and dressers. Jahad's old room he shared with Koran was laced with a new computer, stereo system, and television hooked up to a Playstation; a little something extra for Koran since he was maintaining his straight "A" average and staying out of trouble. The best part about everything, Jahad bought most of the furniture and appliances hot off the street, going through Budda.

Michelle was in the kitchen when he came in rambling through her new refrigerator while singing an old Gladys Knight song. Jahad stood in the doorway for a moment, listening as she held the notes to "Midnight Train to Georgia", almost better than Gladys.

"What up Ma-Duke?" Maybe I should put you on one of my

albums. Son and mother collabo."

Michelle turned from the refrigerator and gave him a warm smile, "Hey boy. I was wondering if you were coming to see me today. I saved a plate for you just in case."

"That's why I love you so much," he crossed the kitchen and kissed her on the cheek, "I got some dough for you too. It won't be long before you have enough to buy your crib. Thought about where you wanna move to yet?"

"Yes, but you might not like it." Michelle said, putting his plate of turkey wings, string beans, mashed potato's, and corn on the cob in the microwave.

"As long as you get away from these slums I'll be happy."

"North Carolina."

"North what?"

"North Carolina. That's where I plan on moving to. I already priced some houses in Raleigh."

Jahad frowned, "Why you wanna move way down south for? I thought you'd say Jersey or Connecticut."

"That's where our roots are. My grandparents were from North Carolina; I imagine we still have family down there. It might take a while to look them all up. Besides, I'm tired of living in the city. Country life will do me good. It will be good for Koran too. I won't have to worry so much."

"That's were you gon' catch beef at. I told Kay something along the same lines. Guess what he told me?"

"What?"

"He said if we make him move he gon' start wilin' for real. He wasn't joking either."

"I'll beat his ass too!" Michelle said angrily.

"I told him the same thing. He said it wouldn't stop him."

"So he expects me to leave him up here with you?"

"Yep. I told him it was up to you. He's been coolin' out since I been home so I don't got no problems with it as long as he keep his grades up."

Michelle held Jahad's eyes with a straight face, "I'll think about it, but if I do let him stay, promise you won't let him get caught up in the street. Promise me Jahad!"

"You know I want the best for him, just as you much as you do. I got him Ma." Jahad replied but would swallow those same words years later.

~~~~

On the way to Janet's apartment, his conversation with Michelle played heavily on his mind. Never once had he broken a promise to his family, but the situation with the Coco Twins could cause him to do just that. If he went through with what he had planned then most likely he wouldn't be around to keep Koran from trying to follow in his backward footsteps. Jahad had never backed down from any beef, it wasn't in his blood to back down. Now for the first time in his life he considered trying to make peace. Not for his own sake, but Koran's.

Entering Janet's building, as he walked towards the elevator, it slid open and the same arrogant Puerto Rican he bumped into months ago stepped out. His entire outfit was Louis Vuitton. Beige Louis Vuitton slacks, black suede Louis Vuitton dress shoes, and a black and beige Louis Vuitton wool sweater. A split second later, Jahad's mouth dropped open when another Puerto Rican walked out looking exactly like the first dressed in regular street gear. Black Iceburg jeans, a black hoodie, black Timberlands, wearing a black and white Averix leather jacket.

Instantly, alarms went off in Jahad's head seeing the two twins. They couldn't possibly be who he thought they were, but there was only one way to find out.

"Ayo Hector?" he called out reaching under his jacket for the gun he took off Manuel earlier.

Both twins snapped their heads in his direction, but the clad in Louis Vuitton answered, "Yeah, and you are?"

A crooked smile creased the corners of Jahad's mouth, "Ain't this some shit... I'm Jah."

José gave Jahad a hatred filled scowl, while hector studied him with a curious smile. José, ignorant to the fact that Jahad already had his gun in hand, made an attempt to pull his gun. Luckily Hector grabbed his arm, in the process saving both their lives. "I don't think that would be a good idea José. Our friend here might not agree with your decision." Hector said keeping his eyes on Jahad, who now held the 9mm beside his leg with the hammer cocked back.

"You know, I could body both of you right now and be done with it," Jahad addressed Hector feeling in his gut that he was the twin to appeal to, "I'd rather go about it another way tho'."

"For what reason would you want to kill us?" Hector asked, his smile turning into a sad frown, "We've done nothing to you."

"C'mon man, you know what's up. Your man beat my man ass, I beat your man ass, and then shit got outta control. That was your mans fault tho'... now from what I heard the Coco Twins ain't to be fucked with, but I feel the same way about my team, so the outcome will probably go something like this. Since we're outnumbered eventually my whole clique will get bodied, but not before we merk alotta your people. Or I could merk both of you right now and put an end to the threat, but then I might have to worry about the police."

Hector nodded, "I see you're a thinker. That may prove to be valuable for both of us since I plan to turn the park over to you anyway."

"You what?"

"You heard me. Just a few days ago, my brother and I were discussing you so it's fortunate we happened to meet before things went too far. And for the record, what happened to your friend Cream wasn't my doing. Certain members of my family felt he was ungrateful after all the gratitude we've shown him and took matters into their own hands." Hector cut his eyes at José.

Jahad looked at José, "Whoever these family members are, I'm pretty sure they know Cream ain't built like that. I wonder why they ain't go at somebody else in my clique? Personally, I think a muthafucka who picks their battles are cowards."

"You Moreno bastard!" José hissed and started towards Jahad. "If it was left up to me I'd kill all you muthafuckas like I..."

"José!" Hector shouted, snatching his twin by the arm, "Act like you have some damn sense!"

"Obviously it ain't up to you scrams, if it was tho' killing us wouldn't be as easy as you think."

"Nobody will be doing any killing," Hector broke in, "Jahad please excuse my brother's brashness. He tends to fly off the handle at times."

José glanced at Hector frowning then gave Jahad one last malicious glare before he stormed out the building. Jahad watched him leave to make sure he wouldn't try to shoot him in the back, then faced Hector.

"So the beef is dead right? I mean, I don't have to worry about your brother going behind your back, doing some corny shit do I?"

"As far as I'm concerned there was never any beef and José is well aware that I want you on our team. So you have nothing to fear?"

"Fear?" Jahad snorted, "Never that. The worst thing that can happen to me is I get bodied. Like I said tho', I won't die easy."

"I'm sure you won't." Hector replied thinking he could kill Jahad tonight if he chose to, "If you don't mind I'd rather get off the subject of killing and death... Call it fate or whatever you want to call it, but we met today for a reason so I say we seize the opportunity. I'm offering you the park as a gesture of my goodwill. Now, it comes with certain stipulations. You have..."

"Ayo, hold up man. Before you get it twisted, you ain't gon' be pimpin' me like you were doing my mans. Another thing, we won't be out there too much longer either. What we doing now is just a stepping stone for something greater."

"And what might that be if you don't mind me asking?"

"The music industry. It's only a matter of time before we blow, so in a few more months you can have the park back."

"That's really not my concern."

"What is?"

"You are. My brother is short sighted. Me, I can see your potential. Now hear me out, for the past few months you've been making money in my park free of charge. I personally held my brother back from..."

"Your park?" Jahad cut him off frowning, "When did it become your park?"

"I said hear me out!" Hector snapped sternly, holding up his hand, "The Park I'll turn over to you and your family, and pull my people out. All I ask is that you buy your product from me. As far as your music, there's no reason for me to put on any airs. I know all about what you have planned; the studio on Webster Avenue, down to the people you bought your stolen equipment from. So I'll be blunt, I want in."

Jahad's answer would decide his fate.

"You want in?" Jahad raised the gun, "I know you ain't trying to put pressure on me. Ain't shit sweet here Duke!"

"No, no. You misunderstood me," Hector said quickly, "I'm speaking about a partnership. I have contacts with some heavy hitters already in the industry who I can turn you on to. Advertisement and promotion, I'll handle. All I ask is for a small percentage; say thirty percent."

Jahad's mind raced wondering how Hector knew so much about him. The implication led to a thought he couldn't fathom. One thing he was certain of though, there was no way in hell he would let Hector get his hand mixed up in his record label. The thought, he kept to himself. The twins, Hector in particular, carried a very dangerous aura, like that of a scorpion, quiet and deadly, despite his polished articulate manner and five thousand dollar outfits. "How you know so much about me man?"

"There isn't too much that goes on inside the Bronx period that I don't know. That's not the issue. Are you gonna let me help you or not?"

"Let me sleep on it. I'll get back at you."

"Certainly." Hector smiled, "Unfortunately the park isn't up for discussion. You said from what you heard that I'm not one to be fucked with. Let me assure you, what you heard is exactly right. It's my product you move or nothing. If I continue to let you do it, before long someone else will try it, then another. That would be a lot of unnecessary murders. I'm sure you understand."

"No doubt, I understand. You still putting pressure on me, only from a different angle."

This was the first time anyone had ever tried to force a decision on him and Jahad didn't like it. Didn't like it at all.

Hector shook his head, "You're looking at it all wrong Jahad. Sometimes you have to bend a little in order to get ahead. Look at what I'm doing, I'm offering you a whole lot in exchange for so little out of respect for who you are."

Warning bells went off in Jahad's head again by the way Hector said, "Who you are". It was on an intimate level like they had history together.

"Put yourself in my shoes," Hector continued, "if you were controlling these streets would you allow someone to move in on your territory without paying taxes. All I expect is that you buy your product from me. I'm going beyond being reasonable."

"On the strength of who I am, right?"

Hector nodded, "And your potential. I shouldn't say this with you having that gun in your hand, but anyone else would be dead now."

"Is that a threat?"

"No, not at all. I'm speaking facts."

"So, if I don't buy my coke from you, what you sayin' is I'm dead right?"

Hector held Jahad's stare without answering, his mind already made up that Jahad would have to die. He had qualities Hector admired, qualities Hector guessed were installed by the same person he himself mimicked. It was those same qualities though, that made him come to his decision. Jahad was too cocky, too head strong, and wasn't willing to bend, not even an inch. This could prove to be a problem in the future. He was also smart enough not to tell Hector no, when it came to a partnership, although it was written all over his face.

"You know, I ain't feeling this shit, I'm a rock with you tho', and don't get the idea like I'm a be your lieutenant either. I'm telling you now, when I say I'm done, I'm done. Now with the coke, I'm paying fifteen dollar a gram for some now. I ain't go no problems agreeing to your prices, as long as the coke is good. If not we gon' have to work something out."

Hector smiled, covering his anger. Jahad acted like he ran the show, "Whatever you suggest. Tomorrow we'll get everything settled."

"No doubt. You want my cell number or should I take yours?"

"There's no need. I'll be in touch."

~~~~

The white CL600 Mercedes Benz, idled quietly as Hector approached, his thoughts on the perfect way to end Jahad's life. Hector wanted him to suffer. Not physically, but mentally, so the pain would be much worse. The most important thing to Jahad he figured was his music. That's where it would begin. Once his dream was destroyed, next would be his friends, then his family. Before he ended his miserable life, Jahad would know the cost of challenging the Coco Twins.

CHAPTER 12

Jahad made it in late to the studio the next morning. After satisfying Janet's demanding sex drive, he tossed and turned, unable to sleep with the conversation he had with Hector nagging at his subconscious. Something wasn't right. For one, Hector knew too much about him; information that could only come from someone close to him. He also had the strange feeling that Hector's interest went far deeper than becoming a partner in his record label. The way Hector said, "Who you are" was something he couldn't dismiss from his thoughts. There was a meaning behind the words, but what? Who was he? The thought played in his mind as the cab dropped him off in front of the studio.

Music assaulted his ears when he opened the door, the bass vibrating off the windows. He was about to tell Atomic to turn the music down until he noticed Eric and Tony in the booth free styling over DMX's 'Stop Being Greedy' instrumental. Razor determined to learn how to produce tracks stood beside Atomic, watching as he worked the control board. Joey, Kwan, and Derrick sat on the couch bobbing to the music with blunts hanging out the sides of their mouths. Jahad listened for a minute, then made a motion to Atomic to kill the music.

"Ayo, Atomic what up?" Eric asked sticking his head out the booth. "I was eatin' that shit."

"Chill Sun, we need to build about some important shit. We gon' lay down our verses after I put ya'll on to what happened last night." Jahad sat on the loveseat across from the couch, "Ayo, Atomic, do me a favor Homey. Run to the Jamaican restaurant and snatch us up some beef patties and shit."

"What up Jah?" Tony asked once Atomic left sitting in the recliner while Eric sat beside Jahad on the loveseat.

"You'll never guess who I bumped into last night."

"Who?"

"The muthafuckin' Coco Twins. I caught their asses coming out of my Shorty's building last night."

"Word!" Derrick said excitedly, "You merk 'em?"

"Nah, check this out tho'. They want me..."

Music came blaring from the two large speakers that sat outside the recording booth. Everybody whipped their heads towards the control board and saw Razor fumbling trying to find the power switch.

"Razor get your ass over here and leave that shit alone before you blow something up." Jahad laughed.

Razor grinned sheepishly, "My fault Sun. I'm trying to get on some DJ Premiere shit over here."

"You can get back to that in a minute. Right now you need to hear this." He waited until Razor was seated on the edge of the couch before continuing, "Anyway, they want me to take over the park, but..."

"Who wants you to take over the park?" Razor asked.

"Hector."

"You seen him?"

"See, if you would have been over here listening, I wouldn't have to repeat myself. Yeah, I seen him. I caught him and José coming off the elevator last night."

"You kill 'em?"

Jahad sighed loudly through his nose, "Razor can I talk man, or do you have something else you wanna say?"

Razor bit the inside of his cheek to keep from laughing, "Nah Sun, go 'head."

"They, well Hector, want us to rock the park. José wants us dead. Hector is running shit tho'. He said he'd pull Manual, Man-Man, out so we can have it to ourselves. All we have to do is cop our coke from him."

"What you tell him?" Tony asked surprised.

"That we'd rock with him. To keep it real, the only reason I did it was because what we trying to do. I don't like that dude."

"You made a smart move, but why you?" Tony asked more to himself. "I mean Man-Man was holding the park all the way down and they see more money fuckin' with him. It's gotta be a catch."

"It is. Hector wants to become a partner with our music label."

"What!" Derrick stood outraged, "How in the hell he know about that?"

"That's a good question. He knows everything tho'. I mean everything." Jahad looked at each of his friends.

Erick shook his head angrily, "Ayo, I know you ain't gon' let this dude move in on us like that."

"Hell nah. I told him I'd think about it. I got a feeling he knows I'm frontin' tho'."

"We might have problems then. Them dudes are use to getting what they want," Tony said.

"So," Jahad shrugged his shoulders, "that's their problem, not ours. In a couple more months we cutting all ties with 'em, whether they like it or not."

Tony looked at Jahad with worry in his eyes, "I'm telling you Jah, the Coco Twins be on some other shit. They gon' be expecting something for letting us rock the park."

"Fuck 'em. They'll get no more than we're willing to give. And they definitely ain't touching no parts of our music. If they wanna go to war, then we'll go all the way. By then we'll have enough dough to put a nice price on their head." So like I said, fuck 'em."

"So it's cool if we go back to the park?" Derrick asked.

"Yeah. That's our spot now. For the time being anyway."

"I'm a bungee now then. Ya'll niggas c'mon." Derrick looked at Joey, Kwan, and Razor.

"A'ight. I want ya'll to keep your hammers on you just in case tho'."

Ten minutes later, Atomic returned with two bags of Jamaican food. After they ate and smoked two blunts, Jahad, Tony, and Eric went inside the booth while Atomic went behind the control board.

"Ayo Atomic, this how we gon' rock it," Eric said putting on his headphones, "I'm a lay my song down first, Jah is coming in after me, then Tone. Don't stop the music tho'. When I give you the cue, start mixing in Jah's beat." He turned to Jahad and Tony, "Ya'll niggas gotta be ready to catch the beat, so stay on point."

Jahad and Tony nodded as music came through their headsets.

"Turn my music down some Atomic," Eric said getting hype. "Yeah, that's it, that's it. Ya'll niggas come in here with me on the hook. One, two, three…"

I'm familiar with the art of war / Automatic 44's / While you niggas steady bumpin' your jaws / I'll put you on pause, rewind you / show your mistakes / show your ass how you ended up food on my plate / I'm familiar with the Art of War / Automatic 44's / While you niggas steady bumpin' your jaws / I'll put you on pause, rewind you / show your mistakes / show your ass how you ended up food on my plate /

I don't play the gangsta' role, yo, I leave that to the phonies/I be myself, fly to death, with a tender Roni/

But keep the gat, keep my strap, never leave me lonely/

Desert Eagle 44, I stay with the homey/Close by my side, just in case you run up on me/Thinking shit is sweet, but nah Homey, you don't know me/I'm familiar with the Art of War, keep it on the low tho'/Four o'clock in the morning kickin' in your front door/Masked up, gloves on, gat in my palm/I'm spittin' real shit, got you thinkin' it's a song/

But test my right arm and you can see for yourself/I did a bid for clappin' dudes, that's bad for your health/Have you wheezin' when you breathe/Bleeding on your knees/Crawling for your life while your trying to cop a plea/But there's no escaping me so save your weak apology/

'Cause I'm familiar with the Art of War / Automatic 44's / while you niggas steady bumpin' your jaws / I'll put you on pause, rewind you / show your mistakes / show your ass how..."

BOOM! BOOM! BOOM! BOOM! BOOM! BOOM! TAT! TAT! TAT! TAT! TAT! BOOM! BOOM! BOOM! BOOM! BOOM! BOOM! TAT! TAT! TAT! TAT! TAT! BOOM! BOOM! BOOM! BOOM!

Bullets shattered the front window, tearing through the studio wall like a fist driven through paper. For the first few seconds, no one had any idea what was going on. Then, as if in a movie, Atomic's head exploded and a fine mist shot through the air, splattering the wall like airbrush paint.

"Oh shit! Get down! Get Down!" Jahad screamed, tackling Tony and Eric to the floor as bullets shattered the thick soundproof glass and tore into the control board, sending sparks shooting in the air like fireworks. While on the floor, he struggled to hold Eric who was desperately trying to get to his feet. Jahad had no idea why. By the sound of it there had to be at least four or five shooters with automatic weapons. The shots were too rapid to be regular handguns.

"Atomic! I gotta see what's up with Atomic." Eric pushed himself up on his hands and knees and snatched away from Jahad, paying no attention to the broken glass that bit into his palms.

"Bring your ass back here Eric! He's dead!" Jahad shouted. His eyes grew wider than saucers when a firebomb sailed through the front window in the direction of Atomic's twisted body, "Ayo Eric, get the fuck out the way!"

Eric pressed on, consumed with grief taking took no notice of the firebomb flying in his direction. He paused right before he reached Atomic to look back at Jahad just as the firebomb crashed into the floor inches from his face and exploded, blinding him with heat, "Aaahhhh shiiiiiiit!" Eric screamed, trying to douse out the flame cooking his face, while fire seeped underneath his stomach and ignited his clothes.

"Goddammit!" Jahad yelled and started out the booth, thinking he could save Eric, but it was all in vain. The only sensible thing to do was put a bullet in Eric's head to end his misery.

Seeing that Jahad was about to make the same mistake as Eric, Tony dived on his back and pinned him to the floor, "Let's get the fuck outta here Jah! If you try that superman shit, we gon' both be in this muthafucka roasted."

"This shit is my fault Tone. I shoulda killed those bastards. I shoulda killed 'em!"

"You won't have a chance if we don't get the fuck outta here! C'mon man!"

By this time, two more firebombs landed in the sitting area, setting fire to every thing in sight. Thick black smoke looking like dark storm clouds rose from the carpet and leather furniture, filling every inch of the studio. The posters caught fire and peeled away from the walls like old ancient scrolls.

Jahad watched transfixed, with an unbearable pain in his heart. Tears of despair, pain, and rage wailed up in his eyes as his goal and last chance to live a straight prosperous life all went up in flames. Before turning to leave, he took one last look at his shattered dream while an unquenchable fire ignited inside him. The same fire that would eventually transform him into the man he was destined to be.

~~~~

It was going on three thirty when Jahad and Tony made it back to Monroe projects. Both smelled of smoke and looked as if they were coal mine workers. Across the street, school kids were streaming out the park as usual, just another normal day. It wouldn't be long before the park turned into a war zone with blood that would never wash from the concrete.

Jahad's one and only thought as he exited the cab was the Coco Twins. More to the point, killing them, although he doubted he would accomplish it today after the move they pulled. Most likely they would be holed up somewhere like the snakes they were. So for the time being he set his mind to killing their workers; all of them if he could manage it with two guns and four clips.

"Ayo Jah, what's up man?" Tony asked following him to his building, "What we gon' do?"

"You ain't gon' do nothing 'cause you ain't getting involved. This shit is my fault so I'm a handle it. If I call you later I'll let you know what's up. If not, make sure my family is taken care of. I mean that Tone; I would do the same for you." Jahad's eyes held a pain so intense Tony couldn't help but feel it.

"You know you don't even have to ask me no shit like that. I'm sayin' tho', I'm coming with you."

"Nah Tone. Just leave man, I got this." He said and raced off toward Janet's building.

Janet sat in the living room painting her toenails when he came in. She rushed out to meet him, wearing nothing but a long T-shirt, a smile stretching across her pretty mouth, with thoughts of seducing Jahad in the hallway until she saw his soot filled clothes. "What happened to you? Your boss had you burning furniture or something?"

He said nothing as he walked past her with a deranged look in his eyes, headed towards the bedroom.

"Jahad, answer me Baby," she gripped him by his shoulder, turning him, "what happened?"

"Now ain't the time Janet." He said through clinched teeth, snatching away from her.

In the bedroom he went straight to his closet and took out his bulletproof vest, two Glock 40 calibers from the top shelf, and two extra clips. The vest he strapped on over his sooty t-shirt before

105

tucking both guns into his waist line. To conceal everything, he pulled on a Timberland hoodie. Janet watched him from where she sat on the bed worried, but silent. The look in his eyes told her now wasn't the time to bother him.

Once he was prepared for war, he walked to the bed and grabbed Janet's hand, "Listen Ma, I got fifty eight thousand in my Timberland box. If I don't come back, make sure my mom gets forty thousand and you keep the rest. If the police come around asking questions, you don't know me. In fact, get all my shit outta here and take it to my mom's crib. I'll meet you there later if I can, a'ight?"

Janet stood and wrapped her arms tightly around his waist, "What you mean if you don't come back? You have to come back!" She cried.

"Calm down Janet," he kissed her tears, "I wish I could explain, but I can't. All I can say is somebody fucked up."

"Please Jah, don't do nothing crazy. Please Baby."

"I ain't got no damn choice. These muthafuckas forced my hand!"

"You do have a choice. You can do whatever it is you plan on doing and risk going to jail or getting killed. Or you can stay focused on what we're trying to build. We're almost there Jah. Don't give up now Baby."

Jahad shook his head to fight back tears, "It's over Janet. It ain't nothing to build no more. Those faggot ass Coco Twins burnt down the goddamn studio and bodies two of my homies, so where is my choice, huh? I don't have a damn choice!" He shouted and ran out the bedroom.

Stunned, Janet stumbled back into the bed, growing instantly cold, "The Coco Twins... Oh my God. No." She ran from the bedroom, intent on stopping Jahad, just as the apartment door slammed. There was something terribly important she had to tell him. She had passed the living room when the telephone rung and froze her in her tracks. For some reason, she had a pretty good idea who was calling. Hesitantly, she answered on the fourth ring.

"Hello?"

"Janet?" Hector spoke her name, calm and quiet.

"Y-yes."

"I need you Janet... I really need you."

CHAPTER 13

The first people Jahad spotted when he crossed the street into the park were his friends sitting at their usual park bench. Hector's people were out in numbers too, crowding the handball court with a few young women from the projects among them, scheming on money for hairdo's and new outfits. Scanning the area, he guessed that there were about twenty-five to thirty people, and if he could he was going to kill every last one of them. He felt no compassion at all. How could he, when the Coco Twins felt none for him. So everybody in the vicinity of the handball court were targets.

First, before he made his move, his friends had to leave the park. He already accepted that he might die today. If he did it would be his own fault, since he didn't kill the Coco Twins when he had the chance. By his way of thinking, his friends shouldn't have to face the same fate because of his mistake.

"Ayo, Tone said he wanted to build with you niggas," he said as he approached thinking up a quick lie, "he's up on my mom's roof waiting."

Razor looked up frowning, "Why in the hell didn't he come out here?"

Jahad shrugged his shoulders, "I don't know, ask him."

"Jah, I thought you said the Coco Twins were turning this shit over to us." Derrick said, pushing himself off the bench, "Man-Man still got niggas out here pumpin'."

"Oh word, Duke out here? Good." Jahad said, and a spark of his menace intent flashed through his eyes, "That's what Tone wants to build with ya'll about."

Derrick nodded, walking off with Joey and Kwan following, while Razor stood in place, his eyes locked on Jahad's face. "Jah what's really up man? The only thing slow about me is the way I walk and something ain't right."

Jahad shook his head back and forth, trying to rid himself of the pain. The vision of Atomic's head exploding, Eric's burning body, and the studio going up in flames was clear as water in his mind. Along with the vision came that same strong urge to strike out at everybody involved, whether directly or indirectly. Looking back at Razor, he saw the one person who would be his best asset in making it happen, "They fucked up Razor, word up, they fucked up fam'!"

"Who? What the hell you talking 'bout?"

"The Coco Twins. They had the studio burnt down and merked Eric and Atomic."

"What!" Razor reached to his waist and pulled out a Beretta 9mm, "Where the fuck they at?"

"I'm sayin', I'm 'bout to body all them muthafuckas over there." Jahad looked over his shoulder at the handball court.

Razor smiled, "Word. C'mon lets kill 'em."

Razor started walking off, but Jahad grabbed his shoulder. "Hold up Sun. You need something to cover your face with, just in case we make it out alive."

"Fuck that, it's on nigga!"

Jahad pulled the hood over his head and drew the strings tight so that only his eyes and nose were showing then followed behind Razor with his head down, hoping he wouldn't draw attention to himself. Razor on the other hand, walked with his gun out to his side without a care in the world of who saw him. The crowds on the handball court were too occupied selling drugs, and shooting dice to notice them until it was too late. From about forty feet away, Razor took off running aiming at the heart of the crowd.

BOOM! BOOM! BOOM! BOOM! BOOM! BOOM! BOOM! BOOM! BOOM! Jahad ran to Razor's right, lifted both his guns, and started picking off those trying to escape.

BOOM! BOOM! BOOM! BOOM! BOOM! BOOM! BOOM! BOOM! BOOM! BOOM! BOOM! BOOM! BOOM! BOOM! BOOM! BOOM! BOOM! BOOM! BOOM!

Bullets ripped into the crowd, slamming a few people back into the wall before they fell to the concrete dead or either holding their wounds, screaming in agony. When Jahad's magazines clicked empty, he calmly stuffed them in his hoodie pocket and popped in two fresh clips. Razor, living up to his name, dropped his gun once his bullets were spent, and started slitting the throats of those too wounded to get away. All around them were dead and wounded people, some trying desperately to crawl away, but there was no escape. Jahad walked through the dead, shooting the wounded in the back of their heads. At that moment, his conscience was filled with something dark and evil... Revenge!

He was on the verge of stepping over a dead body to kill his fifth victim, when a bullet slammed into his chest and lifted him off his feet. Once he hit the ground, he looked up in pain, his vision blurry, and saw Manuel taking aim at Razor who was bent over in the process of cutting someone's throat.

"Razor!" Jahad yelled, lifting his gun, "Dive... Now!"

Without hesitating, Razor dived on top of a dead body, just as a hail of bullets flew over his head. Manuel thinking Jahad was dead, spun around shocked and made the last mistake of his life. Jahad took aim at the center of his forehead, and squeezed off two shots that jerk his head back with enough force to snap his neck. No sooner than he fell Jahad ran over still holding his chest and emptied one of his clips in Manuel's face. Blood, bits of bone fingerprints, and pinkish colored brains splattered the concrete and Jahad's boots before his gun clicked empty.

"C'mon Razor, lets get the fuck outta here." Jahad said looking around paranoid. In all directions the park was empty; reminding him of the day his father was murdered.

"Hold up." Razor called out, crawling on his hands and knees, his tongue hanging out the side of his mouth, still slitting throats with a determined look in his eyes. "Give me a second. I still got a few more left."

"Fuck that, c'mon nigga!"

Reluctantly, Razor pushed himself off the ground covered in blood and followed close behind Jahad. They made it to the edge of the park boarding Story Avenue when two uniform cops came crossing the street towards them with their guns out. Jahad was about to turn and run, but Razor wrapped an arm around his shoulder.

"Give me your gun and front like you hurt."

Jahad looked at him like he was crazy, which he was, "What? You see the damn Po-Po right there."

"Just do it! Give me your gun and grab your chest like you been shot or something."

Playing along, Jahad bent over moaning and slid Razor his gun. To his surprise Razor wrapped his forearm around his neck roughly and pressed the gun to his temple just as the two white cops reached the sidewalk.

"Drop the damn guns, or I'll kill him right fuckin' here!" He shouted, easing his way towards the cops, "I said drop 'em!"

The cops froze ten feet away, their guns pointed at Jahad's chest. In the distance sirens could be heard growing closer with each passing second. Along the Avenue, traffic had come to a stop while people watched with shocked and excited expressions, like they were watching a movie.

"I'm getting ready to try some shit Jah." Razor whispered.

"What the fuck you doing Razor? You..."

Razor swung the gun from Jahad's head and shot the police to his right in the head twice, knocking him back into his partner. At the same moment his partner let off a shot that hit Jahad in the stomach, forcing the wind out of him. Razor used the opportunity to shoot the cop in the throat, and then raised the gun a few inches higher and squeezed off two rounds in his face. A gasp rose from the onlookers as Razor half dragged Jahad across the street through the stalled traffic. Jahad held on tight, trying to catch his breath but to the onlookers it looked as if he were being kidnapped.

By the time they made it to the other side of the street, cop cars were only a few hundred feet away, speeding up Story Avenue in full pursuit. Razor kept a steady pace, helping Jahad along until they made it to Michelle's building.

"You a'ight nigga?" He asked, glancing over his shoulder as sweat poured from his face.

Jahad nodded, clutching his stomach, still too winded to speak.

"Key the damn door then, before I have to body some more cops."

Jahad fumbled trying to get his key out until Razor got tired of waiting and dug in Jahad's pocket, taking out the key. After he keyed them in, he helped Jahad up the stairs, meeting Derrick, Joey, and Kwan, just as they were leaving.

"What the fuck happened in the park?" Derrick asked, looking at their bloody clothes.

"Nothing!" Jahad snapped, leaning against the roof's exit door, feeling as if someone had hit him in the chest and stomach with a sledgehammer. He took a few deep breaths, then looked up at Razor, "Why in the hell you do that stupid shit for? You know the police ain't gon' stop looking for us until they get us or we dead."

"Not us, me." Razor replied, glancing over at the park where more than twenty police cars had pulled up already, along with a fire truck, two news crews, and three ambulances.

"What the hell you talking 'bout." Jahad asked, wincing as he stood up straight.

"Think about it. We killed at least seven muthafuckas so..."

"What!" Derrick, Joey, and Kwan all shouted at the same time.

Razor shot them a scowl, then complained, "Somebody gotta take the fall Jah. You know it's gon' be mad eyewitnesses saying they saw me put the hammer to your head. A lotta muthafuckas saw me merk those cops too. You should..."

"Merk who!" The trio shouted again.

"Shut the fuck up and let me finish!" Razor yelled before turning back to Jahad, "You should be good, if not, I'm a make sure you are. Everybody saw my face, so I'm going down anyway."

Jahad screwed up his face, "Who the hell I look like to let you go down for this shit by yourself. We in this together nigga."

"Nah Jah," Razor smiled sadly, "you held down the last case, remember? I'm a hold this one down."

Jahad shook his head distressed. He couldn't picture letting Razor take the fall for something he was responsible for. If only he had killed the Coco Twins when he had the chance, none of this would have ever happened.

"Check it Jah," Razor said interrupting his thoughts, "you gotta be out here to hold the clique together. You know I'm a hold it down, regardless of where I'm at?"

"So what you sayin'? You gon' turn yourself in?"

Razor nodded, "I have to. I might kill a few more muthafuckas before I do it tho'...On some real shit, I know how much this music shit meant to you and they fucked it up. They took your dream, our dream, 'cause I can't even do my Premiere shit now," he said in an attempt to lighten the mood.

"You don't have to do this shit Razor." Jahad pleaded, "I got some dough in the stash. You can bungee dog, go out west or down south."

"Nah Homey. The only way this shit will work is if I take the case. If not, all the heat gon' fall on you. Just chill Sun, I said I got it."

Jahad's eyes filled with tears. If Razor took the weight, there was no way possible he would ever see the street again. On the other hand he also knew Razor was right, someone had to make a sacrifice, or the police could end up killing them both. Overwhelmed with emotions, he gave Razor a fierce hug. "Ayo word up, I love you nigga! And as long as I'm out here, you know your family don't have to worry about nothing."

"I love you too nigga or I wouldn't be doing this shit." Razor smiled, "Now let me get your other hammer so this shit will add up when I turn myself in. We need to get off this damn roof too. It won't be long before this muthafucka is flooded with cops."

Jahad gave Razor the 40 Caliber, then turned to Derrick, "Call Tone when you leave here and tell him to meet me at my mom's crib. I'ma hit him with some dough for ya'll so ya'll can get your people somewhere safe. The beef is cooking now, so most likely ya'll gon' be targets... where in the hell is Cream?"

"Probably somewhere sleeping that ass whippin' off." Derrick answered.

"Try to find him and let him know what's up. When we leave here, go straight home and get your people packed up. I'll meet ya'll back up here at twelve. If I don't, Tone will. I love you niggas be safe!"

~~~~

Jahad went straight to Michelle's apartment from the roof. Knowing the Coco Twins, they would make the beef personal once they heard about what happened in the park, so although Michelle probably wouldn't like it, they were leaving, even if it meant dragging them out. Entering the apartment, he barely had time to close the door before Michelle, Latrice, and Tony rushed up the hallway towards him, their faces masked with fear.

"Thank God!" Michelle cried running into his arms.

"What's wrong with you?" Jahad asked, pretending to be confused, "What happened?"

"You know what happened!" She snapped, "All those people died in the park. It's all over the news."

"And? What's it got to do with me?"

At that moment, Janet bent the corner from the direction of the kitchen. She looked at him a second as if she saw a ghost, her eyes wide, then burst into tears as she ran to him, "You're alive!"

"Yeah, I'm alive... you told my moms I had something to do with what happened in the park?" He asked frowning.

"Not... Not exactly, but I didn't know what to think Boo."

"Who else you tell?"

"Nobody. I came straight here after you left. What you trying to say?"

"Nothing Janet, just don't ever speak on it again, a'ight?"

"What happened?" Michelle asked, looking at his bloody clothes.

"Nothing Ma... listen, you need to get everybody packed up. I'm getting you outta here."

"Packed up? You're telling me nothing happened, but you want us to get packed up. And where exactly are we supposed to go?"

"Ya'll can stay with my aunt if you want," Tony answered, "she lives out in Long Island. I can set it up with a phone call."

"Do that now and send your family with 'em. Shit is real thick now. Tell her they might be out there for a while, but its five thousand in it for her."

Tony nodded, taking out his cell phone just as it rung, "Yeah what up... I'm already here... Word! Oh Shit!"

"What? What happened?" Jahad asked alarmed.

Tony moved the phone away from his ear, "The police just snatched Razor up in the park."

"The park? What was he doing in the park?"

"Hold on." Tony put the phone back to his ear, "What up with Razor... He did what! What made him do some dumb shit like that for... Oh word, Razor... Yeah, yeah, a'ight one." Tony shook his head as he disconnected the call.

"What up with Razor? He a'ight?"

"Yeah, he good. Derrick said when he left the roof he went straight to the park and told the police he bodied all them people. They got two hammers off him too... Ayo, it's a wrap for Sun."

"I know, but we gon' make sure he wants for nothing. Go 'head and make that call so we can get our people outta here."

Neither Michelle nor Latrice made a motion to move, "What have you done Jahad?" Michelle asked with her hands on her hips.

"I'd rather not say Ma. I know it ain't safe for ya'll to be here, so will you please hurry up and pack."

Michelle stared at him a moment before giving in, "Alright

Jahad, but before I leave this apartment, you're gonna tell me what's going on. I'm serious."

"A'ight Ma, but believe me, it ain't my fault."

"I never said it was. C'mon Trice."

"I'll help you Mrs. Copeland," Janet turned to follow.

"Hold on Janet, I need to talk to you."

A flash of fear sparked in her eyes, "About what?"

"You sure you ain't tell nobody else what you think I did?"

She frowned, "I told you I didn't. What, you think I would turn you in?"

"Nah it ain't like that. I just wanted to make sure... Listen, shit is gonna be crazy hot for a while, so you probably won't be seeing too much of me until everything is straightened out. You took my shit out your crib, right?"

She nodded with tears in her eyes.

"Good. You get some of that dough?"

" No. I put it with your stuff. I don't need any money. What I need is for you to let me stay with you. I think I can protect you." She said seriously.

"You protect me?" Jahad smiled and pulled her in his arms, "I like that. No Sexy, what you need to do is go home and pray for me. Like I said, I'm a be lying low, but I'll be coming through from time to time, so don't have nobody in the crib. Remember what I said about giving my puss..."

"Jahad!" Janet said, embarrassed glancing at Tony.

Jahad laughed tilting her head up so he could look into her eyes, "You know I'm crazy in love with you, right? If there was anyway I could avoid this shit I would, I swear I would, but its outta my hands now. When it's over tho' we gon' make what we got official. How you feel about that?"

"What are you talking about Jahad?"

"I'm talking 'bout marrying you girl, changing your last name to Copeland."

Janet burst into tears on the verge of revealing her secret; the secret that weighed on her conscience like a ton of bricks. She was torn between two halves, her mind in turmoil, trying to decide how to appease both halves. One thing was for sure, she would do everything in her power to keep Jahad alive. How could she not when she was carrying his child? Another secret she kept to herself due to the circumstances.

"C'mon Janet, what is it, yes or no? You got me sweatin' here."

She looked up forcing a smile, "You know I will Jahad. You didn't have to ask twice."

CHAPTER 14

Jahad insisted on walking Janet to the elevator, fearful that she could become a target if the Coco Twins found out about their relationship. This led to the thought of sending her away with his family. While he brooded over her safety, Janet did the same about his. She alone had the power to turn the scales in his favor. All it took were a few words, a few words she couldn't manage to speak. In her mind, a small voice whispered repeatedly, tell him, tell him, tell him, but another voice deep in her subconscious screamed just the opposite, they'll kill you, they'll kill you, they'll kill you. What was strange and unbelievable was beneath her fear of Hector was a fierce love, which only her love for Jahad could compare with.

"Jah," Janet forced his name from her lips when they stopped in front of the elevator, her conscience pushing her to tell him, "I have to... (they'll kill you!)." The voice echoed through her mind, causing her to freeze.

"What up?"

She blinked tears from her eyes, "I want...(they'll kill you) I love you, baby. Don't ever forget that."

Jahad smiled, "How can I forget when you love me so good? Now I want you to go pack up some clothes, so you can bounce with my moms. I don't want to be worrying about you all crazy. I'ma go with you to make sure you're good."

"I can't Jah! I have to stay here to keep you safe," Janet cried pushing away from him, "besides, you can't go nowhere looking like that. You need to change." She looked down at his clothes.

"What makes you think can keep me safe?"

"I can, believe me."

Jahad was about to question her further when the elevator door slid open. Thankful for the distraction, Janet gave him a quick kiss then stepped into the elevator, holding his probing stare until the door closed. For a second, she closed her eyes, trying to relieve herself of the tension, but soon the tears came. Too much weighed on her conscience. She was expected to betray the one person who meant the world to her, a deed she couldn't imagine doing, especially finding out that she was pregnant. Her plan, before everything came crashing down, was to break the news to Jahad over a nice candle light dinner, maybe some wine, although Jahad would prefer a cold 40-ounce of beer. Now she had to use her pregnancy as a gambling piece to use with Hector and Jahad.

Somehow she had to find a way to talk Hector out of killing Jahad. If she couldn't, then as much as it would hurt her, she would have to betray him. Those last few minutes spent with Jahad made her realize exactly where her priorities lay. Jahad was her future, Hector was her past, and although she loved him dearly, deep in her heart she knew his love for her was superficial, while Jahad's love was genuine.

Back at her apartment, she paced the living room floor nervously, trying to work up the nerve to call Hector. Each time she reached for the phone, her hand trembled so bad she doubted if she could dial his number. On her third try, before she could pick up the receiver, the phone rung, causing her to jump.

"Hello?"

"Where is he!" Hector shouted.

"I... I... he's not here."

"Don't lie to me Janet. You'll regret it."

"I'm not lying Hector, I wouldn't." Janet took a deep breath, "Hector you know that I've never asked you for anything, so this one time when I ask you to spare Jahad's life, will you please do it... for me?"

"Spare him," Hector spat, "do you have any idea what he's done?"

"I've heard, but that's beside the point. I'm asking you to do this for me. We'll leave and never come back to the Bronx if it'll make things better. Just don't kill him. Please!"

Right then, Hector knew he could no longer trust her, "What's so special about him Janet? Why are you going against me?"

"I'm not going against you Hector. It's just that... I mean... I love him Hector, and I'm pregnant. I want my baby to have its father around."

The muscles in Hector's jaw clenched, but he wasn't about to let his anger cloud his thinking. Pushing his anger aside, he quickly formed a plan, "You're pregnant? That changes everything then. How soon will you two be able to leave?"

Janet felt a ray of hope. "You'll do it?"

"What other choice do I have? I can't see myself killing the father of your unborn child. He can't stay in New York period though, so when will you leave?"

"Thank you Hector! Thank you!" She cried, feeling as if a weight had been lifted from her chest. Once she told Jahad she was carrying his child, being the man she knew he was the child would come first. "We'll leave tonight, promise."

"Make sure you do. And remember Janet, you owe me one." Hector hung up, then punched in José's number, keeping the conversation short, "Janet's apartment in two hours. Come by yourself, bring your gun."

~~~~~

Jahad took a quick shower after walking Janet to the elevator, washing the blood, soot, and smell of death from his skin. His clothes and boots he put in a trash bag to dispose of later. The bulletproof vest he put back on once he examined the two large purplish bruises on his chest and abdomen. Before leaving the bathroom he said a silent prayer, thanking God for Rahoul because if it weren't for the vest he'd probably be in hell.

Koran sat on his bed, looking down at his shoes when Jahad walked in. Beside him was a pile of clothes and an empty suitcase. Looking up, he gave Jahad a twisted scowl, then focused back on his sneakers.

"Why you ain't packing?" Jahad asked, going to his old bed, where his clothes from Janet's were stacked, along with his boot and sneaker boxes.

"You're leaving again ain't you?"

"No, you are, so get your stuff together."

"I ain't going nowhere!"

Jahad turned from his bed and saw tears in Koran's eyes, his small hands bunched into fists, held stiffly by his side. "C'mon Kay, now ain't the time for the bullshit. Get packed so you can get the hell outta here."

118

"Fuck that!" Koran jumped from the bed and rushed Jahad, swinging wildly, "You ain't leaving me this time! I'm coming with you! I'm coming!"

Caught off guard, Jahad wrapped him in his arms, "Whoa lil' nigga. What you mean? I ain't going nowhere, so why you spazzing?"

"You are! You're going back to jail or you gon' get killed just like dad did. I'm coming with you this time." He pushed himself away and looked up at Jahad defiantly.

"Where you get the idea I'm a get bodied from?"

"I know what happened in the park. I was looking out the window."

"You saw me!" Jahad walked to the window overlooking the park. Police cars and ambulances were everywhere, but from the distance the police looked like small dots. "How the hell you see us?"

"With these," Koran held up his binoculars, "when I heard the shots, I ran to the window. I couldn't see your face too good, but I saw Razor's."

"You ain't tell nobody did you?"

Koran looked at Jahad like he was stupid, "Why would I do something like that for, so you can go to jail even faster."

Jahad sat on the bed beside him, "I ain't going to jail Kay, at least I hope not, and I definitely won't let nobody kill me so stop stressing'. I can't tell you everything, but some niggas fucked up, and I gotta do what I gotta do. When it's over, ya'll can come back. I already spoke to moms and you can cool out with me when she moves. For now tho', I gotta get ya'll somewhere safer."

"You gon' kill some more people ain't you?" Koran asked bluntly.

Jahad was about to lie until he noticed the look in Koran's eyes. The same look he himself used when he wasn't trying to hear no bullshit. "Yeah Kay, I gotta body a few more niggas. Not because I want to, I have to. If I don't, they gon' body me; feel me?"

Koran nodded, "Kill 'em then. I can help. All you have to do is show me how to shoot a gun."

Jahad smiled, "Nah lil' nigga, you know I can't do nothing like that... I never told you this, but I always wanted to go to college. Now you have a chance to do something I always wanted to do. Why you think I stay on you about keeping your grades up. You gon' be that Harvard nigga. So let me do me, and you do you, by keeping your grades up. What you say?"

After a few seconds, Koran nodded, "A'ight, you better not get killed tho'."

"I die hard lil' nigga. Now get your stuff together so you can bounce. Oh yeah, if you swing on me again, I'm a rock your lil' ass."

"Yeah, you can rock me now, but when I get older I'ma rock you back." Koran grinned, going to his closet.

Jahad turned back to his bed in search for a matching outfit and accidentally knocked over his shoe boxes. Heaps of money spilled out onto the floor from his Timberland box, bound by rubber bands in thousand dollar rolls. Catching sight of the money, Koran dropped his clothes and dove to the floor, scooping up money in a frenzy, trying to stuff his pockets.

"Chill lil' nigga." Jahad laughed peeling money from his hands, "Go 'head and pack. I'm a bless you when you're finished."

"For real?"

"Yeah, now hurry up."

From his stack of clothes, Jahad took out two jean suits, some socks, and three pair of boxers. With all that was going on he figured he wouldn't have use for a lot of clothes. As he stuffed his duffle bag out the corner of his eye, he noticed a large brown paper bag sitting at the far side of the bed. The coke. He had close to eighteen ounces left from his last buy. He wrapped it up in a t-shirt and threw it in with his clothes, just as Koran cornered him.

"Let me get my blessin'."

"I ought to bless you up side the head." Jahad said giving him a roll of money. "Don't tell moms I gave you all this dough. Don't be spending it all crazy either."

Koran nodded, his eyes glued to the money.

"Koran, Jahad!" Michelle called out sticking her head in the door.

"Yeah Ma." They both answered while Koran stuffed the money in his back pocket.

"Koran take your suitcase to the living room. I need to have a word with your brother."

Koran cut his eye at Jahad as he grabbed his suitcase, "Don't forget what you told me."

"I got you lil' nigga."

Michelle closed the door behind Koran, "What was that about?"

"Nothing Ma, what up?"

"Tell me what's going on Jahad."

"I'm sayin'... I don't really wanna go there."

"You already went there!" She snapped, stepping in his face, "You came in here telling us we have to leave and I want to know why."

Jahad closed his eyes and sighed, "Some dudes came up on Webster Ave. and hit up my studio. You remember my friend Eric, the dude I use to work with?"

"Yes, your rapping friend."

"He's dead. They killed him and his cousin Anthony. The studio ain't nothing but ashes now. That's what happened."

Michelle gripped his hand, "Who did it!"

"These Puerto Rican dudes. You know I was doing my music thing, well they wanted to get their hands in it and I said no. So to show me they weren't feeling it, they did what they did and I did what I did."

"The park?"

"Yeah, and now I gotta get the Coco Twins, then it'll be finished."

"Coco Twins?" Michelle said confused, "What did those people in the park have to do with whoever killed your friends?"

"The Coco Twins are the bastards who sent them dudes to the studio. The people in the park were their workers. I guess they thought I was gone or something. They slept on the wrong nigga." Jahad's voice was ice cold.

"Close to ten people were killed Jahad!" Michelle shouted hysterically. From what she saw on the news, there was no way possible Jahad would come out of this without going to jail or worse. "If they catch you, you're going under the jail!"

"I'm good Ma, so calm down. Razor went to the park and turned himself in. He's taking the weight for the bodies."

Michelle sat down on the edge of the bed and looked up at Jahad through pleading eyes, "Jahad please listen to me. Come with us and leave this mess alone. Nothing good can come from it. Nothing! They killed some of your friends, you killed a lot of theirs. Leave it at that and let's go."

Jahad shook his head, "You don't understand Ma. They ain't only kill my friends, they killed everything I worked hard for. And they did it just because they could. I ain't do shit to them, nothing…I gotta get 'em!"

"You don't have to do nothing!" Michelle shouted. "You're letting your damn pride get the best of you and it's gonna mess around and get you killed!"

"I won't get killed Ma, trust me," he said turning back to his bed hoping she would change the subject. From his shoebox he counted out twenty, thousand dollar rolls, and put it to the side of the bed then another twenty so Tony could split it with his crew. "This dough should be enough with what you already have to cop your crib. If you need to reach me, I'll be at Mrs. Harris' crib, but I want you to move as soon as possible."

"Ha." Michelle snorted, "If you think I'm moving you bumped your head. Until this mess is over, I'll be right here in New York; since I see you aren't trying to hear one word I'm saying."

"I hear you Ma, I gotta finish it tho'. I mean, look at what they did. Just look at what they did!" He yelled as tears sprung to his eyes.

"I know baby, I know." Michelle stood and hugged him, "You can't let what they did destroy you though Jahad. Your dream was one of many. They burnt down your studio, so what, build another one. You'll be letting them win if you give up on your dreams. Think about that." She said, and then walked out leaving him to his thoughts.

Jahad felt everything she said, but he no longer wanted to pursue his music. The passion was gone; it went up in flames with his studio. Now his craving was for something far greater. Power! And powerful he would become far beyond his expectations.

CHAPTER 15

Jahad waited until Tony left with his family before heading to Emma's with his duffel bag slung over his shoulder, and a Remington 380 automatic in his right hand, cuffed against his side. The hallway was empty when he stepped from the Michelle's apartment. Quiet to the point he could hear his heart beating as his eyes darted back and forth from the staircase entrance to the elevator turn off. He half expected Hectors people to show up at any moment. Paranoia had him so in tune with his senses he heard when the elevator squeaked to a stop on his floor. Seized by fear and a burst of adrenaline, he dropped the duffel bag from his shoulder and took aim at the corner Turnoff. Seconds passed, then Emma returning from her nightly church services turned corner carrying a bag of groceries humming a gospel melody. Seeing the gun pointed at her she froze and dropped her groceries spilling tomatoes and oranges all over the floor.

"Jahad what are you doing!" She shouted clutching her chest, "Put that thing away right now!"

His eyes filled with panic, he swung the gun away, but kept it pointed in the direction of the elevator turn off, "Was anybody on the elevator with you?"

"No boy now put that gun away. What's wrong with you?" Emma kept her eyes or him while picking up groceries.

"I'm in trouble Mrs. Harris. I need your..."

"Shhhhhh! Come on in this apartment we can talk then. Almost made me have a heart attack pointing that thing at me," she scolded under her breath.

Jahad's attention was still focused on the elevator and staircase entrance when Emma pushed the door open and impatiently ushered him inside. Once inside, she secured the lock then led him to a bedroom across from our own. The same bedroom he used to sleep in as a child when she would baby-sit him. Nothing about the room had changed, the queen size bed, made up with the same handmade yellow, red, and blue quilt he used to snuggle up under and the same fluffy white pillows. Beside the bed, sat a large chest, the same chest he hid in when he and Latrice played hide and seek. On the opposite side of the bed sat an antique dresser, decorated with tiny woodcarvings of black angels. Jahad stood in the doorway a second, while the memories washed over him making him forget his troubles for the moment.

"Go on and put your things up. I'll be in the kitchen... are you hungry?"

"I can't eat nothing right now if I wanted to Mrs. H," he replied wearily.

"Well, I have some chicken that I fried last night I'll heat up just in case you get an appetite; some homemade biscuits too."

Left by himself, Jahad went over to the chest, finding it packed with pressed white sheets. From his duffel bag he took out the coke, which was wrapped tightly in Saran wrap and the remainder of his stash and placed everything in between the sheets. The gun he put in his back pocket, not wanting to be far from it. Before putting his duffel bag away he took out a sandwich bag half-full with lime green weed and a box of White House cigars, when it occurred to him that Emma might flip if she caught him smoking weed in her apartment. To his surprise when he walked into the kitchen she was sitting at the dining table smoking a joint the size of his pinky finger.

"I knew it!" He laughed pulling out a chair, "You be in here getting toasted."

Emma smiled and took a long pull from her joint, "It's..." She coughed and blew out a cloud of smoke, "its natural grown herbals from God's green earth. It won't hurt me a bit."

"I can't beef with you," he placed his weed on the table along with his cigars, "I guess you won't mind if I twist up a fatty."

"I don't see how you young people smoke them things. What you call 'em blunts? If you ask me it's a waste of marijuana."

"Believe me Mrs. H., after what I've been through today, I need to smoke a fat one."

"And just what have you been through?"

"You don't want to know."

"Oh, I don't? Obviously you are involved with whatever

happened in the park or you wouldn't be here now. What I need to know is why, because if it has anything to do with those Puerto Rican boys... then I have a story to tell you. Something I probably should've told you a long time ago. I didn't because I didn't think you would get mixed up in the stuff your father was mixed up in, and I feared how you would react."

"My father? Puerto Rican boys?" Jahad asked as the hairs on his arm stiffened, "I know you ain't talkin' bout..."

"Hector and José Sanchez," Emma finished for him, "Go on and tell me what happened."

Jahad sat up straight in his chair stunned, confused, and a bit fearful at the mention of his father's name in the same sentence as the Coco twins. Anxious to hear what she had to say, he recounted everything from the time he came home from Spofford, including his attempt at starting his record label, up until the massacre in the park. He was angry all over again by the time he finished speaking through his clenched teeth.

"So they call themselves the Coco Twins now," Emma said disgustedly, "I know it's a sin to hate and I pray that someday I can rid myself of it, but I hate them boys with a passion. They never should have been born."

Jahad was taken back by the vehemence in her voice, "How you know about the Coco Twins?"

"I'll tell you, but truth be told, that park and a lot of the other drug areas around here are rightfully yours. Although John didn't want that life for you and he was right. You're way too smart to be mixed up in the streets. He used to brag about how you were going to be the first in the family to go off to college."

"You're losing me Mrs. Harris," Jahad frowned, wondering if she was a little too high.

"I'll explain everything, but I have to start from the beginning. And don't mention a word of this to your mother." Emma stared off at the wall a moment with a smile creasing the corners of her mouth as her mind faded back in time, "You know, your father changed my life. This is back in the late 60's before that crack mess came out and heroine was popular. Money Jay, that's what everybody called John back then, and he had it going on as you young people say. To this day I still don't know how he did it, some said he had ties with the Mafia, they controlled all the drugs back then, but the South Bronx belonged to John. Personally,..."

"Hold up Mrs. Harris. Backup." Jahad held up his hand trying to grasp what she was saying, "You're telling me my pops was a drug dealer? I mean come on Mrs. Harris, he couldn't be. Up until the day he was murdered, he went to work every morning at five and was home by four, five days a week. I remember like it was yesterday."

"Oh, John wasn't your average drug dealer. Michelle had no idea what he was into, still don't, I suppose. Not long after he met her, he started working for the Transit System. This didn't stop him from maintaining his business in the streets though; he just kept it a secret."

Jahad shook his head, unable to digest the information. It was too much, the image in which he perceived his father was all a lie... a lie he just couldn't accept. "I'm sayin', how you know?"

"I was there Jahad. Before I got strung on that poison, I was a prostitute until John..."

"Whoa! You were what?"

"Let me talk Jahad," Emma said patiently, "I was a prostitute. Up until my pimp figured I was too old to produce enough money. That's when I started working for John delivering packages. I was doing good for while, then curiosity got the best of me and I went in one of his packages. At first I was snorting, until someone showed me how to shoot up. From there I was a slave to heroin. It's not like these other drugs. When it gets a hold of you the only thing that can save you is God. When John found out, I thought he'd cut me off, boy was he mad." She smiled sadly, "Instead he sent me to a rehab in Virginia, and I found Jesus. Nine months later I came home and he set me up in this same apartment. Didn't let me want for nothing either, as long as I stayed clean. My whole 63 years on this earth I never knew a better man."

Emma failed to mention that John was her lover up until the day he was murdered. Another secret he kept from his family, and one she would never reveal.

"How did he keep all this away from us?"

"Because he had a good head on his shoulders. Not long after he started working, he turned the street side of his operation over to his best friend; all John did was supply the drugs. I'm sure you remember those family outings every Saturday when he would take ya'll to Manhattan. Well that's when he made his pickups. Before I got strung out I would go with him from time to time."

Jahad's mouth dropped open, thinking back to all the trips to Central Park, Rockefeller Center, Radio City Music Hall, and the Apollo Theater. As a kid, he always wondered why they never went anywhere other than Manhattan now he finally understood. He also remembered how his father would disappear for an hour or so, always returning with a medium-sized briefcase. It never occurred to any of them that John was buying drugs. Not their hard-working father.

"If that's the case, why didn't he leave us no money?"

"I suppose he did. John didn't believe in keeping his money in banks. Knowing him like I do, I guarantee he had some stashed somewhere. So don't go thinking..."

"The key!" Jahad shouted, remembering the last conversation he had with his father, "Before pops died he said something about a key, I never asked my moms about it tho'. He never got around to saying what it went to either... my Pops friend, who is he? Maybe he knows or has an idea what it goes to."

Emma shook her head, "He's dead. He and your father were killed the same day. That's what makes this mess with you and them Puerto Rican boys so strange, but I guess it would happen one day. John's partner was..."

"KABOOM! KABOOM! KABOOM! TAT! TAT! TAT! TAT! TAT!"

Startled by the sudden thundering gunshots, Jahad leaped from his chair across the kitchen table to cover Emma. It took a few seconds for it to sink in, that the shots were coming from outside the apartment. Then it dawned on him what was actually happening.

"Oh word, that's how it's going down!" He roared reaching in his back pocket for his .380, "Mrs. Harris chill here until I get back."

Emma gripped his arm, "Jahad don't you go out there baby. Please don't!" She cried, her eyes wide with fear.

"I got to Mrs. Harris. They came to kill my family. They gotta get it!" He rushed off to the front door and paused before opening it to calm himself down. If he ran out in the blind there was a chance he would be killed before he could fire a shot.

"If you go out there I'm coming with you." Emma said behind him holding a large butchers knife.

If things weren't so serious, he would have laughed, "They have guns out there Mrs. Harris. You can't do nothing with that knife, chill here until I get back . . . I will be coming back."

She held his eyes a moment before nodding, "Alright Jahad, but don't let them boys kill you. They'll win all over again."

Jahad had no idea what she was talking about and resisted the urge to ask her what she meant. Her revelations shocking as they were filled him with a sense of obligation to claim what his father once controlled. Even though she didn't say it, he knew the Coco twins were somehow involved with his father's death, which fueled his hatred.

As he eased the apartment door open, he glanced right first, towards Michelle's apartment and saw the door wide open riddled with bullet holes. Cautiously he moved along with his back against the wall, his gun held out in front of him, when a slight noise came from behind him. Turning quickly prepared to fire, he locked eyes with Cream, who was peeping around the corner from the elevator.

"Ayo Cream, what up?" He asked as Cream ducked back around the corner. It only took a second to realize what was going on, "Oh, you slimy bastard! You brought these muthafuckas to my moms crib!"

He ran towards the elevator forgetting all about whoever was in his mother's apartment, but by the time he turned the corner, it was making its way to the bottom floor. His mind still on Cream, he raced towards the staircase just as two Puerto Ricans ran out of Michelle's apartment. The one on his left carrying a Mac-II strapped around his shoulder, the other a 12 gauge pistol grip pump shotgun. Caught off guard by his sudden appearance, they both froze for a split second, giving Jahad the chance to raise his gun.

"POP! POP! POP! POP! POP!"

Slugs from the .380 tore into the Puerto Rican on Jahad's left, his face and neck jerking his head back and sent a stream of blood skeeting from a wound in his jugular vein. As he fell to the floor his finger automatically tightened on the trigger.

"TAT! TAT! TAT! TAT! TAT! TAT! TAT! TAT! TAT! TAT! TAT!"

Bullets sprayed the hallway hitting the other Puerto Rican in his legs and came only inches from Jahad's head before the gun turned upwards towards the ceiling. Thinking fast, Jahad quickly crossed the hallway before his other assailant could recover and shot him twice in the head. For a second he looked around breathing hard surprised he was still alive then Cream flashed through his mind, and he snatched up the shotgun, determined to catch him. He suspected the Coco Twins were getting their information from someone who knew him, which was obvious. What he didn't expect was that it was one of his friends. The same friend he put his life on the line to protect, broke bread with, and considered a brother.

Halfway through the staircase, fear gripped him wondering if Cream had sent killers to Janet's apartment too. The thought made him take the steps three at a time until he reached the bottom floor. Exiting the building he glanced around wildly, expecting to see more of Hector's goons. Instead, and even more frightening, a team of police dressed in riot gear raced towards him coming from the direction of the park. His heart nearly jumped out of his chest as he sprinted towards Janet's building, praying he could ditch the vest and his guns before he was caught. Luckily two teenage girls were coming out of the building as he ran up, so he didn't have to waste time keying himself in. Once inside, he took the stairs straight to the roof taking off his vest, throwing it along with the shotgun, and the .380 over the ledge. He was too tired to take the stairs back down to Janet's floor, so waited for the elevator on the 14th, dreading the idea of going to jail.

If only he could make it to Janet's apartment. He felt like he might have a chance. That was a big "if" with at least 50 police after him, probably already storming the building. The thought of losing Janet made the dread even worse. He couldn't picture himself being without her. If luck was on his side, and he did make it, then maybe he would take Michelle's advice and leave New York. He and Janet could start a new life with the money he had left, once he sold the coke. Then came another maybe, he could pursue his music again. The idea started taking shape in his mind as the elevator came to a stop on her floor. He braced himself expecting to be rushed by police when the doors slid open and let out a sigh of relief seeing no one. Almost there he thought. Then as he bent the corner, his heart shattered along with his trust in women.

Directly in front of his eyes, Janet, the one person who possessed the power to make him change his life, stood in her doorway hugging the man behind all of his misfortune. Hector. José stood off to the side leaning against the wall with his arms folded across his chest.

Jahad watched their embrace through watery eyes while unconsciously reaching to his waist for a gun that wasn't there. His mind screamed, Move! Move! Yet the shock of what he was seeing held him in place.

"Why?... How?...What?..." He stammered, his mind jumbling words together without logic.

All three heads snapped in his direction. José, his face twisted with hatred, Janet looking horrified, and Hector casting a sly smile. Without thinking Jahad started towards them with fire in his eyes. He didn't care if he was killed, actually welcomed it, as long as he could get one of them first, preferably Janet. Hector kept the smile plastered on his face while reaching to the small of his back for his automatic 357. José had his gun out, and in the process of lifting it when the staircase door flew open and police flooded the hallway, their guns trained on Jahad's head. Hector and José quickly slid in Janet's apartment, leaving her standing in the doorway stunned.

"FREEZE! NYPD!" yelled a beefy black cop.

Jahad never took his eyes off Janet as he was tackled to the floor, kicked and stomped in the process, before handcuffs were tightly clamped on his wrist.

"Stop it! Stop it! He hasn't done anything!" She screamed, rushing towards them as they stood Jahad to his feet.

She was only five steps in front of him when he tried his best to kick her, but was yanked backed by the police. "Get the fuck away from me bitch!" He spat venomously.

"Jahad."

"Lady you need to back up, you're interfering with police duty. That's a charge. Besides, he doesn't seem to want your help anyway." One of the cops said while the others roughly shoved Jahad through the staircase door.

CHAPTER 16

From Monroe projects Jahad was taken straight to Central booking where he was charged with two counts of first-degree murder, fingerprinted, then escorted to a small interrogation room. The walls, originally painted beige, were dullish yellow stained by years of cigarette smoke. Two metal foldout chairs set around a square wooden table across from a one-way mirror that Jahad turned his back to; feeling he was being watched.

For nearly 2 hours he sat handcuffed to an iron rail thinking nothing of his charges. He couldn't, the picture of Janet in the arms of Hector was lodged into his memory, prohibiting him to think of anything else. The initial shock and pain was over. In its place a cold numbness, and passionate hatred for the Coco Twins and Janet. It consumed every inch of his being. He was so he caught up in his thoughts he never noticed when the two detectives walked in. The first through the door, a tall white man around 35 with strawberry blond haircut close to his scalp. The other, a average size Puerto Rican pushing 50, his long black hair graying at the temples was pulled back into a ponytail.

"Jahad Copeland, I'm Detective Page," said the white cop, "And, this is my partner Detective Lopez. To make this simple, we're about to ask you some very important questions and we expect some answers." He reached in his shirt pocket and took out a pack of Marlboro's, "Smoke?"

Jahad ignored the offered cigarette, "I can't help what you expect. I ain't got shit to say to you. My lawyer will do my talking."

"That's your right, but a lawyer won't help you," Detective Page said, pulling out a chair while Lopez grilled Jahad hostilely. "We have an eyewitness who will be more than willing to testify that you murdered the two men in building 1835. He also gave us information that makes you an accomplice to the murders at PS 100 School Park. So most likely you'll be charged with the murders of those two officers too. And before you get to thinking that Lateef Wilkins plans on going down by himself, get it out of your head, this is a one shot deal, right here. Tell us what happened before he does and we will see that you get some help when you go to court."

At the mention of Razor's name, Jahad's heart began to race, then he thought about what was said and realized they were trying to get a confession out of him. "Help me? You'll be helping me when you let me call a lawyer."

"Since you wanna be a smart ass, let's see how you like it in bullpen two." Detective Lopez spoke for the first time in a harsh raspy voice.

Jahad had no idea what bullpen two was until he was dragged to a bullpen no bigger than 20 x 20 feet, crowded with Puerto Ricans. Before tossing him in without taking off the handcuffs, Lopez yelled in Spanish that Jahad was in for murdering fellow Puerto Ricans. This led to the worst ass whipping he ever took in his life. Every able-bodied Puerto Rican commended to beating his ass no sooner than the detectives walked off. With his hands in cuffs the attempts he made to fight back were futile. Five minutes later, the longest five minutes of his life, he was dragged from the bullpen, bloody and badly bruised, and placed in another bullpen, full of drunks and drug addicts. The nauseating smell of shit, piss, and unwashed bodies lingered in the air like fog, as he crawled to the back of the bullpen finding an empty spot near a sick heroine addict.

For the first time in his life he felt totally helpless, but he refused to feel sorry for himself. He fed off the pain and forced himself to think, plan, and prepare for what lay ahead. It wasn't hard to figure out who the detectives eyewitness was, which meant Cream had to be dealt with. Once that problem was solved, he could devote his time to planning his revenge on the Coco Twins and Janet. For now though, his main concern was getting back on the street. He was still brainstorming when a guard called him from the bullpen and led him back to the interrogation room where detectives Page and Lopez sat waiting.

"This is the last chance to help yourself, Mr. Copeland," Detective Page said, standing to offer Jahad a seat, "cooperate and will see that you get a good plea-bargain."

Jahad looked at both men scornfully, making no attempt to sit, "I'll tell you what you can do for me. Suck my dick!" He yelled.

Detective Lopez shot out of his chair and slammed a fist into Jahad's stomach. You'll regret it, you Moreno bastard! Trust me, you'll regret it!"

~~~~

Hours later, handcuffed and shackled, Jahad was led outside by three police to a blue, orange, and white bus; his transportation to the notorious Riker's Island.

From Eric, he had heard numerous stories how life was one the Island, now he was about to see firsthand. Fear bubbled in his stomach imagining what he was about to face, then as quickly as it came he pushed it away. Regardless of the circumstances, he would hold himself down. This he was sure of.

The bus stopped at different booking houses on its way to Rikers, picking up prisoners who looked just as miserable as Jahad. The only difference was his battered face. Eventually he dozed off, exhausted from the days events, and the ass whipping he took, waking when the bus stopped in front of the third, fifth story building once they were on the Island. Correctional officers escorted the prisoners from the bus, inside to a bullpen to await dorm assignments. Ten other prisoners were already inside standing around waiting to go to court.

"Ayo Jah!" Someone called out from the rear of the bullpen after the Correctional Officers walked off.

With his left eye swollen shut, a flat lip and speed knots lining his forehead, Jahad spun around expecting another fight. Instead he was greeted by his fencer Budda. To be close to forty, Budda could easily pass for being in his mid twenties. His face and head were hairless except for the neatly trimmed goatee shaping his thick lips and although he was short, his build was thick, framed with muscles.

"Budda?" Jahad said, looking him up and down with his good eye, "What the hell you doing in here? I just saw your ass a few weeks ago."

Budda smiled showing his one gold tooth, "Nah, what the hell you doing here? Somebody fucked you up good."

"Yeah, like 50 Puerto Ricans beat my ass at Central booking."

"Word? What happened?"

Jahad nodded to the back of the bullpen where no one was

standing and motioned for Budda to follow, then related what happened starting with the Coco twins. When he finished Buddha reached in his sock and pulled out a long handmade ice pick, then spit a razor from his mouth. "Take these 'cause you gon' need 'em. Let me put you on to something too, when you get to your dorm put down a demonstration on one of them Germans so niggas can see how you rock. Do . . ."

"Germans?" Jahad asked confused.

"That's what we call Puerto Ricans on the rock 'cause it's so many of them muthafuckas. Now listen, niggas are drawn to strength, not sayin' you gon' be around some weak dudes, but when the time comes, when some Germans try to move on you, and trust me, they will, niggas might hold you down. So handle your business."

"I'm sayin', for what reason would some Puerto Rican's wanna move on me? I ain't did shit to 'em."

"For the same reason they got at me, the Coco Twins. Those muthafuckas got long arms." Budda replied knowingly, "You know this German they call Man-Man?"

Jahad smirked, "Yeah I know scrams, or knew him. He's dead."

Budda smiled, "Good, he's a fuckin' rat. That's what I'm doing here now. We were beefin' over some stereo equipment I sold him, that no good bastard tried to get me; and you know how hard I hustle for my shit. So I robbed his ass, caught him coming out of his building and he turned around and put the damn cops on me on the low. They busted up my whole operation. Five days after I was here, the Coco Twins put the word out and this happened." He turned so Jahad could see the long scar that ran from the top of his head, down to the bottom of his neck. "Three of them bastards ran up on me when I was in the shower, so keep your eyes open. After what you told me I'm sure they gon' want you dead and these crazy ass Germans won't mind doing it."

"No doubt. What up with you tho'? You outta here or what?"

"I should be. They only got me on a possession of stolen property wrap."

"If you touch get up with Tone and let him know Cream is on some bullshit and to handle that."

Budda frowned, "You talking 'bout pretty ass Cream? That's you man right?"

"That's what I thought, until he brought some Puerto Ricans to my moms crib to body me."

"Get the fuck outta here! That bitch as nigga. If Tone don't handle it, I will. That's my word!"

Not too long after, Budda was called out for court; Jahad was orientated, seen by the medical staff, then escorted by two Correctional Officers to his sleeping quarters in C-74. Before leaving Buddha explained how the use of the phone worked. Three phones were in the sleeping area; one for the blacks, one for the Puerto Ricans, and a neutral phone usually controlled by the Puerto Ricans also. Phone time depended on three things, who you knew, how well you fought, and how well you used a razor, knife, or ice pick. Since he was beefing with Puerto Ricans Jahad's mind was made up to take their phone. Walking through the Sallyport leading to his dorm, adrenaline rushed through his bloodstream at the thought of what he was about to do. As he stepped through the entrance of his sleeping quarters, he stopped and took in his surroundings. The phone's Budda spoke of were to his right, next to the showers. On both sides, to his left and right, cells lined the wall, eight on the left, nine on the right. A few people stood outside their cells talking, some posted up in the back of the dorm, all watching Jahad as he walked in. Jahad went straight to his assigned cell, ignoring their probing stares, stored belongings he had, then stepped from his cell to make his announcement.

"Ayo! Who phone time is between four and five on the German phone?" He called out so everybody could hear him, masking his fear with a straight face.

Instantly all the attention was his, even those who were in their cells peeked out at Jahad, who now stood in the middle of the dorm. A second later a huge Puerto Rican walked from his cell near the telephones. He stood close to 6'5" and weighed 300 pounds, if not more, with his long black hair braided in two long braids.

"I run the phone period. You said that shit like you plan on taking my shit or something. You think you built like that?" The Puerto Rican asked, closing the distance between himself and Jahad.

Jahad took a few steps back so he couldn't be seen by the Correctional Officer who stood in the control booth overlooking the dorm while adjusting the razor between his fingers. Through his peripheral vision, he noticed that two of the Puerto Ricans had stepped clear of their cells, watching him closely.

"Nah Duke, it ain't like that. All I'm sayin' is I need to rock the phone around that time." Jahad clutched the razor between his thumb and index finger, "I mean, if that's a'ight..." He swung the razor opening the side of the Puerto Rican's face as soon as he stepped within striking distance.

Surprisingly the Puerto Rican didn't even flinch and try to spit a razor from his mouth, but Jahad, acute to his move, swung a hard left hook that connected flesh to his jaw. Thinking off the ass whipping he took earlier at Central booking, rage took over. Jahad grabbed him by the collar of his wife beater and started ripping his face, repeatedly, releasing mounds of built up fury. After about 15 swings he dropped the razor and threw a series of left and right hooks until the Puerto Rican fell to the floor convulsing, the side of his face looking more like raw hamburger meat.

Still caught up in his own rage, Jahad turned just as the two Puerto Ricans who stood outside their door ran towards him. He quickly snatched the ice pick from his waistline and squared off, forgetting all about the odds, "Bring it muthafuckas."

Taking notice of the deadly intent in Jahad's eyes, the two Puerto Ricans froze. This was only one of the reasons they stopped though. Behind Jahad, without him knowing it, four black dudes stood; all holding pocketknives, giving the two Puerto Ricans the same deadly look.

"The German phone is mine now! Whoever was rockin' on it is dead until you come see me. Whoever don't like it, see me now!" he shouted, then walked to his cell, still on his adrenaline high.

A few minutes later, a tall slim brown skinned dude with Strong West Indian features, wearing a black Ralph Lauren jean suit, his hair braided in four thick cornrows approached Jahad's cell, "Ayo, Carlos, the German you just chopped up, is caked up. If I were you I'd clean his room out before the CO's flood the spot...by the way, that was some pretty work you put in." He smiled, showing two rows of gold teeth with Buck town engraved in red stones.

Jahad studied the guy for a second to see if he posed a threat before replying, "What room was Duke in?"

"Ten, right beside the shower... what's your name, where you from?"

"Jah, from the boogie down... you?"

"Jah, I heard that name before, I'm that nigga Sha'" He said with a slyly grin, "East New York, Cypress projects."

"So you a Brooklyn nigga, huh?" Jahad returned the grin, "How is shit poppin' off in here?" He asked, looking out his cell catching hostile glares from the Puerto Ricans who had gathered around Carlos.

"Get your shit first, then we can build. I want to introduce you to some good niggas too. Oh yeah, don't sweat those Germans. They won't fake no moves since Carlos is out the way."

Jahad nodded as Sha' walked off, thinking, Riker's Island was no different than Spofford. Different place, same rules: Only the strong survived. A motto he lived by.

A smile lit his battered face when he entered Carlos' cell. It was cluttered with food, clothes, sneakers, and an assortment of jewelry. Two Cuban link chains, one gold, one platinum, both with diamond crusted crucifix medallions, to gold bracelets, three gold diamond rings, and a platinum pinky ring. The clothes were all made by expensive designers, Polo, Pelle Pelle, Sean John, Rocawear, Phat Farm jean suits, Gucci, Louis Vuitton velour sweatsuits, Iceberg sweaters and jeans, four pair of sneakers and two pair of Timberland boots. It took three trips to transfer everything to his room, and he took everything including the thick beach towels. On his last trip, he found a box of Gemstar razors and an ice pick stashed in a pair of construction Timberlands. The ice pick he tucked in his waistline along with the one he got from Budda, then made his way to the back of the dorm where Sha' stood with three other dudes smoking weed.

"You get right?" Sha' asked.

"Hell yeah, Duke was caked up for real... good look."

"No doubt." Sha' said, turning to the guys he stood with, "These are my mans, Star, Lord, and Prince... this wild nigga here is Jah from the Boogie Down."

Jahad nodded, taking in their appearance. Star was the shortest, standing 5'7" in his beef and broccoli Timberlands. He wore an army fatigue suit with Congo dreadlocks hanging to the middle of his back and shaping his baby face. Lord, dressed in a brown Timberland hoodie, Pelle Pelle blue jeans, and a pair of wheat colored Timberlands was the biggest weighing a solid 240 pounds, all muscle, an even 6 feet with a short haircut. A long scar ran from his temple to his chin, results of a knife fight his second day at Rikers. Prince, the pretty boy out the bunch, reminded Jahad a lot of Cream, but there was nothing soft about him. He and Jahad stood around the same height and size, but where Jahad was dark, Prince was high yellow, with a short curly Afro. He wore a white Louis Vuitton sweatsuit, white Nike Air One's, looking like he was ready to strut across a catwalk. Sha' went on to explain that Star was from Queens, Forty Projects, Prince from Harlem, Wagner Projects, and Lord from Brooklyn, Bed-Stuy.

"What happened to your face dog?" Star asked looking at Jahad's swollen eye, "I didn't see Carlos get nothing off."

"Some Puerto Ricans got at me at Central Booking."

"Oh word!" Lord chuckled, "Now I see why you chopped Carlos ass up. Damn, they beat the shit outta you Sun," he passed Jahad a lit blunt still laughing.

Jahad screwed up his face, "That shit wouldn't be funny if twenty muthafuckas jumped your ass. I'm lucky, they didn't body me."

Lord laughed even harder.

"At least you got your face back." Prince said punching Lord who was seized by a fit of giggles, "Keep your eyes open tho', those Germans are some sneaky ass dudes."

Sha' gave his friends a thoughtful look, then turned to Jahad, "Ayo, peep it, we be holdin' each other down in here. We saw how you get busy and it's like this, you hold us down, and we hold you down."

Jahad looked at them suspiciously, "You know, I'm feelin' that, right, but what's the catch?"

"No catch." Sha' held up his hands, "We're official niggas, you seem like an official nigga and official niggas should always hold each other down. At least that's how we see it. I mean, to keep it real with you, you probably won't last another day in this muthafucka with these Germans without somebody watching your back. Especially after that shit you did to Carlos. So we can make you stronger and you can make us stronger; feel me?"

A crooked grin spread across Jahad's face, "Yeah you made a good point. Since it's going down like that, let's bus' these down." He pulled the box of razors from his back pocket.

"Nah, you keep 'em, we got crazy guns." Star pulled out a Barlowe pocketknife, with a six-inch blade. Sha', Prince, and Lord followed suit, pulling out their knives.

Jahad laughed, "Shit, fuck the razors, I want one of them."

They all laughed.

By this time the Puerto Ricans had dragged Carlos to the front of the dorm so he could get some medical attention. For any of them to even mention what happened meant an automatic death sentence, being they would be labeled snitches. The word alone meant death.

CHAPTER 17

A day after Jahad made his grand appearance on Riker's Island, Janet, scared for her life made her escape from the Bronx. At the subway station on St. Lawrence she hustled her baby sister through the turnstile while the crowds entering and leaving, eyed her suspiciously. In her eyes was a frantic look, as if she were either on the run, or had done something she had no business doing. Every few seconds she glanced over her shoulder fearfully, half expecting to see Tony or another one of Jahad's friends. By the time she and her sister made it to a bench to wait on the train, she felt somewhat safe until a hand gripped her shoulder. Janet shot off the bench and was about to grab her sister's hand when she noticed the white transit cop.

"Are you alright lady?" He asked, watching her trembling hands.

Janet forced a smile, "Yes... I'm fine." She stuffed her hands in her pocket but couldn't disguise the distressed looked in her eyes.

"You sure? You seem kind of jumpy. Is there something I can help either of you with?"

"No, I said I was fine!" Janet snapped praying he would leave.

"How about you?" He directed the question to the little girl.

"If I wasn't I'd say so. Now leave us alone and go mess with somebody else."

The transit cop gave them another look over before leaving.

Janet was everything but fine. Scared, heartbroken, and desperate was more like it. Her heart had been stuck in her throat ever since earlier that day after she saw Tony knocking on her door. Luckily, his back was turned towards her when she turned the corner from the elevator. Quietly she made her escape down four flights of stairs to her girlfriends apartment with Jahad's words ringing in her ears, "one of my mans will probably merk you." From there she called up to her mother's apartment, three floors above hers, and pleaded that they had to leave. After explaining her situation, Janet's mother, a recovering drug addict, plainly stated that she wasn't going anywhere, but allowed her youngest daughter to leave, then went on to chastise Janet for getting mixed up with the Coco Twins; whom she despised.

Janet's baby sister following instructions went to her apartment, careful to make sure no one was waiting on the floor before entering, and went to Janet's closed where eighty five thousand dollars of Hector's money was stashed in a Gucci shoe box. With the box tucked under her arm, she rushed down the stairs to meet Janet, who by then was on the verge of having a nervous breakdown.

Janet had no qualms about taking Hector's money. If it wasn't for him, she wouldn't be on the run in the first place. Besides, he had so much he probably wouldn't miss it anyway. At one point, she thought of going to him for protection, but changed her mind knowing that would only be digging a deeper hole for herself with Jahad.

"What happened Janet?" Her baby sister asked once they boarded the train, headed for Manhattan. "Why we gotta leave?"

Janet gave her a sad smile, "I can't explain, but we'll be alright."

"I know why!" The little girl hissed angrily, "Mommy told me. It's because of Hector and José. Why you mess with them for anyway? You know they don't like us."

"That's not true. For what reason would they not like us?"

"Don't act stupid, you know why. I don't care though, I don't like them either."

Janet faced the window denying what deep in her heart she knew was the truth. If she allowed herself to believe it, the illusion of the bond she shared with Hector would be shattered and also put her at fault for what happened to Jahad. The thought of Jahad brought fresh tears to her eyes. The only man she could see spending the rest of her life with, now wanted her dead. She understood his feelings, knowing how deeply he felt about loyalty, but he had the wrong impression. She would never betray him. If anything, she put her life on the line to save him. Some way or another she had to contact him, tell him everything and pray that he understood.

"Where are we going anyway?" Her little sister asked pulling on her sleeve, "I don't want to miss too many days from school."

"We're going to Harlem. I have a girlfriend we can stay with until I find…"

"Harlem? We shoulda stayed home then. It won't be too hard for whoever you're running from to find us there . . . who are you running from anyway?"

"Nobody!" Janet snapped, "Why don't you shut up. I have enough on my mind already."

"And whose fault is that?" The little girl mumbled under her breath.

Janet rolled her eyes and turned back to the window. Although she didn't want to admit it, her sister was right. The Bronx and Harlem were too close. Until she had everything straightened out, she wanted to distance herself as far as possible from the Bronx without leaving New York. She had another girlfriend that lived in Brownsville. That was far enough. It wouldn't be for long anyway she told herself. Once she explained everything to Jahad they would be able to come home. At least she hoped so.

CHAPTER 18

Jahad was on "The Rock" (as Riker's Island was referred to by the inmates), thirteen days and still hadn't informed anyone he was locked up. Highly disappointed with himself, he knew his family would be disappointed, especially Koran. He couldn't blame them; he had let them all down. To keep his mind off of it he spent his time getting to know his new friends, researching his case in the law library, and mostly feeding his hatred for the Coco Twins and Janet. Surprisingly, it ran way deeper for Janet than the Coco Twins. Not only did she betray him, she broke his heart and came close to breaking his spirit. Nights alone in his cell the pain of thinking about her being with another man, the same man who destroyed his dream, murdered his friends, and attempted to murder his family made him want to take his own life, just to put an end to his suffering. What made him hold on was the love for his family and his confidence that one day he would make Janet and the Coco Twins pay for every ounce of pain he felt.

Already a plan was forming in his mind. A plan with a lot of variables, but plan just the same. First, Tony would have to do whatever it took to make amends with the Coco Twins. If that could be accomplished it would open the door for phase two of his plan. Gathering information, one of the most important things involved. The last phase depended on beating his charges. So far they didn't really have anything, Cream was his only worry. So basically, everything was in the hands of his friends, Tony mostly, since he was the thinker. Without their help he didn't stand a chance.

~~~~

"Jahad Copeland! Jahad Copeland! Report to visitation!"

When the announcement came booming through the dorms intercom system, Jahad was laid back on his bunk reading Sun Tzu's, 'The Art of War'. Placing the book aside, he sat up confused. No one knew where he was so who could be coming to see him he thought. Unless... he let the thought trail off, refusing to stress himself more than he already was.

"Ayo Jah, they just called you to the dance floor Sun." Sha' said, stopping in his cell, dressed in a wifebeater and two pair of boxers.

"I heard. I wonder who in the hell it is tho'."

"Whatcha' mean? Most likely it's your family. If you think it's the cops bringing you more charges, they do that shit during the weekdays."

"I hope you right."

Since he hadn't bothered to call anyone he had no idea what was going on with Razor. He hadn't been indicted for the murders in the park, so evidently Razor had kept his word. Still, Jahad thought he would have bumped into him by now. Every time he went to the law library, he asked about Razor being there. That was the only time he could see inmates from other houses, but no one heard of him, which was impossible if he was at Rikers Island. Razor would have been chopped somebody up. This sparked the thought of him being in the mental ward or Bellevue, which was definitely possible.

Focusing back on his visit, he grabbed a black and white Gucci sweatsuit to wear but Sha' shook his head, "Nah Sun, you can't rock that on the dance floor, jumpsuit only. They don't want our families to see how fly we get up in here. We should all be out there with you soon. My mans an' dem comin' through to bless me with some new shit they got out there called Purple Haze. It's supposed to be better than dro."

"Word?" Jahad said pulling on his jumpsuit as Prince stepped in his doorway, freshly dressed for his visit, "I'm sayin', it don't get too much better than dro."

"I'm tellin' you Sun, my man said the Purple Haze shit makes dro seem like regular weed. We gon' see tho'." Sha' said, turning to Prince with a grin, "What up homey, your wifey comin' through with Candy today?"

Prince laughed, "Yeah, but I already told you, Candy ain't feelin' your bubbly. You too gangsta for Ma."

"Yeah right. Knowing your slick ass, you probably fuckin' Shorty too."

"Nah, but if I could get away with it, I would." Prince winked, handing Jahad a small bottle of Muslim oil, "Put some of than on

Sun."

"What is it?"

"Black Coconut. It's gon' be mad bitches out there. You might get lucky."

"Shit, that's the last thing I need."

"Oh, you on some fuck a bitch shit, huh?" Sha' laughed.

"More like kill a bitch." Jahad replied bitterly as he walked out his cell.

~~~~

Entering the visitation area, a wave of excitement could be felt stemming from families going so long without seeing, touching, or having their loved ones around. Father's held their children, mother's held their sons, and wives and girlfriends kissed their husbands and boyfriends passionately without a care in the world of who was watching. Little kids raced through tables like they were at a playground trailed by Correctional Officers playing the role of babysitters. Other Correctional Officers thinking they were real cops, watched everybody with hawk eyes in hopes of busting someone passing contraband, some plainly being assholes because it was in their nature to harass people.

"Jahad!" Someone called out over the busy chatter that echoed through the spacious visitation area.

Turning his head in the direction of the voice he saw Michelle, waving her arms from where she sat at a table near the snack machines, positioned along the front wall. Latrice, Tony, and Koran sat with her all smiling, except Koran, who had a twisted scowl on his face. It wasn't until that moment did he realize how much he missed his family. In order to stay focused and think straight, a lot of things he had to push from his mind, like his craving to be with them. Something a lot of inmates did just so they could cope with their time.

"What up Ma-Duke?" Jahad's crooked smile beamed as he approached the table with a warm feeling spreading through his chest.

Michelle stood to hug him and burst into tears once he was wrapped tightly in her embrace, "Why . . . Why didn't you call. . . call me? I thought. . . I thought you were dead." She sobbed against his shoulder.

"I'm good Ma." He rubbed her back in an effort to soothe her,

145

"I'm okay. I ain't want to tell you I was locked up until I figured how to get out."

She pushed away from him frowning, "I don't care where you were, you should have called me. For three damn weeks, I've been worried sick, and when I heard what happened to our apartment I. . ." Sobs racked her body again.

"My fault Ma. I'm sorry." He held her, feeling deeply ashamed for causing so much stress.

"What happened to your face?" Latrice asked, standing to hug him, her brown eyes on the fading bruises, under both his eyes.

Jahad smiled, hoping to break the tension, "I got my ass beat by like thirty Puerto Ricans. Worst ass whipping I ever took in my life. I'm a'ight tho'."

"I'm glad you got beat up." Koran said with the same twisted scowl on his face.

"What you mean you glad?"

"That's what you get for lying to me. I wish I was big enough to beat you up." He kept his head straight, refusing to look at Jahad.

Jahad sighed and pulled out a chair, sitting so he faced Koran, "You know, I understand why you heated. I would be heated too if somebody broke a promise to me, but sometimes certain things can't be avoided. It ain't like I meant to lie to you. Believe me, this is the last place I wanna be. Would you rather have me here tho' or in a coffin?"

Koran didn't answer, although his expression softened a little.

"It ain't like I'm a be in here forever," Jahad continued, I'm coming home."

"When?" Koran asked quickly, finally turned to look at Jahad.

"As soon as I go to trial, they can't keep me in here for holding down the crib. So like I said, I'm coming home. What I need you to do is fallback and keep your grades up like we talked about."

"How can I when I ain't in school?"

"You will be soon. Tone is gon' make sure everything is good at home first. We still got the same deal too. Keep your grades up and you get the shopping spree; you dig?"

"How you. . ."

"I already know what you gon' ask, and don't stress that, stress your grades. I'll handle my end, "Jahad said turning to Tony, "What up Baby Paw?"

Tony stood and gave Jahad a hug, "Ayo, why you ain't let niggas know what was going on? If it wasn't for Budda, we still wouldn't know you got bagged?"

"Word you saw Budda? So he told you what was up, right?"

"Yeah, it's still hard for me to believe tho'. But yo..." Tony grew silent for a few seconds, his eyes mirroring a deep sorrow, "Razor... Razor is gone Jah."

"What you mean he gone?"

"The homey is dead. Po-Po bodied him at the precinct. Said he tried to escape."

Jahad's legs buckled and he flopped hard back down into his chair. Overwhelmed by grief, tears ran freely from his eyes, staining the front of his jumpsuit. Along with his grief, was an intense rage that burned in the pit of his stomach, and eased its way to his heart, yearning to be released. For a while he sat staring off in space, picturing the last time he saw Razor's face.

"You alright Jahad?" Michelle asked, taking hold of his hand.

"Nah, I... I..." He shook his head unable to think straight, "If ya'll don't mind let me build with Tone a minute in private."

Michelle nodded, and then led Koran and Latrice to the snack machines.

"Ayo Tone, I never meant for any of this to happen Man, word up! It's gone too far man and now it ain't no turning back for real. I want you to find out who the cops were who bodied Razor so..."

"What! I know you ain't talking 'bout..."

"Listen!" Jahad snapped, looking around before speaking, "I'm a make all this shit right when I touch the bricks, but I'ma need your help, yours and the rest of the clique. You with me or what?"

"You know I am, but killin' cops Jah. C'mon!"

"If a cop bodied somebody in your family without a reason and you had a chance to get at him, would you do it?"

"Hell yeah, but..."

"No buts, Razor was family and if one of them cops bodied him without a reason, then they deserves to die. Razor would do the same for you. What you need to do is find out if there's any truth to what they're screaming. If so then we'll fallback, if not you know what time it is."

Tony nodded.

"Now check this, you might think I'm buggin' when I say this too, but I want you to start working for the Coco Twins again."

Tony shot up in his chair, "Yeah, you buggin'! After all that bullshit we went through with them dudes, you think I'm gon' rock with 'em like that? They must got you on medication or something in here."

"Hear me out first Sun..." Jahad explained what he had planned step for step. By the time he finished, Tony had a wide grin on his face.

"I'm feelin' that. Word up, I'm feelin' that." Tony's eyes glistened.

Jahad laughed, "I though you would. I gotta get outta here to make everything work and that depends on you too. Something gotta be done about Cream, Sun. Po-Po talking 'bout they got an eye witness and he was the only nigga up there when that shit popped off. His gay ass ran off before I merked those two Germans tho', so he didn't see shit. Lying bastard! I know Mrs. Harris didn't rat me out...O-yeah, I got some coke and money stashed in Mrs. Harris' crib, get that. I'm a need you to flip the coke and get me a lawyer."

"I'll get it soon as I get home, shit is crazy around the way now tho'. Ain't nobody making no money. The police be posted up in the park like they live there."

"It'll cool down eventually. Think you can get back in with Hector?"

"I'ma try. I'll probably have to throw dirt on your name tho'. How I wasn't really feelin' you like that, so forth and so on."

"Do what you gotta do. I was reading a book by this Chinese dude, Sun Tzu, and he said some deep shit. 'All warfare is based on deception.' So I don't care what you have to do, just as long as you get back in with him. That'll open the door for what I told you about."

"Don't worry I..."

"Ayo Jah!" Prince called out from across the room as he walked up with two females, one on each arm.

Turning his head, Jahad locked eyes with the woman on Prince's right. She wore her hair fashionably short, similar to the Halle Berry style, which suited her heart shaped face perfectly. Her complexion, the color of a Hershey's bar, matched her large chocolate eyes that held Jahad's from under long curly eyelashes and arched eyebrows. His eyes moved slowly over her face, pausing at her plush pouty lips did up with pink lipstick, then further down over her apple-sized breast, slim waist, and pear shaped hips in the white Chanel bodysuit she wore. Not once did his eyes waver towards Prince or the strikingly beautiful Dominican woman on his left arm.

"What up Jah," Prince gave Jahad a hug, then turned to the two women, "this is my wifey Karen." He nodded towards the beautiful Dominican of his left, "and her best friend Candy. Candy, Karen, this is my man Jah."

Jahad gave Karen a polite nod, while extending his hand to Candy, "How you doing Miss Candy."

"I'm fine thank you, but you don't look too well." She reached out and brushed her fingers lightly over the bruise under his eye.

"Oh, this ain't nothing Ma," A crooked grin lit up his face, "you should see the other dude."

Candy smiled, "He's kinda cute Prince, bruises and all."

Prince frowned, "You telling me like I wanna get with him or something. You know I don't get down like that."

"Shut up." Candy punched him on the shoulder laughing.

"Prince this is my man... Nah, my brother Tone. Tone, this is my man Prince. We hold down the dorm together."

While Prince and Tone were shaking hands, Sha' walked over with his three visitors.

"What the deal yo... what up Karen and beautiful." Sha' addressed Candy with a grin wide enough to show every last on of his gold teeth.

Karen and Candy nodded while glancing at the three guys with Sha' who had the look of being nothing but thugs. All three wore army fatigue pants, Timberland's and plain white t-shirts.

"Prince, Jah, these are my niggas, Crook, Black Face, and Trigger."

Short and stocky, Crook wore his hair in a tapered knotty Afro, his complexion a dusty brown. Black Face's name fitted him perfectly. He was so dark; his complexion could pass for well done, his features, pure African. Around average height, his nose was so big it nearly stretched across his wide face with long big purple lips to match. Trigger, the tallest of the three standing at 6'3", was only a shade lighter than Black Face; his head bald and shiny like it had been polished.

While introductions were being made, Michelle, Latrice, and Koran make their way back to the table.

"Ma, these are my man's Prince and Sha', and Sha's homey's Crook, Black Face, and Trigger. And these two beautiful women are Prince's wife Karen, and her gorgeous friend Candy."

Candy blushed.

"This is my family," Jahad continued, "Ma-Duke, my sister Latrice, and my lil' brother Koran."

Michelle spoke to everyone then addressed Sha' and Prince, "Will you two young men please do me a favor, and keep an eye out for my son."

"We gotcha Mrs... Ma-Duke," Sha' said grinning.

Embarrassed, Jahad cut his eye at Michelle, "What makes you think I need somebody to look out for me?"

She rolled her eyes looking at the bruises on his face, "You really want me to answer that?"

"I told you I got jumped Ma. You know I can..."

"It's time to break this up." An old white Correctional Officer interrupted, walking up behind Jahad, "You all need to go back to your own tables."

Everybody shot the Correctional Officer a scowl, including Koran.

"Pssss! I'm getting tired of these fake ass cops; word up!" Sha' said angrily before walking off with his friends in step behind him.

Jahad settled back at his table and glanced over at Candy, who gave him a sexy smile and a wink as she walked off, that he returned with one of his crooked smiles. Although he swore off women, for a while Candy had definitely caught his attention a little more than he'd like to admit. He put it off on the fact that he hadn't had sex in three weeks.

Towards the end of visitation, hours later after having to introduce his family two more times to Lord and Star, in turn meeting their family and friends, Jahad stressed to Michelle how he wanted her to move as soon as possible; if not to North Carolina, then anywhere besides the Bronx.

"You think I'm leaving you up here by yourself at a time like this? Them boys must have beaten the sense out of you."

"C'mon Ma, you know I'ma be a'ight. It ain't no reason for you to stay."

"You can talk until your lips fall off, I'm not leaving." Michelle said firmly, "Besides, I don't have enough money."

Jahad wrinkled his face, "What you mean? You should have more than enough."

"I did before I got you a lawyer."

"A lawyer!" Anger seeped into his voice, "After all the time I spent working so you could move, you blew the money on a lawyer. You didn't have to do that!"

"I know I didn't, but I did!" Michelle shot back, "You're in here three weeks without letting me know what's going on. Damn right, I hired you a lawyer. It seems like you could care less what happens to you."

Jahad shook his head, "Ma, you know it ain't like that, but since you already got the lawyer, I got some more dough stashed so you..."

"You don't get it do you, I'm not going anywhere. In fact, we're going home in a few more days. When this mess you're in is straightened out, I'll move."

Jahad stared deep into her eyes and saw where he got his stubborn side from, "So it's settle, huh? Will you do one thing for me then; give Tone a chance to smooth things over with the dudes I was beefin' with. Can you do that?

Michelle smiled, "I guess so... your lawyer should be to see you sometime next week. Emma referred him to me. His name is Vincent Valentino and he's supposed to be one of the best lawyers in the city."

"How much you pay him?" Jahad asked frowning.

"Enough so that he guaranteed you wouldn't spend the rest of your life in jail."

"C'mon Ma."

"Don't worry about it. Just stay out of trouble until it's time for you to go to trial."

"I'm..."

"Attention! Visitation hours are now over. All visitors are asked to leave now." The announcement came blaring through the intercom system.

Reluctantly, Jahad stood all at once, growing depressed, "Listen, don't worry about me. I'm a'ight in here." He said hugging Michelle, "Koran remember what I said about your grades. Tone will make sure you get your gear. And Ma, give me your word you'll chill until Tone says its safe for ya'll to come home."

Michelle patted the side of his face, "I will, and the same thing you told us goes for you. Don't worry about us, concentrate on getting out. We'll be to see you next week, okay."

Jahad nodded as he gave Latrice a hug, "I don't know how many times I gotta tell you, but please stop rockin' those weaves. Rock a bald head if you have too, they're in now." He laughed, ducking a slap aimed for his face.

"Don't pay him no mind Latrice." Sha' said waling up with Prince, Lord, and Star, "Your weave is looking good. I'm definitely feelin' it."

"Thank you Sha'." Latrice blushed, while cutting her eyes at Tony, who wore a frown.

"Ayo, fallback Sha'. Trice is off limits." Tony grabbed her hand possessively.

"Yeah," Jahad said looking at Tony.

"Pardon me Sun. Just giving a compliment where one is due."

Jahad shook his head laughing, "Yeah, you one of them slick ass Brooklyn niggas... Ma, we gon' go 'head and leave before I have to knock one of these rent-a-cops out. I love ya'll, and Tone, handle what we talked about homey."

"Don't stress that, it's done. Ya'll niggas keep your heads up."

~~~~~

Back at the dorm, after a humiliating strip search, Jahad sat on the edge of his bunk, homesick and deeply depressed with his eyes focused on a crack in his dull gray wall, as if he were in a trance. Seeing his family leave evoked the same feelings he fought hard to keep away. Feelings that clouded his thinking and left him feeling hollow inside, save for the rage, he nurtured at the center of his heart. Razor's death fed his hatred, his rage; causing it to fester throughout his being and added another reason for making the Coco Twins suffer.

"C'mon Jah, get off that sad shit man," Sha' said as he and Prince stepped into the cell, "it's happy time nigga." He passed Jahad a freshly rolled blunt.

"Word. This that Purple Haze you were telling me about?"

Sha' smiled, "And you know it. Crook said he paid a buck fifty for a quarter, so you know it's gotta be that fire."

"Shit, for a buck fifty this should make a nigga fly." Jahad remarked, lighting the blunt. He took one pull, started choking like he was dying, and then rushed to his steel toilet to throw up. When he was done, he looked up with a silly crooked grin, his eyes nearly closed, "Ayo, take this shit Sha', before it fuck around and kill me."

Sha' laughed, plucking the blunt from his fingers, "I told you. This that boom right here."

While Sha' took a pull, Prince pulled a slip of paper from his pocket and gave it to Jahad, "You got one Homey."

"What's this?"

"Candy's phone number. She wants you to call her this afternoon?"

Jahad's grin grew wider, "Oh word? What up..."

He was cut off by Sha', who shoved him out the way so he could reach the toilet. "Damn! I rolled this muthafucka too fat. Here Prince, take this shit." He said, wiping his mouth.

"Before you hit that, tell me what's up with Candy," Jahad said making room on his bunk for Sha' to sit, "she one of them money hungry Harlem chicks?"

"Candy?" Sha' looked from Jahad to Prince, "Why you askin' 'bout my shorty for?"

"Your Shorty? Shit," Jahad showed Sha' the slip of paper, "you need to put her in check then."

Sha' laughed, "Ah, damn, you stole my shorty... you uptown niggas man."

"When she become your Shorty?" Prince asked as Star and Lord stepped in Jahad's doorway.

"She ain't know it yet, but I was gon' put the Mack down on her. That's dead now, since slick dick Willie here popped up on the scene. She probably would drained me for my dough anyway."

"Nah, Candy ain't on it like that. She's a hood chick from the Polo Grounds, but she ain't your average project chick."

Jahad pictured Candy's face as he last saw her, then quickly changed the subject when Janet popped in his mind unexpectedly, "Prince where were you getting money at?"

"I had a dope spot on Broadway and a coke spot on St. Nick. My mans still doing their thing on St. Nick. I blew the spot on Broadway up when I caught my case."

"Pass the damn blunt Prince." Star grumbled.

Sha' cut his eye at Jahad and Prince grinning.

"It's crazy hot around my way too. I know ya'll heard about that shit then went don in the South Bronx on Story Ave. It was all over the news."

"That was you?" Prince asked stunned.

"Say word!" Lord said in awe, "That was you bodied all them German? Now I see why they fucked you up at Central Bookin'."

"Whoa, Whoa, Hold up." Jahad held up his hand. Although in the passing week's he had grown close to his new friends, he still didn't really know them and wasn't about to admit to doing nothing, "I never said I did shit. For the record, I'm charged with two bodies. I didn't do that either." He said with a sly smile.

"I feel you," Prince returned his smile; "I didn't body those stinkin' ass Africans on Broadway for trying to shut my spot down."

"Yeah, and I didn't body them niggas in Brownsville. I was set up." Sha' pitched in.

"Well I can't front, I killed the hell outta them niggas on Nostrand, ya'll niggas better not tell on me tho'." Lord said, and they all laughed just as Star took a deep pull from the blunt and showered them all with spittle.

CHAPTER 19

Five days after his visit, Jahad was called to the inmate conference room, which was no bigger than his cell, to meet with his lawyer. Vincent Valentino, dressed in a black five thousand dollar Armani suit, and a pair of six hundred dollar Armani loafers, reminded Jahad of a Hollywood actor with his slicked back black hair speckled with gray, square John Travolta chin, and thin mustache. His olive skin tone enhanced the color of his ice blue eyes set wide apart between a slightly crooked nose. He was pushing fifty, but had the slim youthful body of a thirty year old, standing at an even 6'4".

"Mr. Copeland please have a seat. We have much to discuss." Valentino smiled as he shook Jahad's hand, then reached in his briefcase, taking out Jahad's motion of discovery and placed the thick stack of papers on the steel table. "As you know I'm your lawyer, retained by your lovely mother. My name is Vincent, but all my clients call me Vince, which I prefer. Now from..."

"How much my moms pay you man?" Jahad asked bluntly, taking a seat. For some reason he took an instant dislike to the well dressed Italian.

Not nearly enough, Valentino thought to himself. The only reason he took the case was out of respect for the man he once did business with before becoming a lawyer. This was all a secret and would remain one being Valentino was a man of many secrets. "Since you asked, my consultation fee was twenty five hundred, to review your case, another twenty five hundred, and to take your case, forty thousand."

"Forty five Gee's! Ayo, word to mutha man, I better beat this shit for that kinda dough."

"Well I guess if you don't I better hide, huh?" Valentino smiled, then held up his hand as Jahad shot to his feet, "It was only a joke Mr. Copeland, so don't jump on me. Actually, I would have never taken your case if I felt I couldn't win. My trial record is impeccable, and I plan to keep it that way. I represent... how should I say this... a lot of underworld figures. The press is good for saying I have mob ties because of my Sicilian heritage. The truth is I'm good at what I do."

Valentino winked, and Jahad's feelings slowly began to change, "So you should have full confidence in my abilities. If Gotti would have retained me, he would still hold his title as Teflon Don."

"So you nice, huh Vinny?"

Valentino eyed Jahad curiously a second, "That's strange, only one other person use to refer to me by that name."

"Yeah who was that?"

"It's irrelevant, but nice isn't the word. Great is more like it."

Jahad laughed, "A'ight Mr. Great, so what we looking like?"

"First let me ask you this. Have you spoken to anyone about your case or anything else you may be involved in?"

Jahad shook his head.

"Good. Don't. You never know who's looking for information that may give them leeway in their own case."

"No doubt. What's up with my bond? They talking 'bout I can't get one."

"You can't. Well, I can't say can't but then again I can. I'll give you a sad fact Mr. Copeland. If you were a prominent white male, then most likely you wouldn't be here now. That's our great American judicial system for you."

"I feel you." Jahad said appreciating Valentino's honesty, "So I can look to be in here until I go to trial. What they screaming anyway?"

"Screaming? Who's screaming?" Valentino asked confused.

"Nah man, I'm sayin', what they got against me?"

"Oh, pardon my lack of street slang knowledge... they're screaming that you shot and killed two Puerto Rican males at approximately 6:30 pm, on May 23rd. This was confirmed by, and you didn't get this name from me because I'm not suppose to tell you, a Lamont Ward, who stated he witnessed you commit the murders."

"That's bullshit!" Jahad exploded, "That lying pussy ass nigga didn't see shit!"

"So you didn't do it?"

Jahad stared at Valentino debating on what to tell him.

"Listen Mr. Copeland, anything..."

"Jah."

"Excuse me?"

"Call me Jah. I ain't feeling that Mr. Copeland shit."

"No problem Mr... Jah," Valentino smiled, "as I was saying, anything you tell me is held in strict confidence. It doesn't matter to me if you murdered them or not. I need to know the facts though, so I can prepare the best defense possible for you."

"Oh word? So you sayin' you can't say shit if the judge puts pressure on you?"

"Not a word, and there's nothing he can do about it."

"Since you put it like that, hell yeah I bodied 'em. Those muthafuckas ran up in my moms crib with Mac's and shit and would have killed my family if they were home."

Valentino grabbed a blank sheet of paper and started taking notes, "Were any shots fired in your mother's apartment."

"Yeah, I just happened to be in Mrs. H's crib when I heard the shots."

"Mrs. H?"

"Emma Harris, she lives two apartments down from my moms. I was in her apartment when I heard the shots. I ran out in the hallway and my mom's door was wide open with mad bullet holes in it. That's when I saw Cream, he was..."

"Who's Cream?" Valentino asked without looking up, his fingers racing across the page.

"Lamont Ward's bitch ass. I caught him peeking around the corner by the elevator and ran after him. I thought he was my man too." Jahad said, more to himself as the scene unfolded in his mind.

"He was a friend of yours?"

"Nah, but I thought he was. He's the muthafucka that brought the two Puerto Ricans I bodied to my mom's crib. You know, I grew up with that dude, broke bread with him, use to fight and keep niggas off his soft ass and he brought them dudes to my mom's crib. My moms use to feed his ass when his moms was strung out on that shit, and he brought them dudes there to kill her. I woulda took this shit better if he woulda brought 'em to my Shorty's crib to get at me, but not Ma-Duke." Jahad's voice was laced with pain.

Valentino looked up from his notes, surprised to see tears in

Jahad's eyes, "Jah, you may not believe this but I'm familiar with the life you live, so I'll give you some free advice. Never bound your chain with weak links. Eventually it will break. Now if you don't mind let's continue. You ran after Lamont Ward, towards the elevator..."

Jahad took a moment to let Valentino's words sink in before speaking, "By the time I made it to the elevator, his lucky ass was already on the way down, so I ran towards the staircase. That's when the two dudes ran outta my mom's apartment and shit popped off."

"Did they aim their guns at you?"

"Shit, I ain't give 'em a chance too. If I had, I wouldn't be here talking to you now."

Valentino nodded, reading through the motion of discovery, "Your weapon, I can't find in here where you were caught with the murder weapon. What happened to it?"

"I'm sayin', if it say I didn't get caught with one, why you stressin' it?" Jahad asked suspiciously.

"Come on Jah, I need the facts."

"A'ight man, I got rid of it. Ain't no reason for you to know where."

"You're right, just make sure it doesn't turn up in the cops hands." Valentino looked down at the papers again, "Ballistics state that both men were fatally wounded with .380 Caliber slugs, although one of the men was shot with .45 caliber slugs. How did that happen or did you have someone else with you?"

"Nah. The first dude I hit up, fucked around and hit his man when he was falling. That's what saved my life."

Valentino made a few more notes, and then sat his paper aside, "This is how we can go at it; there's two ways actually. The first is self-defense, which I have no doubts that we can win. You'll have to admit to the killings and personally..."

"I ain't admitting to shit!" Jahad said quickly, "I didn't get bagged with no murder weapon or on the scene of the crime. The only thing they got against me is the statement from Cream, right?"

"Right."

"Don't sweat that then, 'cause he ain't comin' to testify."

"How can you be so sure? You never thought he would turn on you, but he did."

Jahad looked Valentino dead in his eyes, "He ain't comin' to court. I'm 90% sure, so just hold my court date off for a while."

Valentino nodded in understanding, "You remind me of some of my old Italian clients to be as young as you are."

"So I'm good then?"

"Not quite. There's still the matter of the seven murders in P.S. 100 School Park. The DA still hasn't decided whether to indict you or not."

"Get the fuck outta here! How in the hell can they charge me with some shit somebody already confessed too?"

"Really? This is new to me. To be honest, it's not my case, I just happened to catch wind of it. Who's the man who confessed?"

"Lateef Wilkins. The police bodied him right after he turned himself in."

"Did you know him?"

"Yeah, I knew him, he was my homey."

Valentino nodded, "I won't ask if you were involved, but I will say this, and you didn't hear it from me. Lamont Ward is a thorn in your side that needs to be removed."

"So all this shit is coming from Cream. They can charge me on his word alone?"

"Yes, but they wouldn't have much of a case. They won't have one at all if he doesn't testify. You said you were 90% sure, well you need to be 100% sure, or you'll be making my job much harder. So handle your end!"

~~~~

Back at the dorm Jahad called Tony in hopes of hearing some good news. The meeting with Valentino opened his eyes to what he was really facing if Cream wasn't taken care of. Seven counts of murder, the thought alone almost made him physically sick. He'd be a modern day Larry Davis, so to speak. After Tony's cell phone rung six times, Jahad hung up disappointed.

Phone still in hand he decided to call Candy. He had only called four times since receiving her number, wanting to keep their relationship strictly platonic, although each conversation left him wanting more. She always seemed to be on a natural high, infecting him with her jubilant moods. Still, he told himself to be careful. The same thing he was experiencing now with Candy was a repeat of what he went through with Janet when they first met and he had no plans of falling victim to love again.

After dialing her number, the first words out of her mouth when she picked up, made him smile like a five year old with a new toy.

"I hope this is Jah."

"How you know it was me?"

"I didn't but my wish came true?"

Jahad's heart sped up a little, "What if it woulda been your man? You'd be in trouble."

"I don't have a man...yet. I'm working on that now."

"C'mon Ma, so you telling me ain't nobody keeping up the maintenance?"

Candy giggled, "Oh for sho', the maintenance is being kept up. That's all it is though, maintenance. I need a jack of all trades who can do an all around job."

"So you consider me a jack of all trades."

"Maybe. You need to hurry up home, then maybe you can be the King."

"Oh, the King is coming home. I got a lot on my plate tho'."

"Like what, your girl?"

"Picture that. She's the last person I need to see when I get out." Jahad said, meaning just that. Janet was the last person he planned to see after the Coco Twins were dealt with, "I'll be honest with you Ma, I'm a scorned man right now."

"What she do?" Candy asked. Her concerned tone made Jahad want to answer although it sparked his anger to think of what happened.

"I'm crazy loyal to those I care about, so when I'm betrayed it makes me question my own judgment. I mean, trust is real dangerous, especially when you give it to someone who's on some bullshit."

"That's deep, and you're so right. That's what she did, betray you?"

"Yeah, in the worst way," Jahad answered, just as a Correctional Officer walked in announcing mail call.

In jail, mail call is almost as anticipated as visitation, mainly because it's the only thing to look forward to during the week. All conversations stop, a longing gaze tint their eyes, and inmates focus solely on the Correctional Officer, hoping their name will be called. A letter from a girlfriend, mother, kids, or a money order could be the highlight of the day. On the other hand, a Dear John letter or bad news from a lawyer could have the opposite effect. Still, it was something to look forward to.

After three names were called, Jahad's name was called. He suspected the letter was from his mother, but was totally shocked when it bared Janet's name. "Speak of the she-devil. Get me once, shame on you, get me twice, shame on me." He said with a smirk, ripping the letter to shreds.

"She-devil? Who are you talking to?"

"I just got a kite from the chick we were talking 'bout."

"What, she wants you back or something?" Candy asked with a trace of jealousy in her soft voice.

"I ripped the letter up, so I don't know what she wants, don't care. Let's change the subject, she ain't worth talking 'bout. Why don't you do what you do best and make me feel good."

"Oh, I make you feel good? How?"

"Just hearing your voice does the trick, so talk so I can drown myself in your words."

"You made that sound so poetic. Are you a poet?"

"Nah Ma, you brought that outta me." He smiled until it occurred to him that he was lowering his shield, "Let me chill before I let you steal a piece of my heart."

"More poetry. Do I detect a romantic at heart?"

"My romance days are over Shorty."

"Not if I got anything to do with it. And if I do steal your heart, I want more than a piece. I want it all."

Her words sobered him, "I'll be straight up with you Candy, save yourself some time. I'm not the dude for you... I'm sayin'; it's something I'm not getting. I mean, I'm locked up and as bad as you are, there's a million dudes out there who would happily hold you down. What is it about me?"

"You just asked a question I asked myself after our first phone conversation, and I honestly can't answer it. I can't explain it, but I'm drawn to you Jah. Whenever we talk I can feel..."

"You don't want no parts of my heart right now Candy, trust me," he said quickly, having flashbacks of Janet.

"Let me be the judge of that," she replied, then changed the subject, sensing he wasn't comfortable with it.

Two hours later, they finally hung up after Candy made him promise to call her again tomorrow. Considering how she made him feel, it was a promise Jahad looked forward to, despite the warning bells going off in his head. It was only conversation he told himself. He controlled his emotions and would stay in control, even if it meant eventually having to cut her off. Never again would a woman capture his heart, never.

No sooner than he hung up, he called Tony praying he would have some news on Cream.

"Yeah, who this?" Tony answered on the first ring.

"It's me nigga. I got at you earlier, your phone was off or something tho'. What up with Cream?"

"Nothing yet. We can't find him and ain't nobody seen him."

"Shit!" Jahad spat frustrated, "Ayo Tone, you gotta find that nigga, word up. I saw my lawyer today and he could be a real problem. Tell Derrick or somebody else in the clique to stay posted up in his mom's building on some 24 hour shit."

"You sound stressed Sun. Just breathe easy, we gon' get his ass, even if I gotta get at his moms to bring him home, feel me?"

"Yeah, no doubt. As long as he disappears before I go to trial, I'm good... How is it moving with the work?"

"It's still bananas out here. Po-Po ain't as hot, but niggas still gotta lay low to snatch some paper. As far as Hector..."

"You in?" Jahad asked anxiously.

"Nah, not yet. I sent a message through a bitch he's fuckin', that I need to build with him to squash the beef. I been slinging mad dirt on your name around the hood too, so hopefully it'll get back to him that I ain't rockin' with you like that."

"I'm feelin' that, but be careful. When or if, it goes down, see if you'll be able to set up the meeting. If Hector is smart he won't give you that advantage, but if he does, use it. Put the clique in the cut somewhere, so they can hold you down in case he tries some slick shit."

"I know how dangerous Duke is, so trust me, I'll be careful. Just maintain, I got this."

CHAPTER 20

Three weeks after Tony requested the meeting with Hector, it was finally set up at Jimmy's Café; a well known hangout spot for the celebrities on Webster Avenue. Tony knew when he first received the word from the same woman he sent the message through that he was walking into a lion's den. Desperate measures sometimes called for taking desperate chances though. If he succeeded in convincing Hector to make him a part of his crew, preferably a lieutenant, then it wouldn't be long before the South Bronx were rid of the Coco Twins if Jahad's plan worked. If he failed, then most likely the South Bronx would be rid of him.

At precisely four o'clock on a Wednesday afternoon, Tony walked into Jimmy's Café and was seized by fear to the point of almost turning around until he laid eyes on Hector, who sat at a table near the back wall, sipping an Espresso. At different tables on both sides and across from Hector sat Puerto Ricans, confirming Tony's prediction. He had definitely walked into a lion's den, but he was no longer afraid. The mere sight of Hector sparked a hatred nearly as deep as Jahad's. Here was the man responsible for Jahad's incarceration, killing his friends, and destroying their dreams, which were right in their grasp. The chance to make him pay, made Tony feel the risk he took with his life was worth it.

Once seated across from Hector, after he was patted down for a weapon, Tony played the role of a scorned friend placing the blame for everything that happened on Jahad and God bless the dead, Razor. While he talked, Hector listened patiently without interrupting, calmly sipping his Espresso and nibbling on a cream bagel.

"Let me ask you something," Hector's eyes bored into Tony's, looking for any sign of deceit, "what does your feelings towards Jahad have to do with me?"

"Nothing," Tony answered without missing a beat, "I just wanted to make it known that I had nothing to do with the beef. I mean, I got family who I'm afraid to let come home because of the shit Jah started. I ain't trying to see nothing happen to 'em, you know? To keep it all real, if you woulda sent me instead of Cream with some niggas to get at Jah, he'd be dead now."

"Cream?" Hector frowned, "Where you get the idea I was dealing with Cream from?"

Tony's senses warned him that he had possibly made a mistake, a deadly one, "Shit, word is all over the Bronx how Cream tried to set Jah up." He said quickly fighting the urge to get up and run, "I'm sayin', you shoulda known his soft ass would fuck it up. I been knowing Duke since primary school and he ain't built for shit like that."

Hector's eyes never strayed from Tony's face as he took a sip of his Espresso, "You also been knowing Jahad since primary school and if my information is correct the two of you were closer than brothers, so why should I believe you would up and turn on him?"

Hector was sharp, Tony had to admit it, but from the time he sent his message Tony began putting together a plausible story to tell Hector in regards to his involvement with Jahad. Tony was sharp too.

"You know Hector, I see exactly what you trying to get at, but it ain't like that. Yeah, at one time Jah was my man, I had genuine love for Duke. All that changed when he came home from Spofford. He ran the show when we were kids, called all the shots. That's when we were kids tho', shit changed. We were all rockin' with you, then he came along with that get rich shit and fucked everything up."

"If that's the case, why you go along with it if you weren't feeling it?"

"I ain't have no choice. You don't know Jah the way I do. It's his way or no way with no questions asked. I told him when he first came home how it was going down, he didn't wanna listen tho'. I couldn't move on him because of Razor, he was the only one down for that stupid shit. You saw for yourself how they got down together, both of 'em crazy as hell and don't trust nobody. To move on 'em would be suicide."

Hector nodded, he definitely knew how Razor and Jahad got down. Seven of his people were dead to prove the fact. "Okay, so you've made your point. You're not feeling Jahad. Now back to my original question. What does that have to do with me?"

"Like I said, nothing. But before I asked you about getting money in the park again, I wanted to make that known. That and the situation with my family. I ain't stupid, I know to come to you before I try to make any moves. I ain't with that wilin' shit either. I can't make no money wilin'."

"So that's it huh?" Hector smiled, "You wanna make some money. For a second there I thought you were trying to set me up."

"Nah man. When have you ever known me to spark some beef? That's the shit Jah was on and why his ass ain't gon' never see the street again. Me, I'm strictly about making that paper."

"I'm all for you making money, so what do you have in mind?"

"As you know the park is crazy hot right now, when it cools down tho' I wanna be on the scene."

Hector nodded, "We'll pick things up from where we left off. But listen, this time around I expect your complete loyalty. No more jumping sides Tone."

"No doubt, but hear me out first. I generate too much money to be on some hand-to-hand shit. My hustle game speaks for itself."

"So what are you asking?"

"Since Man-Man is gone, I wanna hold down that lieutenant position. When Jah came home all he did was supply the weight. I'm the nigga who came up with the schemes to move it. Like I said, I'm a money maker."

Hector gave the impression like he was unsure about accepting Tony's proposition, but truthfully he needed Tony with Manual and his foot soldiers dead, "I'll take a chance with you Tone, and I'll only give you this warning once. Don't fuck up my money."

"C'mon Hector. Me fuckin' up money won't ever happen."

"Good... Every Thursday go to the Bodega on 115th and Ftelly Avenue for the pick-up. It doesn't matter what time, as long as it's before midnight. My money, you drop off at the cleaners on the corner of 116th and Commonwealth before closing time at five o'clock. You got that?"

"Yeah, I got it. Is there a certain day you want me to drop the dough off?"

"Whenever you're finished. Just make sure all my money is there so we won't have any problems."

"Oh, it won't be no problems. I got this." Tony smiled, meaning it in more ways than one.

CHAPTER 21

Six months flew by without a peek of Cream. The pressure forced Jahad and Tony into a frantic tug-of-war match of wills. Tony was all for sending a message to Cream by any means, even if it meant using his mother. Anything to make him show his face. Jahad on the other hand held back, insisting on using those measures as a last resort. He didn't want to stoop to Cream's level unless it was absolutely necessary, being he knew Cream's mother well. Valentino, on crates and eggs himself, settled the matter by filing a bunch of bogus motions so that Jahad's trial date was postponed for close to a year, giving him time to uphold his end of the bargain.

As the months passed, Jahad noticed a dramatic change in Tony. His usual laid-back persona was gone, replaced with a determined will to see the Coco Twins go down. He had always been a thinker, that's where his success came from in the drug game. What he lacked was aggressiveness. Not anymore. Now he was aggressive, quick to make important decisions on his own, and would put himself in situations where his life could be taken at the snap of a finger. Something he would have never done in the past.

Derrick, Kwan, and Joey also noticed the change; being they were the ones subjected to Tony's orders, which they followed without questions, knowing his purpose. Since Derrick was the hot head, his job was to keep a steady eye on Cream's building in case he tried to sneak home. Tony was leery about having his hustle in the park, fearing that his temper and hatred of the Coco Twins might cause him to say the wrong thing around the wrong people. Joey and Kwan, Tony kept in the park with him when they weren't trying to keep tabs on Hector and José, a job that kept them constantly on the run.

While Tony handled business on the street, on Riker's Island Jahad, Sha', Lord, Prince, and Star (the Five Heads they would eventually be named) formed a bond that would soon ignite one incredible idea; an idea that would make them rich beyond their wildest dreams and feared almost as much as God. Already their reputations were spreading as being official stand up dudes, and dangerous as a whole, or individually. Once a week, sometimes twice, somebody was sent to the infirmary for the slightest infraction. At the same time, they were quick to show love to those they felt were worthy. What made them so much of a threat was a combination of things.

They were all thinkers and planned out every assault before committing the deed. Nothing was done on impulse, unless it was absolutely called for. They were all hustlers, charged with murdering the people who tried to stop them from making money. And most of all, they were all natural born leaders with their own little cliques on the street, who held them down. Sha's clique was Crook, Black Face, Trigger, Killer, and Rugged. Lord's clique was Ruff, Magic, Bullet, Vito, Trey, and Apple. Prince's clique was Muta, Pop, Hammer, and Gift. Star's clique was Flash, Monte, Mooney, Biggie, and Corey. Through visitation, Jahad got the chance to meet them all, and they all seemed to be solid brothers. This originally sparked the idea, but at the time he dismissed it, thinking that it was impossible.

Meanwhile, the Coco Twins still hadn't forgotten about Jahad. In fact, a ten thousand dollar price tag had been placed on his head after the word reached them of what happened to Carlos, who happened to be one of their affiliates. Since Jahad cliqued up with Sha', Lord, Prince, and Star, all potential threats had ceased, being the five were a force to be reckoned with. Ten thousand dollars was enough money to erase a lot of fears though. To make matters worse, Jahad only let the Puerto Ricans use the phone once a day from nine to ten in the morning, causing greater animosity. Something had to be done, but the Puerto Ricans were far from stupid. To move on Jahad while his friends were around would be a suicide mission. So the six Puerto Ricans who took up the hit waited until the other four were at the commissary before making their move on Jahad. The day it happened, Jahad sat in his cell, high as hell, listening to a DJ Clue mix tape when he felt the sting from a razor slicing across the back of his neck, followed by a deep penetrating pain in his shoulder from the ice pick stab that was meant for his neck.

"Here's a message from the Coco Twins!" Someone yelled

behind him.

Instead of standing to face his attackers, which would have been a deadly mistake being there were three Puerto Ricans behind him armed with razors and ice picks, waiting to stab him in the chest, Jahad dropped low and forced his chair out between them while snatching two ice picks from his waist. Spinning he swung the ice pick in his right hand, stabbing the Puerto Rican closest to him in the side, then kicked his chair back into him forcing all three out of his cell. To get trapped inside, he knew would probably cost him his life.

"Let's get busy, you cowardly muthafuckas!" He yelled, stepping out of his cell with both ice picks held out in front of him, in his fighting stance. Blood ran freely from the back of his neck, soaking the white Adidas sweatshirt he wore, but he paid it no attention. His mind and body was focused solely on the three Puerto Ricans. With some people, fear was a crippler, slowed their thinking process. Jahad was just the opposite, fear made his brain work faster, his reflexes sharper.

Seeing the reckless expression on his face, the three Puerto Ricans paused a second before rushing in. Jahad bounced on his toes and sidestepped the first Puerto Ricans swing of a long ice pick, then struck out, stabbing his second attacker in the neck. Blood skeeted from the wound directly into Jahad's eye, just as an ice pick pierced the left side of his jaw chipping two of his back teeth before comin out on the right side.

"Ah Shit!" He screamed when the ice pick was snatched from his jaw. He spit blood and bits of his teeth to the floor and got back into his fighting stance, facing the two remaining Puerto Ricans with his confidence building. Inmates stood inside their cells watching the action, awestruck, too scared to enter the dormitory.

The second time they rushed Jahad slipped in a pool of blood when the first Puerto Rican swung his ice pick and was stabbed in the right side of his chest as he fell to the floor. The pain was so intense that tears sprung to his eyes, but he quickly pushed himself to his feet. Feeding off his rage, he turned the tables and rushed his attackers, stabbing one of them in the eye. Still in attack mode, he faced the last Puerto Rican, then all at once his confidence faded. From the back of the dorm, three more came rushing towards him armed with ice picks. Weighing the odds, he knew he was looking into the face of death. Instead of trying to escape which would have been the logical thing to do, he embraced it.

"C'mon muthafuckas! Ya'll might kill me, but word to my mother, one of you bastards gon' die with me!" He shouted preparing for what he figured was his last battle when out of the corner of his eye he saw Sha' running up with two knives in hand, followed by Star, Prince, and Lord. "Word! Let's even this shit out."

In a matter of seconds, the three Puerto Ricans were on the floor unconscious and bleeding from multiple stab wounds. From there, they turned their assaults on the whole dorm for not helping Jahad. After a few minutes, from one end of the dorm to the other, blood and unconscious dudes were strung out on the floor. Being the action had spread to the front of the dorm, Correctional Officers, monitoring both North side and South side dormitories, saw the brutal attacks and called in the Emergency Response Team, better known as the Turtles. The smallest guy in their squad stood 6'4" and weighed no less than 250 pounds. The rest were bigger than a New York Giant defensive lineman, and fucking up inmates was their specialty. What happened when they arrived wasn't a pretty sight for Jahad and his friends, or anyone else in the dorm, who was stupid enough not to lock themselves in their cells. Hours later they woke up in the infirmary with concussions and broken bones, from there pushed in wheelchairs to lock-up.

The next day, once the pain medication wore off, Sha' was the first to wake up. They were in a sixteen-man lock up with two tiers, eight cells on the bottom, and eight cells on top, locked up beside each other. Each cell held a steel bunk, a small steel table, and a steel sink attached to a steel toilet.

"Jah! Ayo Jah!" Sha' called out from his bunk, unable to move because of the cast on his right leg, "Jah! Ayo, what the fuck happened?"

A few seconds passed and a lot of moaning before Jah answered, "Shit, I don't know. I'm over here fucked up," he called out from two cells over. His left arm was broke in two places, his neck in a brace, his whole face swollen, even his forehead, and he had forty stitches on the back of his neck, twenty-five on his left forearm, and ten on his right shoulder.

"Nah, I'm talking 'bout with you and them damn Germans."

"The muthafuckas tried to body me. The Germans I was beefin' with on the street sent 'em... What up with the rest of the fam', they up here?"

"What you mean, what up?" Prince called out from the cell in between Sha and Jahad's, "Those fuckin' Turtles fucked us up, that's what up." His leg was broke along with his wrist and two of his fingers.

"Uh! Uh! Uh! Uh!" Someone grunted loudly from the cell next to Sha's.

"Who the fuck is that... Lord?" Sha' called out.

"Uh uh!"

"Star?"

"Uh uh!"

"What, you can't talk nigga?"

"Uh uh!"

"Let me find out they wired your shit up."

"Uh uh!" Star grunted painfully, besides his broken jaw two of his teeth had been knocked out and his left leg was broke.

"Ayo word up Man. If I ever see one of them Turtle nigga's on the street, I'm a body 'em on the spot. I don't give a fuck where I see 'em at." Lord called out from the end cell beside Star's.

"You a'ight?" Jahad asked.

"Hell nah I ain't a'ight. They broke both my fuckin' legs and my arm. I'm over this muthafucka lookin' like a damn mummy."

"Well shit, if we fucked up like this, imagine how fucked up those Germans are. They got it twice." Sha' called out, laughing.

"Fuck you Moreno bastards! It ain't over!" One of the Puerto Ricans who like Sha' said, got it twice, yelled from a cell further down.

"Yeah, yeah, yeah," Prince called out dismissing him.

Laid back on his bunk, Jahad felt a wave of gratitude for his comrades. "Ayo, ya'll niggas hear me? I love ya'll for holdin' me down; word up!"

"Go 'head with that emotional shit Jah!" Sha' called out with a smile in his voice.

~~~~

The following week they went up in front of the Disciplinary Board, where they were sentenced to 90 days segregation time, which was good considering the damage they did. During this time, Jahad's original plan took root in his mind, using what he had planned for the Coco Twins as the foundation. All that was left to do was convince Sha', Lord, Prince, and Star that it could work. Being he wanted to keep it a secret and a lot of ears were on lock up, he decided to wait before bringing it to their attention.

Exactly eighty-six days later, they were released back into regular population. After the story circulated how they ran through the whole dorm before the Turtles stopped in, they were practically living legends on Riker's Island. An attempt was made to break them up, send each one to a different housing unit, but they weren't going for it. The promise to cause havoc in whatever house they were sent to held weight with the top administrators. In the end, they were placed back in C-74 in the same dormitory where Jahad once more claimed the Puerto Rican phone out of spite.

Three months after getting off lock up, Jahad finally spoke about what had been on his mind for nearly six months, while they were all in his cell, smoking weed after visitation.

"Ayo, check this out. I'm 'bout to spit some real shit." He said, taking a deep pull from his blunt, coughing a few times before continuing, "We all built like that, right? We all hustlers, we all leaders, and we all in this muthafucka 'cause niggas tried to stop us from eating. Now I had this shit on my mind for a minute, but..."

"What the fuck you talking 'bout Jah?" Lord interrupted, reaching for the blunt.

"Chill nigga, let me finish... the two Puerto Rican dudes I was beefin' with got the South Bronx in a choke hold right now. I got a plan tho' that's gon' dead all that. Now peep this, Prince you had a diesel spot on Broadway and a coke spot on St. Nick, Sha'..."

"Yeah, but..."

Jahad held up a hand to silence him, "Sha' you were getting money in East New York and Brownsville, Lord you were snatching paper in the Stuy, Star, you were doing your thing in Queens. So what I'm sayin' is we take all that shit over. All we gotta do is put our heads together."

No one spoke for a few seconds, then Prince burst out laughing, "Ayo, Sha', what the hell is in these trees? Sun buggin'...how the hell we suppose to take some shit over and we locked up?"

"Hold up Prince. Let's see where Jah is going with this shit." Sha' replied, intrigued.

"Yeah," Star added.

"It's like this, I'ma get the fuck up outta here with help from my man's on the street. I can help ya'll get out too. If I touch before any of you, I'm taking shit over in my hood. That's my word!"

"A'ight, I'm feelin' that," Sha' sat his blunt on the steel table, "but say you or any one of us gets out first. How we supposed to take nigga's spots? Muthafuckas got teams out there Jah. Shit, say we all get out at the same time, we still ain't strong enough to move on nigga's shit. You talking 'bout taking over spots in the Bronx, Harlem, Queens, and Brooklyn? C'mon we only five niggas."

"Wrong," Jahad said with a crooked grin, "together we like twenty deep with our cliques on the bricks. As of now my clique is built like that. From being around you niggas I know ya'll don't fuck with no weak ass dudes. If so, I'm telling you now from experience, cut them niggas lose." He thought about Cream and the advice Valentino gave him. "Like I was sayin' tho', twenty strong niggas are more than enough to move on any team. What we do is plug our mans on the street together and have 'em move as one unit, feel me?"

Prince nodded, warming to the idea, "I see your vision Sun, but it'll take more than twenty niggas, especially if we'll be going against some major niggas. You gotta leave room just in case somebody or a few niggas on our team gets bodied. Another thing, what about startup money? Say we do take over niggas spots, how we gon' supply the work? That's gon' take mad dough."

"I feel you about needing more than twenty niggas," Lord said with a mischievous grin slowly turning the corners of his mouth. "I know the perfect way to get some startup money, tho'. It's how we negotiate with niggas in Brooklyn. We kidnap their asses. We all know big time hustlers in our hoods, shit, those same niggas we were beefin' with. We snatch up their moms or seeds and make 'em pay out the ass."

"Word!" Jahad nodded vigorously, "I ain't even think of that. I was gon' kill them two Puerto Rican bastards and be done with it. Now, I'm a snatch one of 'em up and get a couple hundred thou', then merk their asses. . . That's what I mean by putting our heads together. This shit can work!"

"Yeah, but what about the niggas we gon' need tho'?

Sha' asked, "Prince made a good point, twenty niggas won't do it."

The room grew quiet as everybody started thinking. After about five minutes Star stood and slammed his hand down on the table, "I got it! Where do most live niggas we know come from? Niggas who been through some of the same shit we been through, get busy, and live by the code of the streets?"

Sha' frowned, "What the hell you talking 'bout Star?"

I'm talking 'bout right here nigga. The Rock! We put niggas on the team from right in here. Live official niggas!"

"Oh shit, that's it!" Jahad looked out his window at the recreation yard where inmates were playing basketball and working out on the pull-up bar. "Niggas know how we get down too so they'll rock with us like that. We gotta keep this shit crazy low tho', for real! If we can pull this off a lot a muthafuckas gon' get bodied and what's the use in doing anything if we ain't gon' be on the street to enjoy it. One nigga can sink the whole ship. Look at what Sammy did to the mob. So we gotta keep it low and make sure the niggas we pull are stand up niggas."

Lord nodded, "This is what we do then... the niggas we pull, we don't even let 'em know what's going down."

"I'm feelin' that, 'cause we can't leave no room for even one mistake. This is some serious shit right here, and in the wrong ears it could get us all fucked up in the end. So now that we have all this time on our hands, we use it to watch certain niggas to see if they fit the roster," Jahad said, grabbing Sha's blunt off the table.

"Jah your mans still getting money on the street?" Prince asked.

"Yeah, and guess what, they're hustling for the same Puerto Rican dudes I was beefin' with."

"What!" Sha' screwed up his face, "What type of shit your mans on?"

Jahad smiled, "Nah, check it. My man Tone is holdin' down a lieutenant spot for 'em, at the same time, he's finding out where they rest at, who they fuckin', where they hang out at, and what spots they own. When I come home I'll know exactly where to get 'em at, feel me? That plan sparked this whole idea."

"Word!" Star said, grinning, "That's some ill shit right there."

"Yeah, and ya'll niggas need to do the same thing. Tell your mans to plug in with some heavyweights and do the one on their whole operation. When we touch the bricks we'll know exactly who our target is and how to get at 'em. That shit Lord said about the kidnapping ties in with everything." Jahad turned to Prince, "What were you gon' say when you asked 'bout my mans?"

"I'm sayin', my fam still getting money on the Nick. How about the rest of you niggas? Your fam still out there eating?"

Sha', Lord, and Star nodded.

"This what we do then. The niggas we put on the team, if they get out before we do, whatever borough they from, we'll have someone from our clique pick 'em up and hold 'em all the way down until we get out and do what we do. That way niggas will know it's all the way official, plus our fam can watch 'em and make sure they ain't no crack head Or no shit like that. We all know how niggas get locked up, pick up a little weight, then get on some guerrilla shit."

"Ain't no crack heads in here now is it?" Jahad asked, grinning, looking at his friends who all gave him a scowl.

"We gon' fuck around and jump your ass in here Jah. Ain't no Pooky's in this muthafucka. . . is it?" Sha' burst out laughing.

This is where it all started. In a small eight by ten cell, with five determined hoodlums. Since they were all hustlers, they agreed to call their clique the M.G.'s, which stood for Money Getters. At the time, none of them had any idea how big the M.G.'s would grow, the lives it would affect, or the lives it would take including their own.

CHAPTER 22

After a week of intensive planning, the M.G. structure was finally set, based simply on unity and secrecy. All five cliques were to move as one, dealing with everything they were involved in. All money made would be brought to the table and divided equally, regardless of which cliques generated the most. The question of a rift coming between the clique over money issues was cancelled out. Once the purpose, along with the ultimate goal was explained the logic behind their reasoning would be understood. No longer would they buy from different drug connects. The coke, heroin, and marijuana would be bought from the same supplier, using three M.G.'s, one for each drug. The reason, in case the connect was busted and turned snitch, only one person will go down instead of the whole crew. What they still hadn't figured out was how to go about moving the drugs. Since their structure was based or secrecy, they wanted no M.G.'s involved with the direct drug sales, for fear of drawing attention to the whole organization. While Jahad and the others were still locked up, one person from each clique was chosen to fill their spots until they came home. Tony was filling in for Jahad, Muta for Prince, Crook for Sha', Flash for Star, and Ruff for Lord. A meeting had been set to be held at Muta's apartment in Harlem on 124th and St. Nicholas Avenue where Tony would explain to the other four the strategy he was using with the Coco Twins, also to unite the cliques and lay down the structure.

That afternoon, two hours before the meeting Jahad called Tony wanting to make sure everything was set. Breathing hard like he had been running Tony answered his cell phone after the fourth ring.

"What you doing... fuckin'?" Jahad asked, wrinkling his face.

"Nah Sun, we got this muthafucka... keep your bitch ass still! Hold him Derrick, hold him!"

In the background, Jahad cold hear scuffling and loud grunts,

"What the fuck you talking 'bout... who you screaming at?"

"Cream... hold on Jah!"

"Word!" Jahad said, and began pacing in small circles, his adrenaline pumping, imagining the expression on Cream's face.

On his way to the shower, Sha' stopped, noticing the wild look of excitement in Jahad's eyes, "What up Jah?"

"They got that nigga Sun. They got him!"

"Got who?"

"That nigga..."

"Ayo Jah," Tony spoke back into the phone, "We gon' take this nigga up on the roof and see if he can fly."

"Where you at?"

"In Cream's mom's building. Sucka ass nigga frontin' like he don't know what's up."

"Oh word? Let me speak to him?"

A second later Cream's voice came through in a shrill whine, "Ayo Jah, what's going on? We family man. . .tell these niggas to let me go."

"Let you go? We family? Family don't do shit like you did. Family don't bring muthafuckas to my mom's crib to kill her. Family don't..."

"They made me do it Jah," Cream cried, "I swear to God. They said they were gon' kill me."

"Psss! Ain't that some shit then, 'cause you gon' die anyway you stupid muthafucka. All the years I've known you, I kept it official man. I thought your pussy ass was my brother and you bring niggas to body my family, my family Cream! Ain't no forgetting or forgiving that!"

"Who you talking to Jah?" Sha' asked, edging closer to the phone trying to listen.

Jahad held up his hand just as Tony spoke, "Call me back in like twenty minutes Sun. We gon' get this shit over with."

"Hold up Tone. Give it to him right there so I can hear it."

"You what?"

"You heard me. Put five or six in his head right there."

"Ayo, you buggin' Jah. We. . ."

"Do it!" Jahad yelled with such intensity, some of his cellmates peeked out of their rooms.

"A'ight, A'ight! You buggin' tho'... Derrick hit that nigga."

For a few seconds Cream's pleading cold be heard, then, "BOOM! BOOM! BOOM! BOOM! BOOM! BOOM!" came through loud and clear.

"Oh Shit!" Tony shouted, "Chill nigga! Chill! He's fuckin' dead already!"

Sha's eyes flew open, his mouth forming a large circle when he realized what had just happened.

"What happened?" Jahad asked anxiously as Star, Lord, and Prince rushed from their cells, knives in hand, thinking there was beef.

"Derrick spazzed the fuck out Sun. I got blood and green shit all over my Timbs...shit! Call me back around nine o'clock. I should be back from Harlem by then."

"A'ight... Ayo Tone, I love you niggas man, word up!"

"Yeah, no doubt. We love you too or we wouldn't be doing this crazy shit. Let us get the fuck outta here before somebody comes. One!"

"One!" Jahad hung up and looked at his friends with a crooked grin.

"Did what I think just happened really happen?" Sha' asked, still stunned.

"Yep. That's what you call street justice."

"Street Justice?" Star said, looking from Jahad to Sha', then back to Jahad, "What the hell you talking 'bout Jah? And why you out here screaming all crazy for? We thought we had to fuck some more Germans up and get broke up by the damn Turtles again."

Jahad laughed, feeling ten pounds lighter, "Nah Homey, what just happened is how we all gon' get the fuck up outta here. C'mon to my room so I can put ya'll on."

CHAPTER 23

Over the span of twenty months, twenty people had been recruited, twenty ruthless brother's hand picked by Jahad, Sha', Prince, Star, and Lord. Four were from the Bronx who had heard of Jahad's beef with the Coco Twins. Eight were from Brooklyn; four recruited by Sha', the other four recruited by Lord. There were four from Harlem, and four from Queens. For two and a half months, before they were approached, the twenty were watched closely to see who they associated with and how loyal they were to those they considered friends.

Taking what they were building to heart the Five Heads set the stage for the twenty to be tested by putting hits on each one to see how they handled themselves. The outcome proved that they were M.G. material, being that the dudes who took up the hits all ended up in the infirmary. From there the recruits were approached while they were by themselves by a Head from their borough and offered help with lawyer fees, money, a place to lay their head once they were released, and a chance to get rich without taking too many risk. All that was required was their loyalty to what was already in the making, but couldn't be explained at the moment, and their absolute silence. How it was planned, not one person out of the twenty recruits had any idea of the others who had been recruited nor would they know until they were all on the street together. The purpose behind this was to keep gossip from spreading.

Once they agreed the Heads upheld their promise by retaining Valentino to handle their cases on a payment plan worked out by Jahad, who by this time had become good friends with the Sicilian lawyer. Their friendship sparked over a period of time during Jahad's lawyer visits. Valentino quickly took a liking to the slang speaking hoodlum, noticing beneath the hard surface was a highly intelligent young man who was a lot like his father, and Jahad grew to admire the suave five thousand dollar suit wearing lawyer for his drive and determination to win his cases by any means necessary. To Jahad, Valentino lived by his motto, only the strong survive. To Valentino, Jahad was his ticket back to the life he craved. Having a keen mind, Valentino knew Jahad was up to something. He wasn't helping all these men get out of jail for nothing. It was this curiosity that would eventually pull him knee deep into the M.G. organization.

~~~~

A week before his trial date, Jahad was called for an unexpected visit. He dressed in a pressed jail issued jumpsuit, dabbed on some Muslim oil, then strolled out the dorm walking with a swagger in his step thinking it could be Candy. Over the months since Prince introduced them, Candy had become a genuine friend and that's as far as Jahad would let their relationship go, despite her efforts to take it further. With all he had planned, love didn't equal up in the equation.

As he entered the visitation area, he looked around the crowded noisy room expecting to see his family or hopefully Candy but was totally surprised when he spotted Emma sitting at a table wearing her Sunday's best beside Valentino, who was dressed immaculately as always, in a brown Jones New York suit.

"Hey Baby!" Emma stood as he approached the table, a smile stretching her wrinkled face, and hugged him tightly while Valentino glanced at them from his chair uncomfortably.

"What's up Mrs. H?"

Emma stepped back and looked at him from head to toe, "Look at you, all bunched up with muscles. They must be feeding you good."

Jahad laughed, and kissed her on the cheek, "Yeah, they feeding me a'ight. How you been?"

"Just fine Baby. Tony checks on me once a week to make sure I have what I need. He's a good boy."

Jahad nodded, thinking about the drugs and money Tony kept stashed in her apartment. "What up Vinny? What you doing here? Ain't no bad news is it?" He asked, sitting in the chair Emma pulled out beside her.

"No, no bad news. Everything is looking good with your case." Valentino glanced at Emma, "Mrs. Harris asked me to come. It concerns a conversation you two had together."

"What he talking 'bout Mrs. H?" Jahad looked from Valentino to Emma frowning, "How ya'll know each other anyway?"

"You will know in a few minutes," Emma took hold of his hand, "let me finish telling you the story."

"What story?... Oh, what we were building about before that sh... stuff popped off."

Emma smiled, "Yes. I never got around to telling you who John's partner was. Those two Puerto Rican boys you got in trouble over, he was their father."

A chill ran through Jahad, "What! My pops partner was the Coco Twins pops."

"Yes, Chico brought..."

"Chico?" Jahad asked, trying to remember where he had heard the name.

"That was his name. John and Chico were good friends, way before they became business partners. John was them boys Godfather, they even called him uncle John. You were still..."

"Whoa!..." Jahad, held up his hand, "Why didn't my pops ever introduce us then?"

"He wanted to shield you from the life he led. I don't know the whole story but at some point Chico divorced his wife and them boys went wild. They were around thirteen when Chico started giving 'em drugs to sell. They were already mixed up in the streets anyway. This is when that crack mess became popular in the 80's. In less than a year the Coco Twins as you call 'em, had all their little friends selling that poison, and Chico couldn't have been prouder. For their sixteenth birthday Chico and John gave 'em their own drug spot on Ftelly Avenue. It wasn't enough though."

Emma shook her head with tears swimming in her eyes, "They're evil Jahad, right down evil!"

"What you mean? What they do?"

"They murdered John and Chico," Valentino answered solemnly, "I never planned on telling you any of this since so much time had passed, even after I found out why you were charged with murder. Emma insisted."

Jahad grew quiet as anger slowly crept over him causing his whole body to tremble. Then suddenly a thought occurred to him, "Hold up, you telling me that the Coco Twins bodied both my pops and their pops, right?" He said giving Valentino a twisted sneer, "Well, how in the hell do you know?"

"It's a long story Jahad, one I'd rather not get into, but it's true. Hector and José Sanchez murdered your father. I discovered this a week after his death and notified Emma."

"I don't give a damn 'bout what you rather not get into. I wanna know how you know all this shit 'bout my pops man. You being this big shot lawyer and whatnot. How in the hell could you know?"

Valentino held Jahad's glare a moment then turned to Emma, "If you will, could you please excuse us for a moment Emma." Once Emma left Valentino looked back at Jahad, his blue eyes turning ice cold, "What I'm about to tell you Jah, I ask that you never mention to anyone, not even your closest friend. Do I have your word?"

"C'mon Vinny, that shit you told me about strict confidence, I live by that same code. So yeah, you got my word."

Valentino nodded, then lowered his voice to a whisper, "I met your father back in '68. We were in the same platoon in Nam. I'm speaking about the Vietnam war. Back in those days, I'm sure you heard about racial tension back in the 60's. Well, just so happens, my platoon was mostly black with a few white boys sprinkled in. I was considered one of the white boys, although in Sicily the Italians treat my people much like the blacks are in America. Anyway, and let me say this first. Racism isn't just a white thing, you have black racist too. I saw proof of that in Nam. The blacks, well a lot of them, terrorized anyone who wasn't of color.

Myself personally, I migrated to America when I was ten with my uncle and his family. I grew up as a street kid in Brooklyn, so I wasn't frightened easily. I grew up around the bullies in Sicily and Brooklyn, I was a bully myself at one time." He gave Jahad a little smile, "One day, the same day John and I became acquainted I had a confrontation with this enormous black guy from Mississippi, Bear. My uncle had sent me a food package and Bear had it in his mind to take my food. I on the other hand wasn't about to let him or anyone else take anything from me. In the end, he beat me senseless and took it anyway, but I fought him, something a lot of guys, even some of the blacks wouldn't do. But taking my food wasn't enough for Bear. While I was still half unconscious he decided he was going to take my manhood, and almost succeeded until John stopped him. Later while we were in the stockade, John told me the only reason he stepped in was because I stood up to Bear."

"I'm sayin', what happened? What, ya'll beat him up or something?" Jahad asked, anxious to hear the rest of the story.

"Well, unlike myself, John was an extraordinary fighter, but Bear was just that, a Bear! Six-five, 300 pounds of muscles. John gave him a good run for his money for a while, until Bear grabbed him, then the fight was over. . .well almost over. While he was squeezing the life out of John I grabbed my army issued knife and stabbed him in the back. This only made him madder. He released John and turned towards me with the knife still stuck in his back. When he reached for me, John snatched the knife and started stabbing him repeatedly until some of the other guys pulled him off of Bear. To make a long story short, we were both kicked out of the Army."

"That's when our business relationship started. My uncle, my whole family actually, are friends of friends and..."

"Friends of friends? What's that?"

"The Mafia," Valentino answered with a smile.

"Oh Word!" Jahad sat up in his chair, "So it's true what Mrs. H said about my pops having mob ties?"

"Not exactly. I mentioned what John did for me to my uncle. Sicilians are big on returning favors so my uncle sent me to the Bronx with ten thousand dollars for John. This was a few months after we returned to the states and by then John was selling heroin in the same park he was killed in. Honestly, during that time jobs were scarce for anyone who participated in the war, especially blacks. Hippies were running the country with their self-righteous values, so I figure John was only doing what he had to do to survive. When I offered him the money he asked if I would use it to buy him some good quality heroin. From our time spent in the stockade we got to know each other pretty well and I entrusted him with the knowledge of my family, so he knew I was connected. From there we began meeting in Manhattan for..."

"You were the dude my pops was coppin' from when we made those trips to Manhattan!"

"For a while yes, then I went to law school. My uncle had no idea I was dealing with John, but by the time I went off to school, this was two years later, John was making so much money I informed my uncle and he continued to have someone meet him. So I wouldn't really say that John had ties, although I did want to avenge his death.

During the time my family was caught up in a war with the Leopardi family. After Gotti went down, there were a lot of business interest to be claimed. Anyway, my uncle refused to dispense any of his people, wanting all his forces concentrated on the war. I remembered Emma from their trips to Manhattan and informed her, in hopes that she would have someone avenge his death, but by then she had turned her life over to God and He would handle it. Those were her exact words."

Jahad nodded, "Call me God then, 'cause I'm gon' handle it." His eyes held a hatred so deep, Valentino looked away.

"I figured you would, which brings me to this question. What are you up to?"

"What you mean?"

"In the past few months, at your suggestion, I've taken on twenty four clients. Why?"

"I'm sayin', you a good lawyer and whatnot, so I figured I'd send some money your way. My man still making payments, right?"

"Yes, but I wasn't born yesterday Jah. I normally charge triple for what I took to take your case, and these other cases. I'm only taking them now because I know you're up to something. I want to know why, maybe I can be of some help. Now what's really good, as your fond of saying."

Jahad laughed, "You a funny dude Vinny. But yo', if I tell you its gotta be kept under that strict confidence code you under."

"Omerta is a term I grew up by. It basically means never reveal a secret."

"Ayo, I read that book. Mario Puzo wrote it, the same dude who wrote the Godfather. So yeah, I know what it means. But check it..." Jahad went on to tell Valentino his plans, including every detail so he would have a clear picture. "...That's why I need you to help me get these dudes out, feel me?"

Valentino studied Jahad a moment, surprised that someone so young could put together a structure that could actually work, "I like it, I like it a lot. You planned everything out to the last detail, but you forgot the most important thing."

"What's that?"

"Your finances. Every dime you make must be accounted for, that's if you want to spend it. You won't be able to put it in the bank or make any investments. If you do so without having a liable front to show where your money came from, then all your efforts to remain anonymous will be wasted. The IRS will swoop down on you before you know it."

"Damn! I ain't think of that. It's called the Ricky law or some shit like that, right?"

Valentino laughed, "The R.I.C.O law and it's designed purposely for such organizations as you plan on starting. There are ways around it."

"What up, you gon' put me on or what?" Jahad asked just as Emma returned to her seat.

"If ya'll are finished talking, Jahad there's something I need you to do for me." She grabbed his hand and stared directly into his eyes, "Use the sense God gave you and leave New York with Michelle. We had a long talk about you and we know how thick headed you are, but you need to listen this time baby, for your own sake."

Jahad shook his head, "I hate to disappoint you or my moms Mrs. H. but..."

"You're not leaving," Emma finished for him. "We both came to that conclusion too. So let me say this. I've never condoned killing, still don't, but if you stay you send those two boys straight to hell where they belong. You hear me?"

Jahad nodded, "Loud and clear Mrs. H."

~~~~

Monday, November 12, 2000, eighteen months after the day he stepped foot on Rikers Island, Jahad went to trial. Entering the courtroom wearing a black Ralph Lauren suit, a white dress shirt, and a pair of Stacy Adams shoes selected by Valentino, Jahad scanned the courtroom for his family and spotted them sitting on the front row behind the defense table with Tony. He gave them a crooked smile then glanced at the District Attorney, an old white man with saggy jaws, thinning gray hair and liver spotted skin, who returned Jahad's look with a smirk. Jahad took a seat in the chair Valentino pulled out for him as the D.A. approached the judge's bench and began whispering quietly.

"What up with Duke?" Jahad asked nervously, nodding towards the D.A.

Valentino gave him a sly smile, "Don't worry, it's already in the bag."

"Don't worry! Them muthafuckas might be trying to railroad me or something. Go see what's up."

Before Valentino could stand the D.A. returned to his table and gave Jahad another smirk, "Your Honor, We, the state of New York motion for the case against defendant Jahad Andre Copeland to be dismissed. Apparently the state's witness has disappeared."

"Mr. Copeland you heard the prosecutor. You're free to go. Case dismissed." The judge slammed his mallet against his podium making it official.

CHAPTER 24

Jahad wasted no time getting down to business. He had a quick lunch with his family while they were still in Mid-Town, where he explained to Michelle that he wouldn't be coming home, which caused a lot of bickering, until he told her that his life was still in danger. This was true, but his main reason was so he could put the finishing touches on his plan, a plan that would leave a lot of dead bodies in its wake. From the diner he and Tony left for a meeting at Muta's apartment. Neither spoke as the cab whipped through Manhattan's heavy traffic, both in deep thought, knowing their lives were about to change although Tony's in a totally different direction from Jahad's.

Twenty minutes later the cab dropped them off in front of Muta's building in the St. Nicholas projects. Tony ushered Jahad inside to the third floor, knocked at Muta's door. A minute later, it opened and they were greeted by Muta, Crook, Ruff, and Flash, who all gave Jahad a warm hug.

"The infamous Jah. What's the deal Sun?" Muta passed Jahad a cold Heineken, then put an arm around his shoulder and lead him inside to the living room.

"I'm good homey. What up with you?"

"I'm good. Ready for the rest of the fam' to come home."

"Yeah, me too." Jahad took a sip of his beer and walked to the middle of the living room, "We don't have time for alotta bullshit, so I'm a get down to business. This move we 'bout to make is crazy important because it sets the stage for everything else. We can't fuck it up!" He looked around, making eye contact with each top lieutenant before continuing.

"I know Tone put ya'll up on the two Puerto Ricans I was beefin' with. When I left the street they were like fifty deep. Tone said they've grown a bit, but their people are scattered out so it'll be easy to tear their asses up. Our main concern is taking out their spots. They have a coke and diesel spot on Beach Ave., a coke and diesel spot on Ftelly, and of course the Big Park on Story Ave. They have a money drop-off spot on Commonwealth, and their hands are basically in all the drugs supplied in every project in the South Bronx. So you can pretty much figure out they got crazy dough. That's what we want first, and then we want their asses in body bags."

"From what I understand, both brothers are relaxed right now, José more so than Hector. If they catch wind that I'm out tho' they gon' go in hiding. So the plan is to hit 'em fast, hard, and unexpectedly." Jahad drove his fist into his palm to emphasize his point, "Tone had Joey and Kwan watching 'em for a while now, so we know their routines. Hector keeps a low profile but has kids spread all over by different chicks. José is crazy loose tho'. Monday thru Friday, he's up in Jimmy's Café on some cool-out shit. That's our prize. I'ma snatch his ass up and make Hector pay out the ass. After I get the babysitting fee, it's a wrap for 'em."

He took a sip of beer to wet his throat, "Now check this, around the same time Hector is delivering the money, Muta you take twelve M.G.'s and organize two teams to hit the spots on Beach Ave. Flash, you and Ruff take six M.G.'s a piece and hit the spots on Ftelly. Tone, the Big Park is you. Try to spare the hustlers we can use. Ya'll know how we rockin', gloves and mask. A muthafucka can't tell on who they can't identify. I want ya'll to be here in the morning at eight o'clock so Kwan can take ya'll to the Bronx and show ya'll the spots. Crook, me, you, Joey, Kwan, and Derrick will snatch José up. It's going down tomorrow or either the day after so..."

"Tomorrow?" Ruff said shaking his head, "We ain't had time to plan this shit all the way out yet."

"That's where you're wrong," Jahad wore a scowl, irritated at being interrupted, "we been planning this shit for over a year now. I can tell you exactly what time the beat walkers come through, what cars T.N.T be rollin' in, and how many people the Coco Twins keep in each spot. So the only thing you need to be stressin' is handling your B.I. and getting the fuck outta there. Anybody else got questions?"

"Yeah, what time we moving out?" Flash asked.

"I want everybody in position at eight-thirty. Tone got stolen vans ready for each clique. Ya'll might be packed in there, but it won't be for long. The beat walkers come through Beach Avenue between 8:00 and 8:30, Ftelly between 9:15 and 9:45, Story between 9:30 and 10:00. I plan on snatching José up around 8:30, and setting the payoff time at 9:00 so Hector won't have time to do shit but get the money together. When we get José wrapped up, one of us will page ya'll. The code will be 000. At precisely 9:00 ya'll niggas do what ya'll do and kill everything moving. When ya'll done, dump the vans. It's a couple whips near each spot for ya'll to move in. I want you five to meet me back here. Send everybody else to Brooklyn and tell 'em to lay low."

"How much dough you gon' get off them dudes?" Muta asked.

"I don't know yet, but I'm figuring a couple hundred thousand or so... Ya'll niggas know after we do this shit the streets gon' be crazy hot so stay on point. The only way we get fucked up is if somebody makes a mistake, so try not to make one. We got twenty niggas, twenty wild official niggas, straight off the Rock who know how to get busy so we should be able to pull this off without no problems. I figure by the time the rest of the fam' comes home, our numbers should be right... Muta, you don't mind me coolin' out here until we handle our B.I. do you? I don't wanna risk being seen in the Bronx."

"Nah Sun, my crib is your crib. Somebody's coming through to check for you anyway?"

"Who?" Jahad arched his eyebrow.

"You'll see."

"C'mon Muta, I ain't with that surprise shit."

Muta laughed, "A'ight man, damn! Shorty from the Polo Grounds, Candy. She's coming through. Prince set it up as a surprise."

"Oh word!" Jahad smiled, picturing Candy in his mind. He hadn't spoken to her in a few weeks with all the planning he had been doing. "Yeah, I need some Candy in my life right now."

"Shit you might be too weak to do anything tomorrow," Muta patted his back.

"Picture that. Killing the Coco Twins gon' be better than busin' a nut... Ayo Crook, pick me up tomorrow at seven o'clock. Sha' told me how creative you are. Put something together for José's ass."

Crook gave Jahad an evil grin, "I already got something in mind."

"Cool... Well I guess that's about it then. I'll see you niggas tomorrow after we do what we do." As everybody was leaving out, Jahad grabbed Tony's shoulder, "Ayo, Sun, when you get home do me a favor and get my family somewhere safe. If you can, send 'em back to Long Island with your aunt. I know my moms is gonna have beef with it, but tell her it's only for a few days. Don't let her talk you out of it Tone. You know how she is."

"C'mon your moms is my moms, so you know I'll handle it."

Jahad nodded, "What up with Koran? He ain't been on no bullshit has he?"

"Nah, lil' dude been chillin'. He makes sure I take him shoppin' every time he gets his report card... Ayo, were you hittin' him off for his progress reports too?"

"Nah, just his report cards. Why?"

Tony laughed, "That lil' nigga ran game on me. He said you copped him one outfit if his progress reports were up to par, his slick ass. He's crazy smart tho'."

Jahad smiled, "Yeah, I know. He ain't gon' like it, but when I get this dough together, I'm sending him down south with moms. That's about the best opportunity I can give him."

"That might be a good idea. To be only twelve, he's a little too serious, word up. He ain't into shit normal twelve year olds be into. To be honest he reminds me of you after your pops died and you see how you turned out."

"If he's like me won't shit be able to change him. Circumstances made me what I am tho'... What up with Trice?" Jahad asked, looking Tone directly in his eyes.

"She's good, and before you say anything, yeah, she's my girl," Tony replied authoritatively, stepping out of Jahad's swinging distance, while Muta watched amused, "If you wanna fight lets get it over with now... What's up?"

For a second they stood like two lions posed to fight, then Jahad burst out laughing so hard tears ran from his eyes, "Oh shit Tone! You dead ass 'bout fuckin' me up huh?"

"I'm sayin, however it goes down, whether you beat my ass or I beat your ass, I ain't hurting her no more. She ain't trying to be with no one else but me and I feel the same way. I ain't gon' let your notion of me hurting her keep us apart. In fact, after all this shit is over we're getting married."

"Married!"

"Yeah nigga, married. We been talking 'bout it for a while now. She's kinda shook, thinking you gon' body me or something. She wanna keep our relationship in the dark like we been doing since you came home from Spofford."

"Hold up," Jahad said, screwing up his face, "I thought..."

"You thought I could just turn off my feelings. It don't work like that Jah, not with me anyway." Tony cut his eye at Muta while watching Jahad out the side of his eye in case he tried to swing. "Ayo Muta, if we break up some of your shit I'll pay for it."

"Don't sweat that Sun. I'm a bounce for a while, so talk it out, fight it out, or whatever. Just don't kill each other in here... O-yeah, Candy should be here in a little while Jah, so don't let Tone fuck you up too bad." Muta laughed, as he walked towards the front door.

"So what's up?" Tony asked again, expecting a fight.

Jahad smiled, "Chill nigga, I ain't gon' fuck you up, so you have my blessin'. All I ask is that you never raise a hand to hurt her."

Tony shook his head, "Never that Jah. I ain't no woman beater, that's that coward shit. Besides Trice is my baby so that's something you never have to stress... Now what I'm 'bout to say you might not be feelin', but when this shit is over, I'm out Sun."

"Out? What you mean?"

"Just that, I'm out. I'm moving down south with your moms and Trice. I'm 'bout to be a family man. Trice... Trice is pregnant and I..."

"Whoa!" Jahad nearly fainted, "She's pregnant!"

"Yeah, I'm 'bout to be a Pops," Tony smiled proudly, "I ain't trying to have my seed mixed up in the street, so I'm taking myself out of the streets, you know?"

Jahad ran a hand over his face. Losing Tony wasn't part of the plan, "I feel you Tone, but damn, you know what's going down. I'ma need you nigga."

"I thought about that, and Derrick can fill in for me. Sun can you think a lil' bit now," Tony smiled, but Jahad's face stayed expressionless. "Look at it this way Jah, would you rather have Trice married to a street nigga or a nigga with a nine to five who comes home to his family everyday?"

"A'ight Tone... A'ight man. Why you ain't tell me sooner tho'?"

"So you could try to talk me out of it. I'm smarter than that Jah."

Jahad laughed, "Yeah, you are. I'ma miss your ass man, word

up."

"I'm a miss you too nigga, believe that." Tony gave Jahad a hug just as someone knocked at the door.

Jahad walked down the short hallway, answered the door, and was nearly knocked over when Candy flung herself in his arms screaming like she had hit the lottery.

"You're really out, I thought Prince was lying!" She held him at arms length as she looked him over with her bright eyes, then gave him a passionate kiss while hungrily trying to pull off his shirt, "We have to do something about these clothes."

"Slow your roll Ma," Jahad cut his eye at Tony who stood off to the side grinning.

Candy giggled, smoothing his shirt down, "How you doing Tone?"

"I'm good Shorty. Jah, I'll see you tomorrow, that's if you can make it?"

"I'll make it nigga. Tell my moms I'll see her in a few days... and Tone, congratulations homey. I would say welcome to the family, but you're already family."

"No doubt, and thanks for understanding. Trice gon' be happy as hell when I let her know you ain't gon' kill me."

Jahad laughed as Tony walked out.

"What was that about?" Candy asked, working at the buttons on his shirt again.

"Tone and my sister are getting married." He let his eyes roam over the cream colored Chanel blouse and wrap around skirt she wore once she shrugged off her leather coat and felt a tingle in his groin area, "What we 'bout to get into?"

"I think you know. Since you've been deprived of some good candy, I'm about to give you something real sweet," she said, rubbing her hands over his chest.

The look in her eyes made Jahad's mouth water with anticipation, "I definitely been deprived. I'm feenin' for something sweet and gooey right now Ma."

"Well you're about to get that and some." She reached between his legs and cupped his massive erection through his pants.

~~~~

Two hours later, they were in Muta's guest room, both out of breath after another session of raw sex. With his legs twitching, body slick with sweat, Jahad rolled off Candy panting, his eyes focused on the ceiling.

"Damn Ma, I gotta be careful or you'll have my ass open."

"What you mean?" She asked, propping herself up on her elbows so she could meet his eyes, "Or are you trying to say I won't be seeing you no more after tonight."

Jahad frowned, "C'mon Candy, stop putting words in my mouth. You were there for me when I was locked up, a real friend, so you know I ain't gon' shit on you. But I'm not into all that relationship bullshit. I told you, it don't work for me."

"I'm not her Jah," Candy said quietly.

"Not who?"

"The girl you told me about. I wouldn't betray you."

"You know, she said the same exact thing, it taught me that words are easily spoken. Not sayin' you don't mean it, but on some real shit, you can't say what you will or won't do 'cause you can't predict the future. And personally, at the time I ain't willing to take that chance. I'll always be your friend tho', I mean that."

Candy sighed, "Well at least your honest. As long as you can scratch this itch for me every now and then, I'm cool with it," she lied. Being his friend wasn't enough. The year and a half they spent getting to know one another left her deeply in love and she wouldn't be satisfied until she was his everything. For now though, she would play the part of a friend, and slowly try to worm her way into his heart.

"I'll do more than scratch it Ma. Catch me on a good day, I might lick it." He stuck out his tongue, receiving a giggle from Candy, "On another note, you wanna hit two-fifth with me tomorrow so I can do some shoppin'?"

"Sure, if you want we can hang out at my place afterwards," she said brightly.

"Nah Ma, we ain't gon' start that shit. Next thing you know I'll have my clothes, sneakers, and toothbrush at your crib."

"At least I tried," she laughed straddling him. She took hold of his flaccid penis and felt it swell instantly in her hand, "Seems like you're about ready again."

"Oh word. You trying to get me open for real. Don't be surprised if you get open in the process."

Candy slid back onto him and started rocking slowly until he was sunk in to the hilt, "Open me now."

CHAPTER 25

Crook pulled up in front of Muta's building that cold Tuesday evening at exactly 7:00, driving a black Chevy Tahoe with dark tinted windows. A second later Jahad jogged from the lobby dressed for the occasion in a black Pelle' Pelle leather jacket, a black Sean John hoody and jeans, black leather gloves, black Timberlands, and a black New York Yankee fitted cap. Tucked in his waistline were two Desert Eagle 44's, in his hoody pocket an extremely sharp straight razor.

"You ready to get busy Sun?" He asked with a crooked grin, as he hopped into the passenger seat.

Crook took a pull from a blunt the size of his thumb, gagged a few times, and then pulled off. "I was born gettin' busy. Where we headed?"

"When you get off the Deegan, hit Webster Avenue. We gon' meet Derrick, Joey, and Kwan at a carwash not too far from Jimmy's Café. You know where River Park Towers are?"

Crook shook his head, with his eyes on traffic, "Nah, heard of 'em, don't know the exact location."

"When you drop me off, hit the Hudson River Drive, I'll give you directions. We'll be behind you in 'bout thirty minutes."

"I gotcha. Wanna hit this?" Crook passed the blunt in Jahad's direction.

"Nah, I'm good. You need to chill too. Fuck around and fall asleep."

"This shit keep me paranoid as hell, so don't stress that."

"If you say so... What you got in mind for Duke?"

"Oh, I got some rope, a little gas, a hammer, some nails, a..."

"You wanna crucify the nigga don't you?"

"We can do that if you want," Crook replied dead serious, "What, we gon' nail him to a tree or something?"

"Nigga, you crazy for real!" Jahad laughed, "I wanna see if his ass can walk on water tho'."

"What you mean?"

"You'll see."

A half hour later, Crook turned off the Major Deegan. Streetlights and colorful billboard signs illuminated Webster Avenue as he weaved through the thick traffic, trying to stay ahead of their schedule. Jahad sat in the passenger seat staring out at traffic without really seeing anything, his thoughts tuned into the move they were about to make. If successful, what lay ahead held so many possibilities, so much power, but would it be enough to quench the fire that burned inside him, he wondered.

"Is that the gas station?" Crook asked, nodding towards the Shell gas station they were approaching.

Snatched from his thoughts, Jahad looked up, "Yeah, make a right as soon as you pass it. Derrick should be pushing a blue minivan."

Crook slowed and turned into the carwash connected to the gas station. He parked beside two large coin operated vacuum cleaners, which separated the Tahoe from the light blue Plymouth Voyager Derrick drove.

"You got some duct tape, right?"

Crook reached over the seat and grabbed a white plastic bag, "Rope, hammer, tape..."

"All I need is the tape. You got the directions down, right?"

Crook nodded.

"A'ight. When you get there, park and find a hiding spot in case Hector tries to slide some bullshit in on us." Jahad got out the truck, tucking the tape in his hoody pocket.

"I gotcha... This is it, huh?" Crook grinned excitedly.

"You better believe it!"

Before Jahad could make it to the minivan, the black sliding door opened and Kwan hopped out with a lip splitting grin, "What up nigga!" He hugged Jahad, then stepped back to look him over, "Damn, we missed your ass man."

"I missed your funny ass too." Jahad draped an arm around his shoulder as they walked back to the van.

Derrick leaned over the seat to give him a hug as soon as he climbed into the back seat, "Word up, its good to see you Sun... You know about Razor, right?"

"Yeah, they get it too."

Derrick nodded satisfied.

"You know we gotta celebrate when this shit is over," Joey said with the same lip splitting grin as his brother.

"And you know it." Jahad chatted a few minutes with his childhood friends then got down to business, "What up with José, he still in Jimmy's?"

"Yeah. I just checked a few minutes ago," Derrick answered, glancing at his watch, "It's eight now. He usually leaves around eight-thirty, so we good on time."

"He's driving, right?"

Kwan nodded, "His Benz is parked up past Jimmy's by White Castle."

"A'ight, this how its going down. I'ma post up by White Castle. Derrick you double park beside his Benz or a car length ahead, have the sliding door open. On his way to his car I'ma snatch his ass up. Kwan, Joey, be ready to tie his ass up when I throw him in. When I do, Derrick you take off for Hudson River Drive. You all have celly's, right?"

"Yeah Jah, we know the drill. Tone put us on to everything," Derrick said.

"Just wanted to make sure. After this move, the South Bronx is ours! ... I never got to thank ya'll either for holding my family down. I'm a bless ya'll when I get this dough."

"C'mon Jah," Kwan threw an arm around his shoulder, "We were just doing what fam' is suppose to do."

"No doubt. And I'm a show love how fam' is suppose to show love." Jahad looked at his G-shock watch, "Ya'll go 'head and get in position. I'm a walk around here and see if I can catch a glimpse of this piece of shit. Kwan make sure this door is open and..."

"Breathe easy Jah. I know what to do," Kwan grinned, pushing him out the door.

From a chilly forty degrees, the temperature had dropped in a matter of a few hours to a bone piercing fifteen degrees. Jahad pulled his hood over his head and blended in with the thick sidewalk traffic, scanning everything in front of him through upturned eyes. He had just passed an electronics store, three stores away from Jimmy's Café when he spotted a familiar face leaving the Café escorting a beautiful

Puerto Rican woman. Taking a closer look he saw that it was José and a cold hatred swept through him.

With his adrenaline pumping, he scanned the sidewalk traffic again while keeping a sharp eye on José. Judging the distance between them, he picked up his pace to a light jog, hoping to reach José before he made it to his car. As his feet drew him closer, he pulled the Desert Eagle from his waistline, keeping it concealed under his hoody. His mind raced with each step, debating whether to let José go and try again when the sidewalks weren't so crowded, or take him now. His hatred made the decision for him. Moving quickly he reversed the grip on the gun so that he held it like a hammer, then rushed up, slamming it into the back of the woman's head. As she crumbled to the ground, José turned, his expression confused, unaware that Jahad had his gun trained at the middle of his back.

"What the fuc..." José's words were cut short by a left hook Jahad delivered to his chin.

"C'mon lover boy. I'm your date now," Jahad said, wrapping an arm around José's waist to keep him from falling. Pedestrians watched awestruck, parting the way as Jahad drug him towards the minivan with his head tilted down so his face couldn't be seen. "If you scream or say anything I'm a leave your ass right here with five or six slugs in your chest."

José shifted his balance so he could see his abductor, "You!" He yelled, shook, "I thought... I thought..."

Jahad hit him in the mouth with the gun, "You won't think shit else if you don't shut the fuck up!"

José said not another word, knowing Jahad wouldn't hesitate to kill him.

As planned, the sliding door was open when they approached. Jahad quickly tossed José in, head first, then dived in behind him, "Go! Go!"

Derrick squealed tires as he pulled into traffic, barely missing a yellow cab that was in the process of changing lanes. While Joey and Kwan were busy taping José's wrist and ankles together, Jahad paged the lieutenants and entered the triple 0 code. They sat José up so that he faced Jahad when they finished their work.

"Long time no see. What's been happening Homey?" Jahad said with a crooked grin to disguise his loathe.

José flared at Jahad, "What you want with me?"

"What you think muthafucka? We got some unfinished business to handle."

"We have nothing..."

Jahad slapped José so hard tears sprung to his eyes, "Shut the fuck up and listen! I'm about to call your faggot ass brother and let him know where to pick your sorry ass up. What's his number?"

José looked away.

"Oh, you don't want to talk?" Jahad scowled, reaching in his hoody pocket taking out the straight razor. You think it's a game, huh?" He said slashing José across the face so hard that the razor scraped the bone.

"AGGGGG!" José screamed, trying his best to scoot away, but Kwan pushed him back towards Jahad.

"Now I'm a ask you one more time. You front, I'm a cut your fuckin' ear off. Now what's the damn number?"

"Okay! Okay!"

Once José recited the number, Jahad dialed, then stared out at traffic with his jaws clenched as the phone rung.

"Hola?" Hector answered on the third ring.

"Hola to you too muthafucka," Jahad spat, "I want you to listen and pay close attention to what I'm about to say. I got your sorry ass brother here, hog tied and bleedin' like a muthafucka. If you ever wanna see him again, you'll meet me behind River Park Towers at nine o'clock with a quarter mill'. That's two hundred and fifty thousand, if your stupid ass can't count. You got that?"

"Who the hell is this and what the hell are you talking about?"

"You know who the fuck I am. The same nigga you tried to kill a couple times. The same nigga whose pops you bodied. You know who I am now?"

"Jah... Jahad?" Hector stuttered.

"In the flesh and I'm dead ass 'bout putting slugs in your brother's head unless you come up with the dough at exactly nine o'clock. Not 9:15, 9:05, or even 9:01. NINE O'CLOCK! Come down Hudson River Drive until you see a blue minivan and don't pull up too close 'cause I'm a start blazin'. I want my money in something see through too, in case you try to pull some slick shit. When I get the dough, you get your brother back... Hold on, I'll let you speak to him," He placed the phone against José's ear, "Go ahead, say Hola or whatever that shit is ya'll be talking."

"Hector!" José spoke frantically, "Thank God, this Moreno bastard... AGGGGGG!" He screamed in agony when Jahad cut him down the middle of his face.

"You need to teach your brother some manners Hector. Fuckin' with me, he'll end up looking like Carlos. You do remember Carlos don't you? ... Now as much as I like talking to you I gotta go."

"Wait!" Hector shouted desperately, "I'll have your money, it's no problem. I need more time though."

Jahad looked at his watch. Eight forty. There was no way Hector could make it in twenty minutes.

"A'ight, you have an hour. But if you try some slick shit, your brother is fish food."

"I'll be there, just don't hurt him anymore... Please!"

"That depends on you Hector, it all depends on you. And since I'm giving you some extra time, I want some extra money so double that. Hurry the fuck up too!" Jahad pressed the end button, and then turned to José, "I see your brother loves your worthless ass. That same love is gon' get his ass killed."

"I thought..." José quickly closed his mouth when Jahad raised the razor.

"I see you're a fast learner," Jahad tore off a piece of tape, placing it over José's mouth, then resumed talking, "I know you don't think I'm stupid enough to let you slimy bastards live. You bodied my pops and tried..."

"He did what?" Kwan asked, shocked.

"Yeah, this bastard here and his bitch ass brother were the muthafuckas who bodied my pops that day. You remember the Puerto Rican dude who was dead beside my pops, right?"

Kwan nodded, remembering the day vividly. It was the first time any of them had ever seen a dead body.

"That was this nigga here pops. They bodied him too."

"Get the fuck outta here!" Kwan and Joey shouted in unison.

"Some ill shit, right?" Jahad looked at José, his face masking his rage, "I'm taking everything muthafucka... everything!"

Fifteen minutes later, Derrick turned off the Major Deegan onto Hudson River Drive. Jahad stared out at the Hudson River's blackish waters as light from River Park Towers shimmered off the water like crystals in the sun, his thoughts on the person who caused him the most pain, Janet. Rumor had it that she was back in the Bronx, living with her mother, although none of his friends had seen her. If there was any truth to the rumor, Jahad figured she thought he was never getting out. She was in for the shock of her life. Once the Coco Twins were dead, she was next in line, but he had no plans of killing her. Killing her would be too good. He wanted her to live and suffer as he suffered, feel the pain he felt.

"How we doing this?" Derrick asked once he parked along side the sidewalk bordering the Hudson River.

Jahad looked at his watch, "We got like thirty minutes before Hector should show up. I don't think he'll try no corny shit, but go find Crook and stay low just in case. When he gets here, stay put unless you see something funny or you see me rub my head. If I do come out busin'."

"So what's up with scrams?" Joey nodded at José, whose blood poured off his chin from the slashes in his face.

"I'm 'bout to see if he can walk on water," Jahad grabbed the tape off the seat and wrapped José's face like a mummy, cutting off his air supply.

"UMMM! UMMM! UMMM!" José grumbled loudly, shaking his head back and forth.

"If I were you, I'd try to hold my breath. Better yet, breath out your ears," Joey laughed, opening the sliding door.

Jahad dragged José out by his collar, while he flapped like a fish out of water, trying desperately to breath, "You ready to perform your miracle muthafucka?"

"UMMM! UMMM!"

"UM, my ass," Jahad hoisted him up by the back of his collar and the seat of his pants, "Let me give you some advice, turn over on your back and try to float." With that said he threw José over into the freezing cold water, watching as he sunk upon contact. "One down, one to go," he whispered, turning back to the van.

Twenty minutes later, a powder blue Lexus LS400, parked thirty yards ahead of the minivan, its dim light left on. Jahad's heart raced, this was the moment he had been waiting on. As he stepped out the van, he screwed up his face, noticing that Hector wasn't alone. From the distance, he could make out a woman's silhouette sitting in the passenger's seat. Something was wrong; he could feel it.

"I thought you'd be smart enough to come by yourself. I guess your brother's life don't mean shit to you after all!" He called out when Hector and the woman stepped from the car.

"Where's José? I have your damn money now turn over my damn brother!"

He's up to something Jahad thought, "Who the fuck are you to be making demands? Bring my money, then we can talk about your sorry ass brother."

"It's coming, but I'm not bringing it. You think I'm stupid enough to walk right into your hands so you can kill me? Give me a little credit... Besides, I thought you would want to see your old flame again."

As the woman drew closer holding a large see through plastic bag full of cash, Jahad's mouth dropped on. Walking only a few feet in front of him was the first and last woman he would ever give his heart to, Janet. Her honey blonde hair was cut short, her face a little fatter, but it was definitely Janet.

"You bitch!" He spat, pointing his gun at her head.

"Jah, listen, you don't understand baby," Janet pleaded. Even under the circumstances, she was so happy to see him. If only he would listen, she could explain everything, so much depended on him understanding. Not for her sake, but for their child. "I need..."

"Shut the fuck up!" He hissed, his finger tightening on the trigger. "Open the damn bag and sit it out in front of you... hurry up!"

"Just let me explain. Hector has..."

"Explain what? I'm sayin', what I ever do wrong to you, huh? What the fuck I do to you!" He yelled with emotions thick in his voice. "Nothing! Not a damn thing and you were fuckin' that slimy bastard. By the looks of it, you still are. You think he gives a fuck about you? I gave a fuck about you. That nigga don't..."

"No! No!" Janet cried, shaking her head. "I never cheated on you Jah, never! Hector is my brother."

"Brother? Chico... Chico..." Stunned, Jahad realized where he had heard that from, "Why didn't you tell me?"

"I was scared baby. I didn't know what to do. I tried to talk Hector out of hurting you, I did. He said he would let us..."

"Whoa, hold up," He shook his head, confused, wanting so bad to believer her, "What you doing here now then?"

"If you would listen, that's what I've been trying to tell you. Hector forced me to come. He took our..."

"BOOM! BOOM! BOOM! BOOM! BOOM! POP! POP! POP! POP! BOOM! BOOM! BOOM!"

At the sound of gunshots, Jahad ducked, just as Janet fell into his arms when a stray bullet slammed into her back. Looking up he saw Derrick, Kwan, Joey, and Crook running towards the Lexus, firing at Hector and two other men who had slipped from the trunk. Unable to stand the firepower Hector weaved his way towards the Hudson River and dived in, just as Jahad took aim at his back.

"Goddammit!" Jahad screamed, sprinting towards the rail looking over the dark water, "You better pray you drown muthafucka! If I catch you I'm a torture your ass. You hear me! You hear me!" He roared as tears of rage poured from his eyes.

"C'mon Jah, lets go man," Derrick said, placing a hand on his shoulder.

Jahad turned from the rail and his eyes immediately focused on Janet's twitching body. For a moment, he felt a tug at his heart. If what she said was true, then his hatred had been in vain. Then again, he would never know...

CHAPTER 26

Hector drug himself from the freezing water seconds after Derrick pulled off, shivering so bad, his teeth chattered. Any longer and he would have been dead. For a couple of minutes, he leaned up against the iron rail, trying to catch his breath while sirens blared in the distance, seeming to grow louder as each second passed. Before him, lying near the edge of the street, Janet still twitched, her green eyes blinking sporadically up at the dark sky. To his left the two men he brought with him lay dead, their bodies riddled with bullet holes.

Hector shook his head, void of any feelings for his half sister, as he stiffly walked to his car. Actually, he wished she would hurry up and die. It would save him the trouble of having to kill her. He felt that this was all her fault. If she had set Jahad up like he told her from the start, his twin brother would still be alive; he had no doubts that Jahad had killed him. He stopped when he made it to his car and gave her one last look, cursing the day she was born.

They were never close, stemming from their childhood when Chico left the twin's mother, Angelina, to live with Janet's mother, who happened to live in the same building. Angelina, hurt and full of scorn, began planting spiteful seeds in her twin boy's minds not long afterwards, which caused them to loathe their father at an early age. Two years later, when Janet was born, naturally some of their hatred shifted her way.

It wasn't until Janet's teenage years that the twins started showing an interest in their baby sister. At sixteen, Janet was beautiful beyond comparison, with an entourage of beautiful friends. Seeing the benefits, the twins used her until they sexed every last one of her friends. This started their one sided relationship. One sided because Janet had genuine love for her brothers, while they could care less about her. From then on, she was there when they called, to do whatever, whether it be hold their drugs and money or get close to certain drug dealers they wanted to kill. As the years passed, she proved to be quite useful, then Jahad came along and everything changed. Hector, being the closest to her, began to feel his reins loosen, but figured once he killed Jahad things would go back to normal. The problem was... Jahad wouldn't die.

Hector turned the heat on full blast once he got in his car, then pulled off dialing the number to his lieutenant on Story Avenue. No one answered. His second call was placed to his lieutenant on Ftelly Avenue, where an unfamiliar voice answered.

"Hello?"

"Who's this!" Hector spat angrily.

"I'm detective West from the..."

Hector quickly hung up, then dialed the number to his other spots, getting the same results. His first thought was that he had been raided, until he drove through each spot and saw police cars, ambulances, and body bags lined up along the sidewalk. It was when he drove through Story Avenue that the realization of what had happened sunk in. The park looked like an amusement park, lit up with red, yellow, and blue lights. News helicopters hovered over the scene shining bright white lights over the numerous body bags that were scattered everywhere looking more like mounds of dirt protruding from the concrete.

He pulled into Monroe projects parking lot when fear seized him at the thought of being a marked man. He put the Lexus in reverse and nearly collided with a parked car as he backed out. A deep sense of hopelessness came over him as he drove away. His brother was dead, his drug empire ruined, and he feared for his life to top things off.

Hector wasn't one to be cornered though. His first obligation was to get his kids somewhere safe. From there, he would start planning his revenge, which would be like ice cream in the end, cold and sweet.

~~~~

Six months later, all Five Heads were on the street together and the pandemonium begun. Dead bodies started popping up in the Bronx, Harlem, Brooklyn, and Queens, frequently, but unexpectedly, including the bodies of two police detectives. Drug spots all over the city were constantly being fire bombed and shot up. Some of New

York's largest drug dealers were being kidnapped along with their kids, wives, and mothers, and being held for Kings ransoms. New York's underworld was in a chaotic state of turmoil. What made it even more frightening was no one had a clue where the assaults were coming from. The NYPD, just as confused as the drug lords, brought in help from the FBI to no avail. The Five Heads stay at Rikers Island produced an untamable beast hungry for power. And as a collective, this group would eliminate all flaws, even its own.

Don't think it stops here; this was only the beginning. And if you're wondering what happened next... Koran is what happened next; an untamable beast all unto himself.

The Machine!

COMING SOON
BOSS: Caught Up In The Hustle!

A WHORES CONSCIENCE
COVER REVEAL SOON!

SEND MONEY ORDER/CHECK TO:	**WYNN PUBLICATIONS** P.O. Box 40411 2777 Brentwood RD. Raleigh, NC 27604		

NAME			
ADDRESS			
CITY			
STATE	ZIP		
EMAIL			

BOOK TITLE	PRICE EACH	QUANTITY	TOTAL
BEHIND THE MASK	12.00		
FALSE	12.00		
MY BROTHERS KEEPER PT 1	12.00		
MY BROTHERS KEEPER PT 2	12.00		

THANK YOU FOR YOUR BUSINESS	TOTAL	
	SHIPPING & HANDLING	6.00
	FINAL TOTAL	

www.ingramcontent.com/pod-product-compliance
Lightning Source LLC
Chambersburg PA
CBHW051506170626
46811CB00002B/672